WINTER OF
THE HOLY IRON

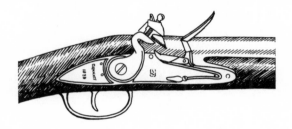

WINTER OF THE HOLY IRON

A NOVEL

Joseph Marshall III

R·E·D
CRANE
BOOKS

SANTA FE

To my parents
and
all my grandparents,
for remembering the stories.

To my great-grandparents
and
great-great-grandparents,
for living them.

Hokahe!

FIRST EDITION

Manufactured in the United States of America
Series format by Paulette Livers Lambert
Text design by Jim Mafchir
Cover painting and text drawings by Gregory Truett Smith
Cover design by R. Suzanne Vilmain

Library of Congress Cataloging-in-Publication Data

Marshall, Joe.
    Winter of the holy iron / Joseph Marshall III. — 1st ed.
      p.   cm.
    ISBN 1-878610-44-9
    1. Indians of North America—Great Plains—First contact with
Europeans—Fiction. 2. West (U.S.)—History—To 1848—Fiction.
3. Teton Indians—Fiction. I. Title.
PS3563.A72215W56 1994
813'.54—dc20   94-9156
                                                      CIP

Red Crane Books
826 Camino de Monte Rey
Santa Fe, New Mexico 87505

Foreword

The hundreds, if not thousands, of native pre-European languages in North America had to adjust to accommodate the many new ideas and artifacts brought over by the emigrants from Europe. In some cases new words were formed; in many cases, existing words were used to help describe new things.

Two trade items which arguably had the greatest impact on native North Americans were liquor and firearms. Native languages did not have words comparable to *gun, flintlock, rifle,* or *ammunition.* But in every instance where the firearm came into intensive contact with a native tribe, a word or phrase was used to describe something or everything about it. Sometimes those words and phrases described an abstract quality attributed to the firearm, and sometimes they described a tangible quality which was easier to perceive.

The firearm came late to the Great Plains, in comparison with its earlier arrival on the eastern seaboard. The Lakota, or Western Sioux, of the northern Great Plains used a phrase which described the gun both abstractly and tangibly. Our phrase for the gun was *maza wakan—maza* meaning iron and *wakan* meaning mysterious, or having a spiritual quality, or holy.

A loose translation of *maza wakan* in English is "holy iron," meaning "iron with mysterious qualities."

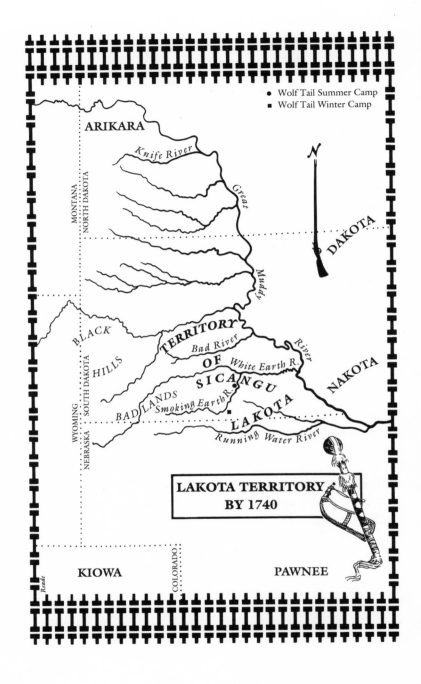

- Wolf Tail Summer Camp
- Wolf Tail Winter Camp

ARIKARA

Knife River

MONTANA
NORTH DAKOTA

Great

DAKOTA

N

Muddy

BLACK

TERRITORY

Bad River

River

HILLS

OF

White Earth R.

NAKOTA

SICANGU

BAD LANDS

Smoking Earth R.

LAKOTA

WYOMING
SOUTH DAKOTA

NEBRASKA

Running Water River

LAKOTA TERRITORY
BY 1740

Reade

KIOWA

COLORADO

PAWNEE

PLACE NAMES IN SICANGU LAKOTA TERRITORY

(in present-day south-central South Dakota)

Past Sicangu designations	Current names
Mnisose (Great Muddy River)	Missouri River
Wakpa Sica (Bad Creek or Bad River)	Bad River
Maka Ska Wakpa (White Earth River)	Big White River
Maka Izita Wakpa (Smoking Earth River)	Little White River
Mni Kaluza Wakpa (Running Water River)	Niobrara River
Wiwila Wakpa (Spring Creek)	Spring Creek

(locations outside of Sicangu territory but still within Lakota territory with Lakota names or designations)

Maka Sica (Bad Lands)	Bad Lands
(Desert Lands)	
(also called the Stronghold)	
He Sapa (Black Mountains)	Black Hills
Paha Sapa (Black Hills)	Black Hills

WINTER OF THE HOLY IRON

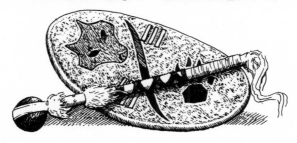

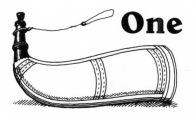

One

It was past midday, and Whirlwind knew he was half a day's ride from the summer encampment of the Wolf Tail Lakota. He glanced up at the low, dark clouds and watched how they hid the sun and cast a cold grayness over the land. He was anxious to see his home and family.

Solitary hunts were good. They helped to appease that part of him that was wild and free. Stalking a white-tailed deer, an elk, or a white-bellied antelope kept the senses and the skills sharpened. Now and then coming face-to-face with the great bear quickened the heart. All of these things only increased his appreciation for life, and being Lakota. But, though each hunt added to his memories, deepened his knowledge, and strengthened his being, Whirlwind never forgot his place as a son, husband, father, and war leader.

The Wolf Tail people, like all Lakota, were wanderers. Not even the oldest man or woman in the encampment could remember a time when they were not. Even before the coming of the horse, they were wanderers, though they had not really chosen such a lifestyle. A people who were of the land must move with the land. To do otherwise was to move outside of the rhythms of all life, because life came from the land.

The buffalo were wanderers, so too the elk and the deer. Without them the Lakota would starve, they would not have warm robes and fine clothing, and their lodges would not be grand and comfortable. So like the hawk, the great cat, the wolf, the short-tailed cat, and the wolverine, the Lakota were hunters. They became wanderers following the buffalo, the elk, and the deer.

It was during the time of the youth of Whirlwind's grandfather that the Lakota had crossed the Great Muddy River and moved west across the prairies. Sicangu Lakota bands, the Wolf Tail people among them, had come to think of the lands west of the Great Muddy River to the beginnings of the White Earth River, and south from the Bad River to the Running Water River as their territory. Within this territory the land provided all they needed for a good life. And within this territory they wandered. Wandering was so deep in their blood now that it was impossible to ignore the yearning to move when it came.

This was the Moon of Falling Leaves, when hunting was good and winter was not far away. It was nearly time for the Wolf Tail people to move to their winter camp. Their summer camp was a day's ride from where the Smoking Earth River flowed into the White Earth River. In several days Whirlwind's people would strike their lodges and move to the winter camp. One reason for moving was to spend the winter in a sheltered, pine-covered valley filled with white-tailed deer, and to let hillsides around their summer encampment replenish the grasses grazed down by their large horse herd. But the other reason was to yield to the stirring in the blood of the wanderer. Even as he rode, Whirlwind could feel a stirring deep in his blood—something that only a wanderer could feel and understand.

Whirlwind urged his horses into a faster walk. The gutted white-tailed buck hanging over the back of the bay gelding showed his ability as a hunter. His senses, sharpened by many, many hunts, had brought him to within easy arrow shot of the buck. Now those same senses were his defense. The Lakota were not without enemies.

He smiled in anticipation of the warm lodge waiting and of the deer ribs that his wife Her Good Trail would roast over the hot coals. BOOM! Suddenly, a thunderous crack of a white man's holy iron stopped the smile. Whirlwind looked east for an instant, in the direction of the noise. Then he quickly guided his horses into a tall plum thicket.

For a short time he kept the buckskin mare and the bay gelding quiet and waited for another thunder-like boom. Memories of his first encounter with a white man's holy iron swept through him like a spring flash flood. He had nearly been killed by such a weapon, four winters ago where the Smoking Earth River flowed into the White Earth River. Whirlwind had killed the white man who had shot at him with that long, smoke-blowing weapon with the thunderous noise. It was the first such weapon and the first white man he had ever seen, though he had heard stories of both. Since that time, he had kept the weapon he had captured hidden in his lodge. And since that time, he had not seen another white man. Whirlwind considered that the chances of seeing one this day were good. But he also realized that the holy iron he had heard could be in the hands of a Kiowa, Pawnee, or Arikara warrior. Those people were enemies of the Lakota. If they had holy irons, life for the Lakota would take a bad turn.

There were no more shots. Whirlwind glanced about, peering intently between the thick branches of the plum thicket. Except for the rustle of fleeing deer through a nearby grove, all was quiet.

Whirlwind dismounted and tied the horses to a branch. With quick, practiced motions he pulled his bow from its case, strung it, and nocked an arrow. His eyes swept all around and glanced at the buckskin mare. She was alert but quiet.

Sometimes it was only necessary to be a hunter. But most times, like now, it was necessary to be a warrior. The hunter provided for his family and his people. The warrior protected them. A Lakota warrior could not turn away from anything which was even the smallest threat to his people. It did not matter if such a thing was faced alone or in the company of other warriors. It had to be faced. The people had to be protected. And Whirlwind considered anyone with a holy iron in his hands to be a threat and an enemy. He patted each horse gently and slipped out of the thicket. He went east, moving silently from thicket to tree, from tree to washout, to another tree. A lifetime of stalking wary whitetails enabled him to move with deathly silence. Past another large tree, he flattened behind a rotting log. Ahead, at about the distance of a strong arrow's cast, about two hundred long paces, stood a tall grove of cottonwoods. Whirlwind studied the area and picked out a route to the edge of the grove. The trees in that grove could hide anything. Even a white man could find a hiding place there, he decided. It would be wise to scout it.

He kept hidden behind the log and lay motionless to the count of fifty. There were no unusual noises, but he thought he could smell ash wood smoke. Turning on his side, Whirlwind looked back toward the thicket where the horses were hidden. He had heard stories of men who had forgotten to look at their back trail. Such foolishness was not the way to live long enough to be an old hunter and warrior. The horses were quiet.

Whirlwind turned his attention back to the cottonwood grove and decided to wait and watch. His eyes kept to the area around the grove, but his ears searched in all directions for any noise that did not belong. After a time he saw a meadowlark fly into the grove and alight on a low, gray branch. Sometime later a young coyote approached with cautious, hesitant steps. The young four-legged's manner in testing the wind told Whirlwind that something might be in that grove. And when the young coyote lost his nerve and trotted away, the warrior was certain that something was amidst the cottonwoods. It was time for a closer look.

He again studied the route he had picked out earlier before he moved away from the cover of the log, a route that was nothing more than low spots. Keeping to the low areas and using shrubs and tall grass to hide himself, Whirlwind made it to the edge of the circle of cottonwoods. He paused for a time to listen again. He remembered the hollow, clicking sounds the white man's holy iron had made before it belched smoke and cracked like thunder on that day nearly four winters ago. One did not forget such small things when life itself was on the line, when death was in the wind. To Whirlwind, the thunderous noise of the white man's holy iron was the voice of death—death not only for a human being but for what it meant to be a true warrior. A true warrior was one who did not need weapons as the basis for his being and his strength. A true warrior understood that real power came from knowledge, skill, and wisdom; any weapon he might use only added to that power. The holy iron was not a creation of the Lakota, and it had a power that could lead a man to think that such a weapon was all that was needed to be a warrior. For Whirlwind, a man without the true power which comes from knowledge, skill, and wisdom was not a warrior. Such a man might forsake the old ways, just for a new and different thing. That was why he had kept the weapon hidden, and silent, in his lodge for these four winters.

He stared through wavering stalks of buffalo grass, knowing that he would have to go into the grove to see what was there. Whirlwind stood, so slowly that it was hard to see motion. Then he flattened himself next to an upright hollow trunk. From there he could see the body of a man through the fork of a large cottonwood. A long, eye-sweeping, sound-searching pause revealed nothing beyond what he had already seen and heard.

The thunderous voice of the holy iron had not spoken without a reason. The first time he had heard that voice four winters ago, the trapper's holy iron had sent an iron ball tearing through Whirlwind's shirt, between his ribs and left elbow. Death had come that close. Now, it seemed, it had come to this grove.

The one who had been killed by the holy iron could be easily seen. His killer could not. The warrior's senses went out in all directions. Eyes probed for the slightest sign of anything out of place. Ears took in every noise, from the soft rustle of a mouse to the distant cackling of a blackbird. Nostrils flared as the warrior tested the breezes, knowing that fear and anger stimulated the sweat and scent glands of four-legged and two-legged prey and predator alike. For a long while, the warrior stood against the hollow trunk until he was satisfied he was the only hunter in the grove of cottonwoods.

Wolf-like gliding steps took the Lakota warrior further into the grove until he blended with an old tree. Only a slight breeze moved, ruffling the pale hair of the man face down in the sand of an old watercourse.

Whirlwind shifted for a better look. The body was not a Lakota. Though the face was burned by the sun, the features were plainly those of a white man. A dead one, from the look of him—killed by the weapon with a thunderous voice, Whirlwind thought. There was no sign of breathing. A quick sniff caught the odor of warm blood.

He crossed over a small rise to the body, putting down his bow and arrows. Powerful wrists easily turned over the buckskin-clad form. A faint moan caught the warrior's ear. Eyelids fluttered below him, bringing a flash of color to the dirty, bearded face. The white man was still alive.

Whirlwind sat back. There was no threat. Yet he still had to consider what to do about this sudden circumstance he had not anticipated.

He stared hard at the smelly, motionless form. A large patch of fresh blood over the man's right hip told a story but still left a mystery to ponder. This white man had been shot with a holy iron, but who was the shooter and where was he at this moment? Whirlwind glanced around. There were tracks nearby, many of them. And he could see how this white man had crawled for a little ways, leaving little furrows in the earth and a trail of blood.

An uneasiness crept into the ever-watchful warrior. There were stories about these hairy-faced men—men, if they were, beginning to come into Lakota country. Some of the Wolf Tail people had once seen a black robe, a kind of holy man—an angry, high-minded one. Whirlwind himself had seen only one white man, and it was a bad remembrance—a trapper Whirlwind had had to kill.

That encounter had made him the envy of other warriors, though the envy was not for the killing. It was because of Whirlwind's capture of the trapper's weapon, a weapon which cracked like thunder and killed at distances far beyond the reach of the bow. Though Whirlwind now owned such a weapon, he did not like it and kept it hidden in his lodge. The holy iron was trouble.

The memory of that past fight with the trapper helped to bring a decision to this moment. Whirlwind would have nothing further to do with this white man. Someone had shot this man, and the shooter could still be nearby . . . with his holy iron.

After picking up his bow and arrows, Whirlwind stood and walked toward the edge of the grove without a backward glance. Then he heard a word spoken in Lakota, his own tongue! The warrior spun around, an arrow nocked on the bowstring.

A pale hand wavered and fell. The white man spoke feebly. "Who are you?" he said, in Lakota! The warrior stood above the man, ready to shoot the arrow. A coarse, raspy noise came from a parched throat and cracked lips. "Who are you?"

Looking down into cloudy blue eyes, Whirlwind stood for a moment before replying, uncertain of what he had heard. "I am Whirlwind," he said. "I am Lakota."

The blue eyes lost focus. The raspy voice hissed once more. "Help me. I am hurt."

Sunset found Whirlwind hidden deep inside a thicket of willows, near the bank of a creek which flowed into the Smoking Earth River. The horses were standing just behind him, tied to the base of thick willow stalks. A low fire was burning in a deep, narrow pit dug in the sand. A strip of deer meat hung over the flames. It was not the meal Whirlwind had anticipated for this evening, but it smelled good and he was hungry.

He was angry, too. Whirlwind could not understand why he had hauled the man out of the cottonwood grove. He doubted if the man would live through the night. If he was right, then the problem of what to do with him would be solved. Still, Whirlwind did admit that he was curious about this Lakota-speaking white man.

White men were not altogether a new thing to the Wolf Tail people. They had been encountered now and then in Lakota territory, and there were stories about them. A Lakota band living near the west banks of the Great Muddy River had been visited by a group of white men about ten winters ago. The leader of that group had told that they were from a land across a vast, angry water—a land of many white men.

As a boy, Whirlwind had also heard stories about white men from his grandfather. Walks High, his father's father, had seen several in the lake country far to the northeast across the Great Muddy River. Grandfather Walks High was himself just a boy then, nearly eighty winters ago. Furthermore, Walks High's father had told him of how some of their people had been driven from the lake country by the Ojibway, who had traded furs to white men for holy irons. With their new weapons they had driven the allied people—the Nakota and Dakota—south and westward. The third part of the alliance, the Lakota, was already living on the prairies west of the Great Muddy River during that time.

The Lakota once lived in the frozen north country south of a great body of water. Leaving their homes in that north country, for reasons now long forgotten, they wandered south and west. For many winters they lived and traveled in a heavily forested land, until they came to a region of very large and very small lakes. The large lakes were deep and angry. Many people were lost in their waters. The smaller lakes were numberless and filled with fish. This area came to be called the Land of Smoking Waters because the cold water of the many lakes sent clouds of mist to hang low in the sky among the trees.

The Nakota and Dakota came from far to the southeast of the lake country, where they had been forest dwellers and had cultivated crops. After being displaced by more war-like peoples, they eventually found their way to the lake country and there met the people from the north. At that time the groups which met did not call themselves the Lakota, Dakota, and Nakota. Although they spoke different languages, they found reasons to live in friendship. After a few generations, their languages and their traditions intermingled, and they became one nation. From the words for *allies* and *friends* came the new names for the three main groups that were now one nation—Lakota, Dakota, and Nakota. Life in the lake country was good, until their Ojibway enemies traded with white men for holy irons. As they were driven south and west by the Ojibway, the Lakota remembered their roots in the frozen north country and looked for wide-open land. Likewise, the Dakota and Nakota erected their lodges along rivers and in valleys where they could plant crops. They stayed east of the Great Muddy River while the Lakota crossed and inhabited the open prairies.

Even as Whirlwind recalled these stories and ate his roasted deer meat, a man was moving cautiously through some trees two valleys away. A dark figure in dirty buckskins stood in a cottonwood grove and studied the tracks in the sand of an old watercourse. Moccasin prints and horse tracks were plain to see. The man fingered his heavy flintlock as he glanced furtively about and stroked his beard with a thick hand. Leaves fluttered helplessly to the earth, and buffalo grass swayed with the wandering breezes. There was rage in the man's cold, gray eyes. He walked a ways until he found two sets of hoofprints leading off to the east. Sharp, angry words rumbled from his dark, meaty face as the man kicked at the earth.

Whirlwind felt the breeze shift direction as he ate his meat. He let the fire go out. A bright flame in the dark of night was a signal for trouble to come. The trouble he did not want to see this night was in the form of a faceless one who had shot a white man. A slight moan came from the form beneath the deer-hide robe. The warrior glanced in the direction of the noise and then stared grimly off into the darkness. He pulled his lance, bow, and the quiver of arrows to within easy reach. He recalled all that he had seen on this hunt. Herds of numberless antelope. Several fat bears as they prepared for the long winter's sleep. Elk in the midst of their ancient rites of mating, assuring that a new generation of their kind would walk the Earth. Once again, the breeze changed direction. It came from the east now, and was cold. Whirlwind pulled a deer-hide robe over his shoulders.

The dying firelight revealed the worry in the warrior's intense, dark eyes. His vigilant glances into the rapidly fading daylight searched for answers to unknown questions as much as for a faceless enemy. The wounded, Lakota-speaking white man was the reason for those unknown questions. Perhaps in him who caused the questions would be an answer. Perhaps that was what had driven the warrior to rescue the white man from the cottonwood grove. Still, the white man, or at least his kind, was an intruder, a stranger. This white man had encroached on Lakota territory, and he had also intruded into the land of the bear, the elk, the antelope, and many other beings.

As if in response to the warrior's thoughts, the white man loosed a long, pitiful moan. Whirlwind's eyes narrowed as he looked away. He tried to bring a hardness into his warrior heart, wondering again at the wisdom of helping the wounded man.

He could ride away now and leave the man to die, as he nearly had earlier. But a warrior was not a killer. There was room for compassion in a warrior's heart. Further, over forty winters of experience told him that this white man in Lakota territory would not touch only one warrior's life. This was something that would touch all of the Wolf Tail people. Therefore, the people had a voice. He would trust in that and take the wounded man to the Wolf Tail village.

Whirlwind looked toward the horses. They were quiet, so he turned and stared into the darkness at nothing in particular as he let his ears search the sounds of the late autumn night. Beneath his robe the warrior's black hair hung loosely almost to his waist. He was taller than most men, and his body was trim and hard. The life of a hunter and warrior had strengthened and shaped his body as well as his instincts. For the moment, he sensed no immediate danger. He leaned back against a thick clump of willows and closed his eyes.

The breeze was still from the east, and it carried the far-off voice of another hunter. A wolf. Its song was strong, and it brought a smile to the face of Whirlwind.

Two

A long arrow's cast west of the village, Whirlwind came to a grove of willows. It was nearly sundown. Early this morning he had cut poles and built a drag to carry the white man. The extra load slowed his pace. That and stopping to check his back trail several times turned a half day's ride into a full day's journey.

He waved to the sentinel hidden near a dead tree. The young warrior trotted over to see the curious thing under the deer robes on the drag poles. "What is it?" he asked.

"A white man," Whirlwind replied. "I found him in a grove of cottonwoods yesterday."

Whirlwind looked over the village as he let the horses pick the way through the willows. Rising smoke from evening cooking fires stretched upward like giant, red lances painted with soft hues by the departing sun. Fifty-four lodges stood in a circle on a high bench west of a river bend. Tall, slender lodgepoles crisscrossed into the sky. Blackened smoke flaps seemed to float above the lighter lower half of the lodges. People were all about, and meat racks and low willow shades stood here and there. War horses were already picketed for the night near the doors to some of the lodges.

Sentinels surrounded the encampment, well placed and carefully hidden. Enemy raiding parties were nearly always roaming the fringes of Lakota territory. About a ten days' ride to the north, just past the territory of the Hunkpapa

Lakota in the Knife River country, were the Arikara. To the
south, past the Running Water River, were the Pawnee. Far
south of the Black Hills were the Kiowa, who had been
pushed out of the prairie country by the Lakota.

Now and then, a daring war party rode far into Lakota
territory. Watchfulness, therefore, was necessary for survival.
Only last spring a Pawnee raiding party from the south was
turned back. Vigilance and many good warriors were the
reasons for victory that day.

Some of the people glanced curiously at Whirlwind, but
only a few. A man coming into camp with a deer hanging
over a pack horse was not an unusual sight. It was autumn,
the Moon of Falling Leaves. The hard prairie winter was
waiting just behind the sharp breezes, and hunters were
coming and going every day. Even the war leader had to feed
his family.

An old warrior worked at a fire next to his lodge. A wise,
deeply lined face framed by two thick, gray braids wrapped
in otter skins looked intently at the weapon in his hands.
Spotted Calf was putting the last touches on a new, sinew-
backed bow. Dark, knowing eyes scanned the limbs of the
weapon. Strong, skillful fingers felt along its surface. Finally,
taking up an antelope leg bone, he rubbed the belly of the
bow in long, even strokes. After many, many strokes, he lifted
the bow and looked closely at it. A smile sparkled in Spotted
Calf's dark eyes. The old warrior was satisfied with the
weapon. This bow, and two others, had been a summer's
work. One bow was a gift for a grandson. Walks High, named
for Spotted Calf's father, was twenty winters old and already
a strong warrior with six eagle feathers on his war lance. The
other two bows had been made for an old friend, Catches,
in exchange for a horse. Spotted Calf's bows were much in
demand, and many came to sit at his fire to learn his skill.

A half-coyote dog across the fire sat up to look intently
at an approaching rider. Spotted Calf knew it was his son,

Whirlwind, just from the way the man sat on his horse. A smile faded from the old warrior's face when he saw the body on the drag poles behind the bay. He put aside the bow and labored to his feet.

"Who is it?" Spotted Calf asked.

"I do not know who he is," Whirlwind replied, dismounting. "But I do know what he is." Grabbing the man's hair, the warrior lifted the head to show a dirty, bearded face.

"Hah!" the old man said, half in alarm. "A white man. Is he alive?"

"He was when I last stopped to rest the horses."

People began to gather as word quickly spread that Whirlwind had brought home more than a deer. Most of the people in the Wolf Tail band had never seen a white man. But they did know that their war leader had almost been killed by one nearly four winters ago.

Concern clouded Spotted Calf's face.

"He was alone when I found him, after I heard the sound of a holy iron being shot," the son explained. "I found him in a grove of cottonwoods. I would have left him, but he asked for my help . . . in our language."

Fierce whispers went through the crowd. A hard look flashed through the old man's eyes. A white man speaking Lakota was something unexpected. Even strange. Some ten winters past, a white man and his sons had traveled up the Great Muddy River and had camped for a time where the Bad River flowed into the Great Muddy. All the men in that group spoke only their own language.

Still, things changed. The old ones knew that best of all. Word came now and again from the east side of the Great Muddy about bearded, pale men from unknown places. The Dakota and Nakota had seen some near the Grandfather River to the southeast and near Spirit Lake up in the lake country. It was said that some of the white men were strange holy men who wore black robes. Others of them were fur traders.

Circling Bear, one of the oldest men among the Wolf Tail people, often told the story of how a relative of his met two white men near the Great Muddy River nearly fifteen winters ago. It had been during an especially hard winter, and Circling Bear's older cousin Comes Alive and two companions had ridden to find a buried cache of dried fat, or tallow. Because their horses suddenly scented something near the cache site, the three men approached on foot. To their surprise, two white men were digging up the buried fat. According to Comes Alive, the white men were gaunt and hollow-eyed. They ate the fat even as they pulled it from the cache. One of them had a holy iron, but they still fled at the sight of the three Lakota—taking some of the fat with them. Comes Alive took pity on them and stopped his companions from chasing the two hungry white men.

Circling Bear called the whites *wasin icu*—Fat Takers. He generally considered them to be a strange, puzzling, and inept people. "We are hunters," he would say, "and they are scavengers."

Rumors and stories about encounters with such people were one thing. But the presence of a white man in a Lakota village was much more worrisome.

Curiosity grew. Spotted Calf motioned for a boy named Red Legs and sent him after his old friend Stone, the medicine man.

A tall, young warrior and a woman with dark, sparkling eyes came through the crowd. The warrior looked expectantly to his father. The woman, Her Good Trail, gave her husband a shy smile and took the lead rope to the bay pack horse. She would wait to hear about this strange thing. Now there was a deer to be skinned and cut up.

By the time the medicine man arrived the white man was on the ground next to Spotted Calf's fire, covered with a deer-hide robe. Whirlwind had asked his son and two other warriors to stand guard. If the man were to suddenly come to life and become wild, someone would be ready for him.

Stone gazed down at the man, but his dark eyes gave no sign of reaction. Like Spotted Calf, he wore his below-waist-length hair in two fur-wrapped braids. But unlike the hair of his good friend, the medicine man's hair was nearly snow-white, giving his dark, deeply lined face many shadowy edges—as if it had been chipped from stone. He tightened his handhold on the robe hanging over his left shoulder and turned a questioning gaze to Whirlwind.

"He still lives," the war leader said. "He spoke to me after I found him. He spoke to me in our language."

Stone next glanced toward his old friend Spotted Calf. "We need to talk about this thing," he said. Kneeling, he pulled aside the robe and the injured man's shirt to look at the badly festered wound. "He might live," the medicine man said.

Whirlwind looked at the two men he respected most, his own father and the medicine man. Both were nearly seventy winters old and had been boyhood friends. As warriors they had both put themselves in danger many times for the sake of the Wolf Tail people. In his own boyhood, Whirlwind had held them in awe. They were both strong of body and daring in action, easily capable of exploits other men would not attempt. Like the time Spotted Calf jumped from the back of one galloping horse to another, and when Stone sneaked into a Pawnee camp alone to rescue his younger sister. Now, as a mature warrior himself, Whirlwind was still in awe of his father and the medicine man—in awe of their knowledge and wisdom. But there was something else that Whirlwind also often felt in the presence of Stone. It was not something more, simply something different—something that Whirlwind had never felt in the company of any other person, man or woman.

As the medicine man covered the wounded man, Whirlwind glanced briefly at Stone's face. Whirlwind could not sense Stone's feelings about a white man being among the

Wolf Tail people, but there was that feeling, a stillness, like a sudden quietness in the middle of a storm.

It was dark. The evening was cool. Her Good Trail took roasted deer ribs to her son and the other guards. There was still no word from the council lodge.

The people had dispersed slowly. But over the course of the evening, many had come to look at the white man. After Stone had looked at the wound, he had asked two women, Walks Far and Yellow Earrings, to remove the man's clothing, wash him, and pack the wound with a poultice he had given them. The women did as they were asked, teasing each other good-naturedly as they worked and carefully hiding the man's nakedness from curious eyes. Through it all, the white man moaned occasionally. Now he was a thin, naked form beneath the deer-hide robe.

Walks Far tied up her pouch of herbs, laid it aside, and looked across the lodge to her cousin Yellow Earrings. Over their many winters both women had tended to many injured hunters and wounded warriors. Though they had teased one another as they tended to the white man, something was bothering Walks Far. A feeling had come upon her even as she first saw the wounded man's bearded face—an unwanted, unwelcome feeling like being covered with a heavy buffalo robe on a hot summer day.

"Cousin," she said to Yellow Earrings. "I am suddenly afraid."

Yellow Earrings, her hair nearly as white as Walks Far's, paused to cast a worried glance toward her cousin. Walks Far was not given to talking lightly of such feelings. "What is it, Cousin?"

Walks Far shook her head. "I do not know. Something about the white man, perhaps."

"He is wounded. He cannot hurt anyone. Three good warriors watch him, even now."

Walks Far nodded. "I know. I am not afraid of him. I think I am afraid of what he brings with him."

Yellow Earrings reached to add a few small twigs to the fire. She waited for them to catch fire before she spoke again. "I saw no weapons."

"I know, Cousin. But it is not what is in his hands, but that which is in his heart. In the heart of his kind, I mean."

"What can that be? I have heard that white men are a pitiful people. The old man Circling Bear calls them Fat Takers. What can they have in their hearts?"

As she pondered the question Walks Far listened to the varied sounds outside her cousin's lodge for a few moments, savoring the sounds of life. Nearby she heard children's voices and running feet. In the next lodge a mother's lullaby rose in response to a baby's soft whimper. A warrior cleared his throat as a war horse stamped his feet. In the distant trees, a dove cooed his love for his mate. She thought of her son, High Hawk, and his family and hoped they would return soon from their journey to the north. She let go of their images and glanced at her cousin's worried face, shaking her head. "Death," she said. "They have death in their hearts."

Yellow Earrings studied her cousin's face for a heartbeat or two. She remembered that it was Walks Far who had heard the owl, the messenger of death, two nights before the warrior Brings Three Horses had died in a blizzard. "Perhaps," she said, "our war leader should not have brought one of them here."

"Our war leader did not do wrong. Time will show that he did right. But the darkness over my heart makes me fear for our people. It is a darkness that makes me feel cold. The coldness of death."

The two old women looked briefly into one another's eyes. Both over seventy winters old, together they could count nearly one hundred fifty winters of life. They were both widows, each having lost an only husband over twenty winters past. Death was no stranger.

Yellow Earrings turned away and reached for a small rawhide case. From it she drew a braid of sweet grass. "My son brought this to me from the Knife River country two winters ago," she said. "I think this is a good time to burn some for a smudge, to purify ourselves and keep all the bad things away from this lodge." Walks Far smiled and nodded as she watched her cousin hold the end of the braid in the flames until it turned to glowing embers. Soon thick, sweet smoke rose in a swirl above the fire. They reached into it and pulled the smoke toward them. Many thoughts whirled in Yellow Earrings's mind, but it was a sudden flatness in her cousin's eyes which worried her—a dull flatness seen in the eyes of a dead person. Yellow Earrings began to mourn for her cousin, even as she wondered what the wounded white man had brought to them all.

Walks High looked at the man with amused disdain. "He does not look strong. Truthfully, he looks dead."

"Perhaps it is better that he dies," Lone Elk said. "I think he may be like the one who almost killed your father."

Red Lance agreed. "But this one has no holy iron," he pointed out. "Maybe he is no warrior."

Walks High pondered that for a moment. "That man with the holy iron was not a warrior. He had a canoe full of furs and was traveling to the Great Muddy. Perhaps he thought my father was trying to take the furs."

"He did think that he could kill a Lakota warrior with his holy iron," Lone Elk said. "Maybe, in their ways, it is the weapon which makes the warrior."

Walks high shook his head. "I do not know. But I do know that his holy iron is a strong weapon. My father says it sends a small iron ball when it makes the loud sound. The ball flies faster than arrows, and it can reach farther."

The two young warriors marveled at Walks High's description of the power of the holy iron. Such a weapon could bring another kind of power to the person who owned it.

"Why," Lone Elk asked quietly, "does your father not use the weapon? Why does he keep it hidden away?"

Walks High thought for a moment, recalling the answers his father had given to the same question. "My father is already war leader of the Wolf Tail Lakota," he said. "And we all know that a leader among the Lakota does not tell other warriors what to do. He does not tell anyone what to do. He advises in the way he thinks is best. Then he must do what he thinks is best. If he is wise, then the people will follow him. If he is right, warriors will follow him onto the warpath." He paused to glance briefly at his friends. "My father said that the holy iron is a fearful thing. Many warriors envy him for having it. Fear would follow envy if he were to use the weapon. But he says fear and envy are not as good as respect. My father would rather have warriors follow him because they respect him as a man and as a warrior. He does not want to be feared because of a powerful weapon."

Red Lance and Lone Elk nodded respectfully. Walks High's words were true. The path of a warrior, onto which each of them had firmly planted their feet, was not easy. It was harder still to wear the blue robe of a war leader. They understood the wisdom of Whirlwind, coming through the words of his son. That which made the warrior was inside the man. That which was inside gave meaning to the words, the actions, and even the weapons. Without that, even the most powerful of weapons would eventually fail him who depended only on such power to acquire meaning and status.

At the head of a narrow gully, nearly a half day's ride from the village of the Wolf Tail Lakota, a dark figure was hunched over a low fire. Dry brush had been carefully placed to conceal the small night camp. Further down the gully, two matched bays were picketed in a stand of oaks.

A rabbit was roasting over the coals. The big man in dark buckskins slowly rubbed the barrel of the long, heavy rifle. Eyes narrowed as he considered the events of the past two days. They had been largely unsatisfactory. There had been no Spanish gold coins among de la Verendrye's things. He had searched, ripped everything apart. Not finding any gold coins was a surprise, but a missing body was even more so. De la Verendrye must have hidden the gold coins in his clothes somehow. But someone had taken the body, as the tracks in the cottonwood grove showed.

The big man stared angrily at the rabbit sizzling over the flames as a disturbing thought poked at the edges of his mind. Maybe de la Verendrye was still alive! The tracks in the cottonwoods were of moccasins and horses' hooves. De la Verendrye did speak some heathen language. Perhaps he had talked someone into rescuing him. If he were alive, there was something else to consider. De la Verendrye might think of revenge and might be able to persuade someone to help him. There was no choice, then, but to eliminate that possibility. Tomorrow was another day. There would be time to plan, time to scout the village near the river. After all, de la Verendrye could still have those Spanish gold coins, too—one of which had accidentally fallen to the ground that day at the camp near Running Water River. De la Verendrye had been very quick to retrieve it and stash it away.

The man slapped the flintlock—de la Verendrye's flint-lock. If only he had bothered to reload and shoot a second time!

The naked man under the deer-hide robe kept his eyes closed but moaned a little. He was awake. Despite the heavy, pressing pain in his side, he paid close attention to the three young warriors. He understood their language, though he spoke a slightly different form of it. The man did not recognize any of the warriors as the one who had rescued him.

The relatives of these people lived east of the Great Muddy River. From those people, the bearded one had heard of these Titunwan Lakota—the People Who Dwelled on the Prairie.

The bearded one had heard the words *maza wakan* and knew they meant "holy iron." He learned that one was hidden somewhere. He needed that weapon, for without it he could not carry out revenge against the man who had tried to kill him—the man who had taken his horses and furs. The hot, heavy pain of his wound made him angrily envision the face of the man who had caused his anguish. Henri Bruneaux! A countryman whom he had come to trust! He could vividly recall the moment when he had heard the noise behind him and had turned to see Bruneaux aiming the flintlock—at him!

Bruneaux had appeared out of nowhere one blustery, gray afternoon while Gaston de la Verendrye had been making camp just north of the Running Water River. That had been sometime in March, two or three weeks after he had crossed the thawing ice of the Great Muddy River. It was good to hear one's own language, and de la Verendrye had easily accepted Bruneaux's story about having been robbed by Indians of everything he owned, noting that the other man especially lamented the loss of his flintlock. That was understandable. This was an unforgiving land, and a white man without a gun was an easy mark for Indians who generally had no liking for white men. Moreover, a white man who had not the slightest idea how to provide for himself without a gun would soon fall prey to his own ignorance.

"It could have been them Omaha, or Pawnee, too," Bruneaux surmised. "I didn't hear a thing. They came in the night. Took my weapon and my flint and striker. That was three days ago. My food was gone, and I was wondering what to do. Then I heard one of your horses snort. Thought it was Indians so I hid. I couldn't believe my eyes when I saw you! Good, huh! And you are French, too!"

It had been over two years since de la Verendrye had heard his own language. Perhaps it was the brotherhood of a mother tongue, more than anything, which had caused him to easily accept his fellow Frenchman. It had not been a conscious decision to trust that big, hulking man with the darting, gray eyes, but trusting him had nearly meant his own life.

One morning, Bruneaux had simply said, "I should do some of the hunting." It had been a natural thing to hand him the flintlock, shot bag, and powder horn. Yet that simple act had taken de la Verendrye close to death and brought him to this moment of uncertainty. But he was certain of two things. He now hated Henri Bruneaux, and he had heard the words *maza wakan,* holy iron.

Through narrowed eyes he carefully peeked at the three young warriors sitting close to him. Each was smoothly muscled. Each was dressed in finely tanned leggings, breech-clout, and fringed shirt. Their moccasins were decorated with fine quillwork. But he knew, from living among the Dakota, not to be fooled by the finery of their attire or their outward calm. These young men were full-fledged warriors. The Dakota, who were stalwart warriors themselves, spoke with respect about their western Lakota relatives.

Among the Dakota the bearded one had found a life vastly different from how other white men described "those savages." He was politely accepted among them, and he found them to be anything but savage. To the Dakota, family was much more than parents and children. It extended to grandmothers and grandfathers, aunts, uncles, and cousins. Children were revered and patiently indulged, and the entire family had an influence on their rearing. That was quite a contrast to the constant fear of his own father's heavy disciplinary hand and his mother's icy remoteness. The only peace he had found at home was in his tiny loft below the rafters of the small cottage. But as he got older and taller, and had to stoop to fit in his loft, there was no more peace. In its place was a yearning to find such peace again—somewhere.

The Dakota were not outwardly curious about the bearded one, he recalled, except for some quiet, discreet questions from several young men he had gotten to know a little. The Dakota were curious about his flintlock, however. They had heard about such a weapon, but most had never seen one. Because of it he had been taken on many hunts. Once he had brought down a buffalo with the flintlock at about a hundred paces. There was a great feast after that, which was his fondest memory of his time with the Dakota. He was sad to leave them, but it was their own stories of vast, open prairie lands to the west of the Great Muddy that had stirred a yearning deep inside him. Now he was here in this encampment, which was much like the Dakota encampment where he had stayed two winters. Although he did not know these people, he recalled that the Dakota respected these Lakota, and that was somewhat reassuring.

The bearded one knew to remain quiet for the moment. Even at his best he would be no match for even one of these warriors. Though wide awake, he was weak and his wound throbbed fiercely. He chose to feign sleep.

In the council lodge, the old men of the village sat around a low fire. Among them were the more experienced warriors and leaders, those with strong reputations. One of these was Bear Heart, Whirlwind's rival and loudest critic.

At the back was a round flat stone. On it was a small bundle of sage and a pipe. The pipe, with a blackened shale bowl and a long stem of ash wood, had already been smoked.

Although the thing being discussed was not often talked about around the council fire, there was still an air of calm in the lodge. These were men who had lived long and seen much. In the face of each man, behind the dark eyes, were the stories of many hunts and battles. Together, they faced this new concern as they had each hunt and each battle. Each man brought to it the power of his being and his experiences. As their fathers and grandfathers had done before them.

Circling Bear, with long, gray hair wrapped in otter skins, looked at Whirlwind. "I have been concerned about white men since four winters ago," he said, "when a white man almost killed my nephew. Before that happened, we had only heard about such people from others who had seen them—except for our brief encounter with one of their holy men, the black robe. The one who was angry."

Heads nodded. They all remembered the black robe.

"It is plain to me," Circling Bear went on, "that the white-skinned people are different. Their ways and their thoughts are things we do not know. So I am wondering if my nephew was wise to bring one of them into our village."

A few heads nodded in acknowledgment of Circling Bear's words.

Bear Heart, a member of the Wolf Warrior Society, was especially loud in his affirmation of Circling Bear's words. His loudness was a surprise to no one since it fit with the hard edge of anger that always seemed to be a part of him now. Even on the warpath, he was known to break the bow of any young warrior who made a mistake simply out of youthful eagerness or ignorance. "Grandfathers," he said, "I agree with those words. Until we know what they are, it would be better to think of white men as enemies. I would not bring any white man into our village. And I would have left this one with an arrow in his heart, as a sign to all the others of his kind."

A silence filled the council lodge for a few heartbeats. Everyone knew that Bear Heart's words were more a criticism of Whirlwind's deeds than they were advice for something to be done. Though never openly discussed, Bear

Heart's dislike for Whirlwind was well known among the Wolf Tail band. Since the lance of the war leader had been passed to Whirlwind, Bear Heart did not attempt to hide his anger at not having been chosen.

Stone cleared his throat and glanced briefly around the lodge, but at no one in particular. "We are one Lakota village. We are the Wolf Tail people," he began. "But the Lakota people are strong because we are many villages. Our strength comes from that. Yet it also comes from knowing about our enemies. These new people, these white men, may turn out to be bad enemies. They may turn out to be friends. But we do not know now what will happen tomorrow. And we do not know much about them, except to be careful.

"A white man who speaks our language is a very new and strange thing. I, for one, think that our war leader did the right thing to bring him here. We could learn much from this white man—if he lives. If the white men do become bad enemies, we will know something about them. It is better to be prepared, because I think there are many of these white-skinned people. And, as we all know, knowledge is a warrior's best weapon."

An old, old man named White Crane was quick to agree. "My friend is right," he said. "If more and more white-skinned men come to our lands, there will be no choice but to deal with them. We need to know if they are many or few. We need to know if they are good or bad."

Bear Heart spoke up again. "If he lives, perhaps this white man could tell us something about the holy iron kept hidden away by our war leader. Since he is a white man, he should know how to make it shoot. Perhaps he can show us that it is nothing to be afraid of."

Stone held up a hand, and held back the anger that darkened his stare. His voice was calm. "We do not sit here to make judgments about the actions of any person, man or woman, among our people," he said, as Bear Heart dropped his eyes to the fire but kept a hard set to his mouth.

Whirlwind, meanwhile, kept his silence.

"It is our purpose," Stone went on, "to look for the right road when it comes to all the tomorrows ahead of our people. And, yes, I think that the white man, and all that he is and has, may be part of tomorrow's road. The holy iron may become part of our lives because it is part of the lives of white men. And I have listened to our war leader's thoughts about the holy iron. He and I have talked of it many times over the past four winters, since he was nearly killed with one near the White Earth River. Perhaps it is time for him to speak those thoughts to all of us now."

An air of expectancy filled the lodge. A few of the old men cleared their throats. Bear Heart stood and threw a hard, challenging stare into the eyes of Whirlwind before he stalked angrily out into the night.

The war leader of the Wolf Tail Lakota stood to speak. "Grandfathers," he began, "thank you for allowing me to speak." He paused to gather his thoughts. "Four winters ago, I had to kill a white man. I approached him in friendship, and he shot his weapon at me. I did not let him shoot at me again. There was no way to know whether he was a good man or a bad man. Or a man at all, in the way we know men to be. But I do know that he took me to be a bad man, because he did not wait for even one heartbeat after he saw me before he took up his holy iron and shot it. Since that moment when death nearly took me, I have often wondered why he tried to kill me. Did he shoot at me because of what was in his heart? Or did he shoot at me because of his weapon? Did he shoot at me because he knew he could kill easily? Did he shoot at me because he felt his weapon gave him a right to kill?

"These questions are always with me. Sometimes they haunt my sleep. Still, I do not know the answers to them. Until I do, the holy iron will remain hidden."

A chorus of low but firm affirmations flowed through the lodge as Whirlwind sat back down. White Crane nodded emphatically and looked around. "We cannot forget that the Ojibway drove our people from the lake country, after they traded with the white men for holy irons. As I think of it, the holy irons turned the Ojibway from warriors into killers. Our war leader has spoken well and clearly. Perhaps we can find some answers from the white-skinned one he has brought among us—if he lives."

Whirlwind stepped out of the council lodge and walked across the camp circle to his father's fire, where the white man was being kept. He knelt to warm his hands. The autumn night had grown chilly. The war leader nodded toward the white man and spoke quietly to the three young warriors. "If he lives, I will talk with him. And if he dies . . . he dies."

Sometime in the night Yellow Earrings awoke. She pushed aside her covering robe and sat up to tend the fire. A handful of heavy twigs would assure there would be coals when dawn came, to help start the outside cooking fire.

Faint light returned inside the lodge as the twigs burned. The old woman could hear her cousin's even sleeping breaths. Outside it was quiet, except for the distant wail of a screech owl telling of the night's chill. Through the open smoke flaps above, a few flickering stars could be seen in between the lodgepoles. Yellow Earrings stared at the stars and whispered a soft prayer: "Thank you for this fine woman, my cousin, Grandfather," she said. "Thank you for making her a part of my life. The way of her life path is known only to you. But wherever you take her along that path, I ask that you always hold her in the hollow of your hand."

Three

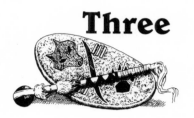

The sun was already above the horizon, but the early morning air was still crisp. Off in the far, hazy distances of new day, grouse were drumming. The encampment of the Wolf Tail band was already awake. Old ones stood or sat outside their lodges, savoring the clean coolness of the air as they watched their village stir with new beginnings. Here and there, boys took horses to the river for a first drink. Between the willows and cottonwoods on either side of the gently flowing stream, narrow clouds of mist hung just above the water. The Smoking Earth River was living up to its name.

Beneath a pile of deer-hide robes next to the lodge of Spotted Calf, there was some movement. The bearded one knew he could not feign sleep for too long. The pain in his right side had subsided to hot throbbing. He was hungry, and he wanted to find a more comfortable position without arousing curiosity.

The guards had been changed, and the three new ones appeared no less competent than the first group. A sudden awakening could be dangerous. The bearded one moaned a little, as if having a bad dream. One of the warriors glanced at him and then turned away again.

Several warriors were gathered in a small clearing just west of the village. They watched intently as Walks High tried his new bow. The target was a hand-sized piece of dry bark set against a low sandbank. Walks High was about thirty long paces away. The first arrow hit barely a finger's width above the target; the second one split the bark in two.

"*Hokahe!*" Spotted Calf was pleased.

Walks High sent four more arrows. All six shafts were grouped in a space no larger than the size of a leaf.

Standing quietly in the group of warriors, Whirlwind smiled to himself, quietly proud of his son's marksmanship. Although all the boys and men in the village were skilled with the bow, as a group the deadliest marksmen were the old men. A lifetime of shooting had elevated their skills to that level.

Walks High smiled and caressed the limbs of his stout, new bow. "It is strong and shoots a fast arrow," he said to his grandfather. "Thank you for this fine thing."

The old warrior waved a hand. "It is nothing. I am glad it works," he said. Inside, the old warrior glowed. It made the heart sing to see such skill in a young man. But even better, it was good to see that a gangly boy had grown into a tall, strong warrior—one who so resembled the old warrior's own father that Spotted Calf had insisted quietly that Whirlwind give the boy the good name of Walks High.

The old man glanced toward the group of warriors watching from the side and immediately saw the pride on Whirlwind's face. It seemed like only yesterday when Walks High, as a small boy named Swallow, had followed his father everywhere with his bow and arrows in one hand and a small war club in the other. Over the years they had become as close as a father and a son could be, closer even than Whirlwind was to Spotted Calf. They had become so close that Walks High used the same gestures as his father, and at a distance, it was sometimes hard to distinguish one from the other, except that Walks High was taller.

One evening last spring, Whirlwind had remarked to his father that his son's recklessness in battle worried him. Spotted Calf clearly remembered that moment and his reply to Whirlwind. "You caused me and your mother the same worry," he had said. "It would seem my grandson follows in his father's footsteps in many ways."

"Then I shall try to leave a clear path," Whirlwind had replied, "because he will go much further than I ever will."

Spotted Calf let the pleasant memories fade as he picked up a large dirt clod. "Get ready," he called to his grandson. He tossed the clod. It flew in an arc as high as the top of the lodgepoles, and as it went into its downward curve, it suddenly shattered into many small pieces. The flight of the arrow had been barely visible. Even as the pieces of dirt fell to the earth like hailstones, Walks High had a second arrow on the string.

The old warrior smiled. It made the heart sing to see such skill.

"Grandfather!" A thin, strident voice came from the edge of the village. It was the boy Red Legs. "Grandfather," he called, "the white man has come back to life!"

The bearded one leaned against a willow backrest, keeping a wary eye on a young warrior wielding a stone-tipped lance. "I will sit still," the man said to the warrior as he clutched his throbbing side. "Do not hurt me."

Good Hand, the warrior, kept a steady gaze on the white man's face, and the lance in his hands did not waver.

Whirlwind found his way through the gathering crowd and looked to Good Hand. "He sat up a little while ago," Good Hand explained. "He asked for a backrest. When we gave him one, he jumped to his feet. I thought he was trying to run, but he could not. He is weak. And naked."

Whirlwind's eyes smiled.

The bearded one gathered the deer-hide robe tighter around his middle, aware of the many pairs of staring eyes.

Her Good Trail came to her husband's side and handed him a breechclout, leggings, shirt, and a belt. "We all know he is male," she said. "He does have all the right parts."

Whirlwind smiled openly. He took the clothes from his wife and held them out to the white man. "If you are strong enough to walk, you can dress yourself in my lodge," he said firmly. "Then we will talk."

The bearded one took the clothes and wondered if he could walk. Even the slightest movement quickened the throbbing in his side.

Whirlwind motioned to Good Hand, and the warrior pulled back his lance and held out a hand to the white man. The bearded one accepted the offer. After the first few shaky steps, his slight dizziness subsided. With the warrior Good Hand's help, the bearded one managed not to stumble. Fortunately, Whirlwind's lodge was not far.

The curious gathered outside of Whirlwind's lodge. Inside the cozy home, Gaston de la Verendrye gnawed on an elk rib, his first meal in three days as far as he could figure. Now that he was beginning to recover, he was becoming more aware of his predicament. Being the only white man in a Lakota village made him nervous. De la Verendrye could see the crowd outside, and he guessed they were waiting to find out what Whirlwind would do with him. Strangely, though he was uncertain what would be done *about* him, he was somehow certain that nothing would be done *to* him. He might be politely asked to leave, but, based on his knowledge of the Dakota, he felt he would not be hurt. The people in one Dakota encampment, east of the Great Muddy, had been kind to him, as well as patient. The Dakota and Lakota were people of the same nation, after all. Still, he did not know these Lakota as individuals. It was possible they might not be as tolerant of a white man as some of their Dakota relatives. A quick glance toward the warrior at the back of the lodge offered no clues. The warrior's face was polite but inscrutable. There was nothing to do but wait and hope for a good outcome.

When de la Verendrye had finished eating, Whirlwind took out a pipe. He assembled it and filled the bowl with red willow bark as he studied the white man. He was the strangest guest to ever sit in this lodge; he was small and looked pitiful in Whirlwind's old buckskins.

This white man was darker than the trapper he had fought with four winters ago, though they had the same pale blue eyes. But the eyes of this white man were alive. The eyes of the other had stared lifeless toward the clouds after Whirlwind's arrow had pierced his heart. That dead white man taught Whirlwind not to trust the one now sitting across the fire.

The warrior pulled a twig from the fire, shook off the ash, and lit the pipe with the glowing ember. The pipe drew well, and Whirlwind sucked on the stem, sending smoke to the top of the lodge. Then he gazed evenly at his guest. "My friend," he said, holding up the pipe for the white man to see, "in my lodge, this is the way to the truth. You have accepted a place to sit in my lodge. You have eaten food prepared by my wife. In return, I ask for the truth. Perhaps you know something of Lakota ways, since it seems you know our language. If that is so, then you know that in the same way that the smoke from this pipe rises to the sky, the truth must rise out of us so that the Great Mystery can see it."

Gaston de la Verendrye felt weak. Although the weakness was mostly due to his wound and the lack of food and water for several days, suddenly mere uncertainty about his circumstances gave way to outright fear, making him feel even weaker. With vulnerability, images of the past surfaced.

He had had some regrets over leaving his home in France, but he had never regretted coming to this new land. The stories of a distant cousin traveling to America had stirred his blood and had given rise to his own yearnings. At first his father had ridiculed his dreams. But, in the end, he helped to book passage across the ocean for his youngest son. "Remember the parable of the prodigal son in the Scriptures," he had said. "Your inheritance, small though it is, is buying your dream. But if you do return one day, do not come home empty-handed." That had been his father's good-bye. His mother had said nothing and only brushed back an unruly lock of his hair. From the back of the cart that took him away, he had watched them fade into the distance until they blended in with the grayness of their small stone cottage—with the tiny loft which had been his place of refuge.

No one seemed to know what had happened to his distant cousin, Sieur de la Verendrye, in this new land. But Gaston de la Verendrye had not come in search of a relative. He had come to escape being a farmer and in pursuit of his own adventures, which he had found. Eight years after landing on the shores of America, he had come to the territory of the Dakota people, just southwest of the lake country. Now he watched as his Lakota host smoked the pipe. It reminded him of his first meeting with the Dakota.

Most among his own kind had nothing good to say about the people who already inhabited this new land. But, perhaps owing to his youth and innocence, Gaston de la Verendrye largely disregarded the airs of superiority so readily taken on by white men. He was intensely curious about the native people, who seemed so at ease in the wilderness. Three years ago he had watched from the deck of a barge on the Mississippi as a hunter stalked and killed a deer on the shore. The hunter had not disturbed a leaf and had made an unerring bow shot from a distance of over sixty cloth yards. De la Verendrye learned later that the hunter was probably one of the Dakota people. Four days after that he collected his wages from the barge master and headed into Dakota territory.

Taking a chance that the Dakota would be more curious than antagonistic toward a lone white man, he killed a deer and carried it to the edge of an encampment. After several warriors surrounded him, he carefully gave the sign that he had come to trade.

A few, silent, anxious moments later, one of the warriors stepped forward and nodded.

"I will trade the deer," de la Verendrye signed.

The warrior nodded again.

"For a place to sleep," de la Verendrye signed again. "And to learn your tongue."

The group of warriors exchanged amused grins. Then the first warrior motioned for de la Verendrye to follow him. Only then did de la Verendrye see the other warriors, nearly a dozen, emerge from concealment and lower their drawn bows. And only then did he realize that his heart was pounding heavily.

Two years later, he said good-bye to them with a heavy heart. He regretted leaving, but it was their stories about the wide-open prairies west of the Great Muddy River and others of their own kind living there which had stirred de la Verendrye's yearning to further explore. But as the warrior White Hare reminded him, ". . . when we leave, we say 'I will see you again.' "

The Dakota had given him a home, and he had learned their language. After that, he began to appreciate the meaning of their stories much more, especially the stories about the lands of their western relatives the Lakota west of the Great Muddy River. The Lakota were buffalo hunters and formidable horse-mounted warriors. Now he sat face-to-face with a Lakota warrior, one to whom he owed his life.

De la Verendrye was afraid.

He suddenly realized that the warrior was holding out the pipe toward him and quickly took it before his host might think him ill mannered. Sucking on it nervously, he nearly choked on the smoke. "I will speak the truth," he said to his host.

"Good," replied the warrior. "I am called Whirlwind. I do not think you remember when I first told you my name."

"The name my father gave me was Gaston," the white man began. "Our family name is de la Verendrye. At sixteen winters I left home. My father arranged for me to travel across the great water, so I left my home in France. That was ten winters ago. Eight winters ago I came to the plains. I worked on a flatboat on the Grandfather River. I left and came to the lands of the Dakota and the Nakota. It was among the Dakota that I found a home, and after two winters with them, I learned their language. It is much like yours, except for some words. The people I lived with called themselves Isanti. They are a good-hearted people."

Whirlwind nodded. "Yes. The People Who Make Knives. I met some of those relatives as a boy. We camped near the Great Muddy. One of my cousins married into their circle and lived among them for many years. He came back after his wife died."

After a quiet moment, Whirlwind brought the conversation back to the present. "I found you in a bad way," he said. "I thought you were dead. How did it happen that you were shot?"

De la Verendrye cleared his throat and gathered his wits. He rubbed his beard and began to take up his story again. "I crossed the ice on the Great Muddy River before the great thaw was over. It was the Moon of Snow Blindness. By the time the thaw was over I had a camp just north of the Running Water River. There I met a man from my country across the great water. His name was Bruneaux. He was robbed by Omaha, he said. We both wanted to travel west and thought we could help one another. I began to trust Bruneaux. We had been coming west for nearly seven moons. Then one day he went hunting with my holy iron but sneaked back into camp. I heard a noise and turned to see him aiming my own holy iron at me. After that I can remember nothing—until I saw you looking down at me." De la Verendrye paused.

Whirlwind gazed at the white man through narrowed eyes. "Why would your friend shoot you?" he wondered.

De la Verendrye carefully leaned against a backrest. Each new throb of pain asked the same question. He shook his head. "I do not know. But I do know that I judged him to be a better man than he was. We were from the same homeland."

Whirlwind smiled slightly. "There are some among my own people who do not think I am worthy of the place I have among them. Yet I do not fear for my life because of their thinking. Your kind must have strange ways."

De la Verendrye nodded. "Yes. It would seem so."

"Tell me," the warrior said quickly, "was there some . . . trouble between you and your friend?"

"If there was, I do not know what it was. The only thing I did not like about him was his boasting. He is a very big man. Strong, too. He boasted many times about how he could scare other men. Maybe he was trying to scare me. I do not know."

"Then you must own something that he wanted," Whirl-wind surmised.

De la Verendrye deliberated for a moment. "Furs," he replied, "and two horses."

Whirlwind contemplated the white man's answer for some moments. "Yes. Horses are worth much. And I learned that furs are also. To some men. But there is another thing."

"My holy iron," said the white man.

Whirlwind glanced at Her Good Trail as she busied herself quietly and then gazed inwardly at something known only to him. "Yes," he finally said in a low voice. "The holy iron. It seems to bring out things . . . in some men."

De la Verendrye looked quickly out the door, remembering the remark he had heard from one of the young warriors guarding him last evening—that this warrior had a flintlock somewhere. He cleared his throat softly. "A holy iron is worth much," he said. "I trapped for many furs in a land called Kentucky to trade for one—the one Bruneaux used to shoot me."

"You traded for that weapon honorably, it seems. The

man who shot you with it did not take it honorably. What made him do it? Is there something about the holy iron that I do not know of?"

The white man was puzzled. "I do not know," he said.

Whirlwind looked long at the man. His story did have the ring of truth. But could he trust him? He thought not.

White men were an unknown thing. Even the enemies of the Lakota were something known. The Arikara. The Kiowa. They could be expected to act in a certain way, do certain things. This could not be said about white men.

Were they many? Or were they few? Did they have other powerful weapons like the holy iron? Whirlwind measured the man across the fire. As the old men had said, perhaps these things could be learned from this lost one. But he would have to be closely watched.

"I will ask some of the young men to build you a small shelter," he told the bearded one. "You may stay among us until you are well. You need to rest so you can heal your wound. And then sometime we will talk again."

De la Verendrye looked at Her Good Trail. "Thank you for the food," he said. "And for the clothes." She smiled but kept her eyes on her work.

"You will stay in our lodge until your shelter is ready," Whirlwind added. "It will not take long to build."

Bear Heart inspected the arrow he had just finished making. He yielded to a sense of disgust and threw it to the ground, pushing himself against his willow backrest. The arrow's sharp stone point sliced into the ground, and it quivered for barely a moment before a hand reached down to grab it. A dark form blocked the sun, and a deep voice spoke. "Well, my friend. Clearly something bothers you."

The man's features were hidden in shade from the low sun just behind his head, but Bear Heart recognized the voice. It was Caught the Eagle, a Mniconju Lakota. One of the People Who Plant by the Water. He had married into the Wolf Tail band and had become a strong voice in the Wolf Warrior Society. Bear Heart nodded a greeting and waved a hand toward the backrest close to the door of his lodge. Caught the Eagle took the seat and handed the new arrow to its owner. "Could it be that you are not pleased with the old men and their thinking about the visitor among us?"

Bear Heart nodded slightly, taking a moment to let his anger fade before he spoke. "It is good that you came," he said to the older man. "There are things we must talk about."

Caught the Eagle leaned back and waited. He was the guest at Bear Heart's lodge. The polite thing was always to let the host speak what was in his heart and mind. He could see the anger leaving Bear Heart's face, making him look somehow younger than his forty winters. Sometimes when the hardness left his face, his eyes grew bright like those of a playful boy. But Caught the Eagle knew that those times came less and less often. The dark scowl that clouded Bear Heart's face these days hid the pleasantness of his features and showed the color of his heart. The warrior Good Hand had once told Caught the Eagle how Bear Heart had ridiculed Spotted Horse one time until the younger man hung his head in shame and sneaked away from the war party—all because Spotted Horse's mount had stepped into a prairie dog hole covered over with thick grass. Such a thing could happen to anyone, at any time, a thing that, in Caught the Eagle's thinking, was not worth hurting anyone. But hurting, shaming words seemed to be Bear Heart's way now. Still, Caught the Eagle remembered a time when Bear Heart had been one of the most thoughtful and patient men he had ever known. Perhaps there was still some of that alive in him. He glanced at this friend through narrowed eyes and hoped that he was right.

Both men were dressed alike, in a tanned buckskin shirt decorated about the shoulders and down the sleeves with rows of braided porcupine quills, leggings, breechclout, and summer moccasins. Like all members of the Wolf Warrior Society, both wore their hair loose, although Caught the Eagle's hair was slightly longer, reaching just below his waistline. Bear Heart had two thin braids, one just ahead of each ear.

Caught the Eagle heard a slight rustle as Light Haired Woman, Bear Heart's young wife, approached them with a bowl of tea in each hand. She smiled shyly and handed one to each man, but to the guest first. Then, just as quietly, she left them.

Bear Heart's eyes darted back and forth as he sipped his drink. "It is not my place to question the thinking of the old men," he said to Caught the Eagle. "But I did tell them that I would have left the white man with an arrow through the heart—if he has one."

The older warrior nodded. He knew Bear Heart had not invited him here to talk about the old men. "I would have done the same as our war leader," he replied evenly.

Bear Heart glanced sharply at his guest. His eyes flashed, yet he spoke calmly. "Perhaps I am the only man foolish enough not to fear the white man." A slight smile tugged at the corners of his mouth.

Caught the Eagle did not stop the smile that came to his lips. "I do not think you are foolish. I do know that you have courage. But I have seen a fire in your eyes ever since High Hawk passed the lance to Whirlwind. You know it is our way to honor the wisdom of the old ones. And it was they who asked High Hawk to pass the lance of the war leader to Whirlwind. Perhaps the old ones know that the fire in your eyes is because of the anger you always carry in your heart. So what are we to speak of? The white man or our war leader?"

"Both!" replied Bear Heart, ignoring the rebuke from the other man. "Yet the more important thing is what will happen to our people because Whirlwind brought the white man to us."

"What can one wounded white man do?"

Bear Heart looked around at the circle of lodges. It was near sundown, and people were busy finishing up various chores before daylight faded. Night sentinels had already taken their positions around the encampment. Some warriors were leading war horses in from the corrals to be tied at picket pins next to the lodge doors. The warrior looked at his guest and shrugged. "Perhaps it is not what the white man can do but what someone else does not do."

Caught the Eagle stared down into his tea. He knew what Bear Heart was driving at—the holy iron.

"Tell me, my friend," Bear Heart went on, "where do you think Whirlwind's holy iron is? In his lodge? Hidden somewhere in a gully?"

Caught the Eagle waved a hand. "What a man does with anything that belongs to him should matter only to him."

"Yes! I agree! But a holy iron is not a simple thing, like a shirt or a knife." Bear Heart gestured with clenched fists. "A holy iron is a strong thing. It is power. A man would be foolish not to use that power. We do have enemies. A war leader should remember that. If the old ones had chosen me as war leader, I would use the holy iron to show our enemies how powerful we are! I would not hide it and act like a dog with my tail tucked under!"

Caught the Eagle finished his tea and placed the empty bowl at Bear Heart's feet. "Our enemies already know we are powerful. We have shown them that without a holy iron. And we must not forget that our way of being warriors was handed down to us from a time long before we ever knew there was such a thing as a holy iron. I remember what my father taught me—that the real power of a warrior comes from within. In my mind, a holy iron can never do that for anyone. Tell your wife she makes good tea," he said, rising. He paused a moment before leaving and cleared his throat. "If I wanted to know about Whirlwind's holy iron, I would go talk with Whirlwind."

Bear Heart's eyes narrowed as a darkness passed through them. He smiled. "I will tell my wife that you thanked her for the tea," he said.

As Caught the Eagle walked away from Bear Heart's lodge, he could feel the angry warrior's eyes on his back.

It was sundown, and the bottoms of the clouds in the western half of the sky were splashed with red hues. The Wolf Tail village was beginning to shed itself of a busy day when one of the sentinels to the north announced people coming in. It was the family of High Hawk, returning from their visit among relatives living to the north along the Great Muddy River. High Hawk was once the war leader, but he had passed the lance to Whirlwind some five winters ago.

Among the returning family was a slender young woman named Sun Rise Woman. She was a favored young daughter, just past her sixteenth winter—one who had cast hopeful glances in the direction of Walks High. Those glances had not gone unnoticed by the young warrior. After all, Sun Rise Woman was one of the most beautiful young women among the Wolf Tail Lakota, indeed among all the Lakota. Slender and delicate, with glistening dark eyes and a smile that could chase reason from even the most sensible man, she was the object of much yearning. But it was only with Walks High that she stood under the elk-hide courting robe, at the door of her mother and father's lodge.

Both families were in favor of such a match. Sun Rise Woman's mother and grandmother were among the Only Ones, an honored women's society whose members had married and stayed with one man. And the Only Ones did not take another husband after losing their first. A young

woman from such an upbringing would add much to the
family of a young warrior who would, one day, be an important man. The old ones smiled as they talked of the prospects
of such a match, one which would bring two honored
families together. Each family's go-betweens had visited
several times now, and the bride price of twenty horses had
been agreed to. A time and a place for the wedding would
be the next thing for the go-betweens to discuss.

Young Red Legs and his best friend Windy Boy carried
the news of High Hawk's return to the corrals. There, Walks
High, Red Lance, and Lone Elk were teaching a tall, sturdy
colt to respond to a jaw rope.

"Well," teased Lone Elk, "I suppose I should go home
and get my good elk robe ready. There will be a long line of
hopefuls in front of High Hawk's lodge. Is there anything
you want me to tell her, once she comes to meet me under
the courting robe?" he asked, glancing at Walks High.

Walks High smiled. "Tell her she is worth more horses
than Lone Elk can ever own."

The friends laughed together, for it was known among
them that a bride price had already been negotiated. The
whispering among the women told that a new buffalo-hide
lodge was nearly finished. And a new batch of lodgepoles,
peeled and drying in the sun since midsummer, was ready.
On the day that Sun Rise Woman and Walks High would be
joined, the women of the Wolf Tail village would raise the
new lodge for them, and there would be feasting and much
dancing. But that day was yet to come, and there was still
time for Walks High's friends to tease him.

Walks High called the two young boys over and put a
soft, snow-white plume feather in Red Legs's hand. "Take
this to Sun Rise Woman," he instructed. "Tell her I am
happy she has returned." Red Legs and Windy Boy dashed
off to perform their important chore, while the three
friends led the colt back into the pens. From there they

could hear the pleasant exchanges as High Hawk's family rode into camp.

Just inside the doorway of Whirlwind's lodge, the bearded one woke up. He had slept for most of a day. Though not yet fully awake, he could hear the commotion outside. Someone had returned from a journey, he guessed from what he could hear. As he was about to sit up, Her Good Trail and a young woman entered the lodge. They went to the back and grabbed two painted rawhide cases. The bearded one turned his head in time to see Her Good Trail untie a braid of wild turnips hanging from a pole.

De la Verendrye waited for the women to leave before he sat up. He silently cursed Bruneaux as sharp spasms of pain accompanied his every move. He listened to the voices outside. As he had surmised, someone had returned from a journey, and a feast would be prepared. The Frenchman smiled, remembering some of the stories he had heard on the Mississippi: The Indians of the plains were savage and bloodthirsty—godless people who would sooner kill a white man than look at one. But his years among the Dakota had taught him otherwise. They had accepted him and let him in among them, though they could easily have killed him that first day he had come to their encampment. Then there was the Pawnee woman who had been taken captive by Dakota warriors during a raid into the south country. She had been made to live with an old woman, to help care for her. But in time, when the Pawnee woman was given a chance to return to her own people, she declined. After her adopted mother died, two Dakota warriors escorted the Pawnee woman safely back to her own country.

A sudden bolt of pain reminded him that it was a white man—a countryman—who had tried to kill him. It was a Lakota warrior who had saved his life. Now, in this Lakota encampment, a feast would be prepared for no other reason than the safe return of some of their own people.

De la Verendrye winced as he twisted to look around the interior of the lodge. Then he noticed a small, dark object at the top of the inner dew liner, where the turnip braid had been. A cold feeling went through him. He realized what he was seeing. Unbelievably, it was the butt of a long muzzle-loader!

He thought back to the conversation between the young warriors at the fire last night. Whirlwind had captured a gun some years ago. But he had never used it, choosing, instead, to hide it. It would make sense that he would hide the weapon in his own lodge.

De la Verendrye glanced out the door. The noise and activity were on the south end of the encampment. For the moment, a wounded white man was apparently of little importance. He gritted his teeth against the pain and went to the back of the lodge.

It was better than he could imagine. The muzzleloader was encased in hide and tied securely to the lodgepole. He felt it from the outside, through the dew liner. It hung muzzle down, and at the bottom he felt what he thought was a horn for powder and a bag of shot. His breath came rapidly as his eyes flashed and darted.

The Frenchman crawled back to his bed near the door. He briefly wondered why a warrior like Whirlwind did not use that weapon. Perhaps, he thought, he does not know how to load and fire it. He had to think of a plan, a way to take the weapon without being noticed. Bruneaux, he surmised, was still travel-ing west. He would be thinking that de la Verendrye was dead and, therefore, not expecting anyone to follow him.

The bearded one glanced at the gun again. Things had changed, it seemed, in his favor. Bruneaux would pay, and soon. There was the means, hanging in the lodge of a Lakota warrior, to make that back-shooter pay. Anyone who valued a gun above a man's life deserved to be punished. All that was necessary for revenge now was patience, and a plan.

He looked out the door again and saw a slender girl with shiny, black braids. She was the most beautiful female de la Verendrye had ever seen. He sat up involuntarily, in spite of the pain, pulled by the girl's beauty. De la Verendrye stared unabashedly and allowed himself a reckless thought. "Perhaps," he whispered, "there is a reason for me to stay here. After I take care of Bruneaux!"

In the dense undergrowth, a long stone's throw from a sentinel standing far to the west of the Wolf Tail encampment, a pair of hard eyes stared toward the maze of lodgepoles. It was all he could see of the village, but he knew that the man he had been tracking was there. Somewhere in that village, among those heathens.

De la Verendrye! A young pup with his holier-than-thou ways! He should be dead! His bag of Spanish gold coins should be hanging from Bruneaux's belt!

"I will have your gold, my onetime friend," hissed the man coiled in the shadowy undergrowth. "I have your musket, and it will help me get your gold! Hiding among them heathens will do you no good! No good at all!"

Bruneaux sighted the flintlock on the head of the Lakota sentinel. A smile creased his dirty face as he exulted in the knowledge of what the weapon could do to that Indian's head. He lowered it and crawled away. Bruneaux had no desire, for the moment, to kill the sentinel. It was de la Verendrye he wanted. And the gold.

Four

I t was near the end of the Moon of Falling Leaves, and the breezes were sharp and cold. Days were growing shorter. There was a change in the winds and a restlessness in the village of the Wolf Tail Lakota. It was nearly time to move to the winter camp. The meadows and hillsides around this summer encampment were mostly grazed down by the large horse herd. Moreover, though this valley allowed for cooling breezes to move freely and provide relief during summer heat, it also allowed winter's winds to move just as freely.

Winter camp was only a few days' travel south, along the same river. There, where Spring Creek flowed into the Smoking Earth River, were tall, pine-covered hills which blocked the winds and offered shelter for black-tailed and white-tailed deer. And south from there, in the sandhill country, was a favorite wintering area for a large herd of buffalo.

Each season had its own face, its own dangers, and its own pleasures. The Wolf Tail people were ready for the winter. Good grass had fattened the horses, and the autumn hunts had been successful. Winter was a time for long visits and storytelling while the blizzards howled outside. It was a time for cleansing, to prepare the spirit for the renewal of the cycle in spring. The old ones talked about these things as they watched the last of autumn slip away. And everyone felt the change in the winds because it touched the wanderer in them—that part of them that not only wandered over the land, but through the seasons of their lives. Just as their footsteps wandered over the land, so their spirits wandered through their own individual journeys. Some crawled, some walked, and some flew.

Sun Rise Woman and her grandmother, Walks Far, were north of the village digging medicine roots. From a rise they could see the circle of lodges on the high flat just west of the river's bend. The old woman looked up at the sky and knew it was time to go home.

"We should have brought a horse," Sun Rise Woman said. "We have come far from the camp."

Her grandmother smiled. "I would much rather walk than try to mount a horse," she said. "Walking is one of the things this old body can still do."

Sun Rise Woman returned her grandmother's smile. "Yes, you are right. But perhaps we have come too far," she said, glancing toward a thick grove of oaks off to the northwest. "We have come far past the sentinels."

The old woman finished wrapping her bundle of roots and took her granddaughter's arm. "I'm ready," she said. "We'll be home before the sun sets."

Just beyond the eastern edge of the village, the warrior Bear Heart stared intently into the face of the bearded Frenchman. De la Verendrye was dozing against a willow backrest just inside his brush shelter. The warrior tossed a pebble against his chest.

"I am called Bear Heart," the man told de la Verendrye.

The Frenchman could only sit and wait to see what would happen. He had seen the dark stares this warrior had cast in his direction several times during the past six days. Bear Heart had the same air of strength and confidence as the war leader Whirlwind, and four eagle feathers tied into his hair told the story of his courage on the warpath. But de la Verendrye also detected arrogance in his demeanor.

"I hear you understand my language," Bear Heart went on. "But I do not care about that." He paused, keeping a steady gaze on the Frenchman's face. "There is something else you know, and for that, I will make a trade with you."

De la Verendrye was puzzled. "What do you mean?" he wanted to know.

The warrior's eyes narrowed. "Four winters ago, our war leader captured a white man's holy iron. Since then, he has kept it hidden and has not used it. I do not think he knows how to use that weapon."

De la Verendrye blinked nervously. The drift of this warrior's words made him visualize a man standing on the edge of a cliff. He was that man.

"I know that you know how to use a holy iron," Bear Heart continued. "And you will teach me."

The Frenchman cleared his throat. "Do you have a holy iron?"

"Soon I will have one. I will trade ten horses for Whirlwind's holy iron."

"And he will trade?"

A hard look flashed across the warrior's black eyes. "It will be difficult to turn down ten horses," he said. "But I offer you something even more, to teach me how to use the holy iron."

De la Verendrye was barely breathing.

The black eyes of Bear Heart bore into the Frenchman. "Your life," he said. "You will teach me how to use the holy iron, and I will let you live."

The Frenchman listened to the soft rustle of the departing warrior's footsteps. The pain in his side intensified. But considering Bear Heart's life-and-death proposition, it seemed minor. By the time de la Verendrye finally glanced toward the edge of the encampment, the warrior was nowhere to be seen. But his words still echoed in the white man's mind.

Since he had moved to the shelter built for him on the east edge of the village, he had been considering how to get his hands on the flintlock in Whirlwind's lodge. Now, if Bear Heart was able to trade for the weapon, de la Verendrye's hopes for revenge were gone. But he somehow felt that Whirlwind would not be easily swayed by ten or twenty horses.

Though his wound was healing, he was still not strong enough to travel, especially on foot. And even if he were, he was not equipped to survive on his own. His only weapon was a stone knife Her Good Trail had given him, to cut up the dried meat she had also given him. Survival itself would be moment to moment without proper weapons. Eluding any pursuers, like Bear Heart, would be very difficult. Furthermore, de la Verendrye remembered how a bear had mauled one of the hunters from the flatboat on the Mississippi. For the moment de la Verendrye was trapped here and could see no way out.

A pair of cold, gray eyes peered at the two women as they walked slowly past a shadowy thicket. Bruneaux had heard voices and stayed motionless behind a clump of soapweeds. Thoughts of finishing off de la Verendrye temporarily vanished as he caught a full glimpse of the younger woman. The girl's beauty confused him for a moment, and all he could do was burrow into the tall grass behind the soapweeds to stay out of sight.

Bruneaux had seen several Indian women, but none had been nearly this beautiful. A girl this beautiful had to be important to someone, more important than de la Verendrye was to the people in the girl's village.

A plan began to take shape. Perhaps a trade could be arranged—the girl for de la Verendrye. No! The girl for de la Verendrye's gold! First, he had to capture the girl and the old woman. They were moving off now and approaching a rise. Beyond that rise the land was too open to seize them, so he had to cut them off before they reached that rise.

Sun Rise Woman heard a muffled grunt and turned her head in time to see the dark shape hurtling toward her. Her shout of warning was stifled by a smothering hand which clamped over her mouth.

Walks Far felt smothering pressure on her back as a foot pressed her hard to the ground. From the corner of her eye she could see Sun Rise Woman's feet kicking at the air as she struggled with whoever held them both. A large foot in the grass next to the old woman's face wore a moccasin that had not been made by Lakota hands. The end of a long weapon touched the old woman's head.

"Grandchild," the old woman said softly, "do not fight. Be still."

Sun Rise Woman knew that the long dark weapon pointed at her grandmother's head was a holy iron. Walks High had described such a thing to her. She ceased struggling. Without a sound, her captor lowered her easily and pushed her down beside her grandmother.

Bruneaux took a step away from the two women and held a finger up. "Shh! Quiet!" he hissed. "I do not want to hurt you, but I will if you cry out!"

Sun Rise Woman helped her grandmother sit up. They both stared at the hunched-over man pointing the weapon at them. He had a large, round face covered by a thick beard. He wore dark, sweat-stained buckskins, and he was big—bigger than any man in the Wolf Tail village. It was easy to see the strength in his thick arms and legs, but it was his wild, gray eyes that held more menacing, unspoken threats. Although the women could not understand his words, they could feel the cold spirit in the dark figure standing over them. They knew who he was. They had heard that the wounded one brought back by Whirlwind had been nearly killed by another white man. This white man!

Sun Rise Woman stifled her fear and moved closer to her grandmother. The white man was motioning and pointing to some trees back up the trail they had just followed. He wanted them to move.

"On your feet! Get up!"

Walks Far squeezed her granddaughter's hand. "He wants us to do something," she whispered. "Stand up, I think."

"Shh! Hurry now!" Bruneaux glanced nervously toward the encampment, and motioned again toward the trees.

The old woman softened her whispers even more. "Stand up and walk. Be strong! One of the sentinels is sure to see us or hear something."

The women stood and started walking cautiously in the direction the white man was pointing.

"That's it! That's it! Keep walking! We shall find a place to hide you! Then . . . !" He suddenly realized he had to consider several necessary steps in the chain of events he had just set in motion, such as where to hide his captives, how to contact the people in the camp, and how to tell them of his captives. Jumbled and unconnected thoughts whirled in his mind, but there was no turning back. He shoved the women to move them along faster.

Walks Far knew that the further they went away from the village, the more hopeless their situation would be. If something happened now, there would be a chance her granddaughter could be saved. The coldness of this white man's spirit was extremely frightening, and the old woman knew he could do unspeakable things. Suddenly, Walks Far squeezed the girl's hand and ducked sharply off to the left. She was able to gain a few precious steps before the white man reacted.

Bruneaux muttered in surprise. The old woman was running back toward the camp. She was trying to warn someone! He raised his weapon and took aim. At about the same instant he realized that firing the weapon would be unwise, he heard the girl gasp. His huge fist caught her on the jawbone, and she bounced once as she hit the ground, unconscious. Then he turned and caught up to the old woman in a few strides. He swung the flintlock and hit the old woman just behind an ear. The weapon's thunder-like blast tore through the trees and echoed down the river valley. In his excitement, he had squeezed the trigger!

For a confused moment he stared down at the body of the old woman. Her eyes stared blankly into the grass.

The boom of a holy iron echoed through the valley of the Smoking Earth River. For a few heartbeats, it brought everything to a stop in the encampment of the Wolf Tail Lakota. Faces turned northward toward the sound—a sound not unlike thunder, yet different. Women instinctively gathered children to them while glancing uncertainly at one another.

The warriors reacted in a heartbeat. Whirlwind was out of his lodge before the last echo died away.

"This way! This way!" A sentinel to the north shouted toward the village and sprinted down a slope in the direction of the sudden thunder-like clap.

"Wolf Warriors!" Whirlwind shouted. "Take your weapons and ride to the north! Everyone else, stay and guard the camp!" Many members of the Wolf Warrior Society were mounted before the war leader's shouts faded, since most already had their war horses close by. Twelve warriors galloped from the village, each of them carrying a lance, war club, buffalo-hide shield, a bow, and a quiver of arrows. Behind them, other mounted warriors began forming a circle around the camp. Old warriors also gathered their weapons and stood among the women and children, ready to escort them to safety at the first sign of a direct assault. Outside the camp, sentinels stayed in their hiding places, looking for the enemy and ready to spread the alarm.

Sun Rise Woman thought she was in a deep, black hole, struggling to reach a faint, faraway light. She felt herself being lifted and then dropped across something hard. The darkness faded a little, but the pain in her head throbbed like a crashing drumbeat. She realized she was hanging head down across the withers of a horse. Her lip was already swelling from the sharp blow which had snuffed out her scream, and she could taste blood in her mouth.

She caught a glimpse of the man as he mounted the horse. His close-set gray eyes were wild with fright and confusion. Fear and anger mingled with her pain as she stared at her captor. The image of her grandmother suddenly running away was frozen in her memory. What had happened to her?

Bruneaux whipped the horse into a gallop. He had turned the other bay loose, hoping to fool any pursuers. The loose bay, with lead rope dangling, followed for a time and then stopped. Bruneaux was riding the taller and faster of the matched bays he had taken from de la Verendrye. His only intent was to get as far away from that village as fast as the horse could gallop. There would be pursuers, he was certain.

Bear Heart and Whirlwind were the first to spot the body of Walks Far, the mother of High Hawk. Even before Whirlwind dismounted and knelt at her side, he knew she was dead. The war leader stood and looked toward the young warrior Good Hand.

"Nephew," he called. "I must ask you to do a difficult thing."

Good Hand looked at the body of the old woman and nodded. "I will take the news to High Hawk and his family."

Bear Heart dismounted and gently closed the old woman's eyes. Then with a murderous glare, he looked to the north. "No honorable enemy kills old women," he hissed. "We will find the hateful thing who has done this."

Whirlwind looked again at the gash on the side of the old woman's head. "She was not shot with a holy iron," he pointed out. "But we all heard one go off. Perhaps someone else has been hurt or killed. It would be wise to look around."

The war leader stayed with the woman's body as the other warriors quickly scattered themselves about. Walks High rode up and dismounted, his face tight with worry. "This grandmother always has Sun Rise Woman with her," he said. "It is not like her to be this far from camp alone."

"The others are searching around now," Whirlwind told his son. "We will wait and see what they find."

Walks High nodded grimly, keeping himself under control and trying not to think the worst.

A young warrior, one of the sentinels, came running through the trees. Spent and breathless, he stared at the body as he caught his breath. "Uncle," he finally said to Whirlwind. "I heard a scream . . . and then that noise. After that, hoofbeats to the north. Two horses. But I could not see anything."

The young warrior suddenly recognized the old woman and looked as if he wanted to cry. "You have done well," the war leader told him.

The young warrior shook his head, tears in his eyes. "If I had been more watchful, perhaps she would not be dead."

"In that case," replied Whirlwind, "we are all to blame. But we must remind ourselves that death is a part of life. All the blaming in the world will not change that."

The young warrior knelt quietly down beside the body of the old woman. He gently touched her gray head. "Grandmother," he whispered, "this is not the way for one like you to leave this world."

Good Hand returned with the High Hawk family, and with the news that Sun Rise Woman and her grandmother had left sometime after midday to dig medicine roots.

Walks High looked helplessly toward the north. Whirl-wind leaned toward his son and spoke softly. "She is alive . . . or we would have found her body, too."

Whirlwind and Bear Heart gathered the warriors. One of them had caught a bay horse with its front legs entangled in its lead rope. Another had found a set of tracks, indicating that one horse was moving north at a gallop.

Whirlwind spoke to the warriors: "We must prepare to move out quickly," he said. "Four warriors will go east, staying north of the river. Four will go west, and four will go north." He glanced at Bear Heart. "It would be good if you could pick three and go east."

Bear Heart nodded.

Whirlwind looked toward another Wolf Warrior, Caught the Eagle. "You know the country to the west," he said. "I do not want this enemy to escape by turning back to the south."

Caught the Eagle nodded. There was fire in his eyes. Walks Far had given his oldest daughter her name. "Cousin," he said, "he will not."

"I will go north," announced Whirlwind. "My son and my nephews Lone Elk and Red Lance can ride with me, if they choose. Everyone should be prepared for several days of hard riding."

The High Hawk family gently loaded their grandmother onto drag poles. As an elk robe was pulled over her face, Long Shawl and Walks Straight, High Hawk's wife and youngest daughter, began to weep. Their deep sobs and piercing wails were as much for the lost daughter as they were for the gentle old woman. And every warrior who heard hardened his heart against a faceless enemy and resolved to be the one to catch him . . . despite the cost.

Solemn faces met the small, sad procession as it entered the encampment. More women added their voices and gathered around the mourning family. The drag horse was pulled to a halt at the High Hawk lodge. Nearby, Yellow Earrings came out with a robe already draped over her head. When the warrior Good Hand had ridden to the High Hawk home, with the burden of his chore easily seen on his face, she knew his news was about her cousin.

Yellow Earrings wept. Her soft sobs belied the searing grief in her soul. Tears streamed down, following the deep lines in her face like a river following the depressions in the land. She gently pushed her way through the other weeping women until she came to the hide-covered body of her cousin. Reaching under the hide, she took an already cold hand into her own. "Oh, Cousin! Do not hurry when you reach the other side. Wait for me! We will travel that road together as well."

The bay was spent. There was no choice but to rest him. Bruneaux coaxed the horse into the shade of a high cutbank along a towering ridge. It was a good vantage point from which he could see clearly in three directions. He dismounted, tossed the girl against the bank, and tied her wrists and ankles together. Satisfied that she could not run, he sat back to look at her.

She was young and slender, and with the darkest eyes Bruneaux had yet seen on an Indian woman. He guessed that she had not yet known a man. But his dark thoughts were pushed aside by the confusion of the moment.

He glanced back down the long slope. There was no one following his trail. "I thought there would be a regiment of savages on my tail by now," he said to the girl, not caring that she could not understand him. There was fear in her eyes as she watched his every move.

He climbed up on the ridge above the bank and looked to the south. Except for a few antelope off to the southwest, nothing was moving. He watched for a time and then jumped back down into the shade. Confusion and uncertainty overpowered him so suddenly that he was frozen into a dark, motionless coil. Indecision stopped his hand in midair, as he started to scratch his beard. After several moments, a plaintive bleat came from his mouth. His eyes blinked rapidly for a time. Only now, as he sat in the shade of the cutbank, did the gravity of his predicament take hold. And, at the same time, he also suddenly realized that he did not know what to do about it. A breeze surged up from the crest of the ridge to the north and past the white man, the girl, and the horse. A little ways to the east, it culminated in a small but furious whirlwind. The dust stinging his eyes shook the man from his lethargy.

Not knowing what else to do, he stood and walked to the horse, which was still panting with his head hanging nearly to the ground. Bruneaux had no comfort for the worn-out animal. From the skirt of the saddle he untied the powder horn and shot bag. There had not been time to reload the gun, after he accidentally squeezed the trigger, smashing the old woman's head.

Bruneaux returned to the shade and looked at the girl. "Because of you there could be a regiment of savages on my tail," he said. "But maybe you will have some use after all. If you be important to someone, and I wager you are, then I hold the odds! Someone may come for you, I wager." He crawled toward her, and she shrank back from him. "If they do come, likely they'll be moving careful. They have to be, 'less they don't give warm spit about what happens to you. But I have a feeling that you are very important to someone. They will be very careful, and that gives me the strong hand." He reached out and stroked a long braid lying across her chest. She recoiled from his touch. "And I will win! I have the thing to do it—this!" He raised the flintlock and stroked her shoulder with it. "Then, maybe I will take you with me, after I shoot one or two of your heathen kin. Maybe you be Bruneaux's woman!"

Bruneaux leaned back and loosed a self-satisfied chuckle. His own sudden outburst of thin logic and the girl's reaction to him bolstered his shaky bravado. With a sense of confidence, he carefully checked the weapon before he reloaded.

The flintlock was his lifeline. Only gold gave him more of a sense of power. But a gun was a way to have gold, and other things as well. He had been without one for a time after someone had sneaked into his night camp and took his. Omaha, most likely, since he had been near their country. Or Pawnee, maybe. But now he had a gun again, and a horse. He was powerful again.

"I think we will head northeast," he said to the girl. "Up into Canada, maybe. I can do trapping up there, if them fur traders are still there. They be English, but they pay good I hear. Yes. It will be Canada. Bruneaux will go to Canada, with his gun and his woman."

Sun Rise Woman could not understand his words, but she knew he had lost his mind. For certain, he had not bathed in many days. She was almost as repelled by his smell as she was afraid of those wild, gray eyes.

She massaged her swollen lip from the inside with the tip of her tongue and could still taste blood. It made her fear rise again, but she struggled to look past it. Her grandmother was safe, she hoped. No doubt she would have shown Walks High's father where the white man had jumped them. That meant that there would be warriors following the tracks of the white man's horse. Perhaps they were all around this ridge even now.

Bruneaux climbed back up the bank to survey the area. It was rough country and a hard climb up the long slopes which converged in a river valley. But he had gained the flats now, and the hills were not as steep.

He was about to climb down when he detected movement just below the crest of a ridge far to the south. A dark spot shifted against the gray slope, moving steadily upward. Then the spot split in two, then three, then four.

Bruneaux knew they were from the girl's village. He slammed the ground with his fist and cursed, startling the horse.

Sun Rise Woman stared at the man and stifled her gasp. They were here! She quietly strained against the cords around her wrists and ankles, but they were too tight to escape. Silently she slid away from the white man and deftly scooped up loose dirt with her hands in order to help when the fighting started. Sun Rise Woman curled up against the cutbank, hiding her handful of dirt behind her knees.

Bruneaux cautiously peeked over the bank. He watched to see if there were more than four riders. No more appeared, but as they came closer he could see that each rider was on one horse and leading a second.

Panic rose in his throat. The four riders would have fresh horses once they spotted him. After that it would only be a matter of time until they caught him. Bruneaux looked down at the gun in his hands. It was his only hope. With it he would have to cut down the odds.

Five

Black as a cloudy, moonless night, Bear Heart's eyes held de la Verendrye motionless. The Frenchman barely noticed the bay gelding the warrior held by the lead rope. He found no comfort in the fact that the warrior carried no weapons. Among these Lakota, he was learning, a man's demeanor could be just as menacing as a drawn bow.

"Our war leader says this could be your horse." Bear Heart's voice reflected the danger in his eyes.

De la Verendrye's mouth was suddenly dry. The bay was one of his horses. He nodded silently.

"We know that he was left behind by the one who killed the mother of High Hawk. Would that be the man you traveled with?"

De la Verendrye nervously cleared his throat. "Yes," he said. Then he quickly told the angry warrior, "He was the man who tried to kill me, too, and took my horses and my weapon." Since the gunshot from a meadow to the north of the Wolf Tail encampment, he had waited anxiously. Something in his gut told him it had been Bruneaux. Now he desperately wanted this warrior to understand that the one who had killed the old woman was not a friend.

"That is what our war leader told me," Bear Heart said coldly. "That killer of old women may not be your friend, but I think he came here because of you. In my mind, you are also to blame for the death of High Hawk's mother."

De la Verendrye's legs weakened. He nearly protested, but he knew such a response would be a sign of weakness to Bear Heart. So he remained silent and tried to return the warrior's stare. But after a moment, he dropped his gaze.

"I am giving you your horse," the warrior said, "because the old ones say it is the proper thing to do."

"Thank you."

Bear Heart tossed the lead rope to the white man. "I do not agree with them, but I will do what they ask. I myself do not think you should be given any kindness. You have brought bad things with you. The only good and useful thing you can do is show me how to use the holy iron." The warrior saw the question in the Frenchman's eyes. "No, I have not forgotten my words about the holy iron. It would be wise if *you* did not make the mistake of forgetting them. After we catch the killer and send him to the next world as a worm, I will be back."

De la Verendrye nodded, knowing it was the only safe thing to do. The warrior walked away to join three others waiting nearby. They were already mounted and equipped for the warpath. One of them was holding Bear Heart's horses and weapons. In spite of his fear of the warrior, de la Verendrye was drawn to him. He was splendidly attired in quilled buckskins. There was purpose in his stride, and he had the same air of strength and confidence as Whirlwind. Tall and slender and handsome of face, he moved without wasted motion. Though his attire was a bit gaudier than that of other warriors, and it seemed like an unspoken boast, Bear Heart gave the impression that he could back up his image with swift, strong action.

Bear Heart and the three other warriors prepared to depart. Each rode one horse and led another, the war horse. Each man carried an unstrung bow, slung across his back and resting slightly on the horse, in its hide case attached to a quiver bristling with arrows. A round buffalo-hide shield and a short, stout war lance were tied at the withers on the neck rope of each war horse. But no weapon was as menacing as the anger in the heart of each warrior—an anger which smoldered like a black fire in their eyes.

Bear Heart took the ropes to his horses and swung easily onto the back of a tall black. In a few heartbeats, he and his warriors faded into the willows, but de la Verendrye could hear them crossing the river. Part of him felt sorry for Bruneaux. De la Verendrye knew one of the warrior groups would catch him—Whirlwind's, Caught the Eagle's, or Bear Heart's. It was only a matter of time. The best Bruneaux could hope for was to prolong the inevitable. If it were Bear Heart who caught Bruneaux first, de la Verendrye suspected his fellow Frenchman would die slowly and painfully. But no matter who caught him, de la Verendrye would be robbed of his chance for revenge.

Bear Heart's group was the last of the pursuers to leave the camp. Caught the Eagle's was the first to leave, heading west. Whirlwind's was going north. Together they numbered twelve Wolf Warriors, any one of which was more than a match for Bruneaux. But Bruneaux had the flintlock and enough balls and powder for fifty shots. The Wolf Warriors generally understood that the range of the gun was far beyond that of even their strongest bow, but they did not know what that meant in terms of specific distance. That lack of detailed information was to Bruneaux's advantage. Face-to-face and hand to hand, or within bow range, any one of the warriors could dispatch Bruneaux easily, but some of them could be wounded or killed trying to get close.

De la Verendrye looked the bay over. He seemed to be in good shape. Of the matched pair, this one was the shorter and had the most endurance. A sense of helplessness gave way to anger as the Frenchman again recalled Bruneaux's brazenness. In a heartbeat, he decided to ride after Whirl-wind's group.

De la Verendrye's only weapon was Her Good Trail's flint knife, and he only had enough food for a few days. If he didn't catch Whirlwind, he would be in serious trouble. The wound in his side was still throbbing, and that could slow him down. But before any more doubts clouded his mind, de la Verendrye grabbed the small bundle of food along with his deer-hide robe and prepared to leave. He looked west toward the main part of the encampment. Warriors formed a rough circle by positioning themselves just beyond the outer ring of lodges. Some stood and some sat, but all had their weapons and horses ready. At the southwest edge of the camp, a crowd gathered outside the High Hawk family lodge. De la Verendrye knew that Stone, the medicine man, was inside that lodge preparing the body of Walks Far for burial. A twinge of guilt gnawed at him.

Bear Heart was right. That old woman didn't have to die. Bruneaux was probably looking for the man he thought he had killed. De la Verendrye guessed that High Hawk's mother and daughter surprised him, and Bruneaux decided that stealing Sun Rise Woman was better than killing his former traveling companion. The old woman was in the way, and Bruneaux's solution was to kill her. Of course, Bruneaux would not likely have been here at all if he had not been intending to finish off de la Verendrye. Bear Heart was right.

De la Verendrye forced himself to look toward the lodge of High Hawk. These Lakota had showed him kindness and hospitality, as had their Dakota relatives east of the Great Muddy. They had taken him in, given him a warm and comfortable shelter, and provided him with food. All this from a people who were thought of as savages by every white man he met. Yet here and in the village of the Isanti Dakota he had been shown more kindness than he had in eight years among his own people. In return, he had brought them trouble. There was no consolation in the knowledge that to cause trouble had not been his intention.

The eerie silence in the encampment deepened his guilt. Even the children and dogs were strangely quiet. De la Verendrye led the horse northeast along the river's edge. He was fairly certain that no one would stop him. At the moment there were other things more important to these people than a strange white man. In a willow thicket out of sight of the camp, he mounted the horse with some difficulty. A sudden cool breeze prompted him to wrap the deer-hide robe around his shoulders. He pushed the last stubborn vestiges of doubt from his mind as he rode after Whirlwind.

The boy Red Legs approached Spotted Calf. The old warrior, sitting in front of a backrest warming himself at the fire, noticed the boy's pinched face. He motioned for the boy to sit down across the fire. "What is it?" he asked.

Red Legs gathered a robe around his waist and shrugged. After a moment he glanced toward the lodge of the High Hawk family. "What happens when someone dies?"

Spotted Calf put more wood on his fire and studied the boy's face for an instant. "Part of the person leaves," he said, "and goes to another place."

The boy looked more confused. "Which part? Where does it go?"

The old warrior smiled. "The spirit," he said. "There are two halves to each person—the body and the spirit. The body, which you can see, is of this world, the world that we can see around us. The spirit, you cannot see. It comes from a place you cannot see, and when the body dies, it goes back to that place. When the spirit leaves, the body dies but stays here."

The boy stared into the fire and pondered the old man's words for a time. He glanced toward the High Hawk lodge and returned his gaze to the fire. "Does everyone have a spirit?" he wondered.

Spotted Calf nodded. "Yes."

"What about animals? And trees. Do trees have a spirit?"

The old warrior nodded again. "Everything has a spirit. Trees. Birds. Buffalo . . . everything. That's how we are all related. We are all related because we are all born into this life. Some of us grow from a seed. Some of us hatch from an egg. Some of us grow in our mother's womb. It does not matter how we are born. We are all given life. Then we live. Then, one day, we die. That is how we are all related, because it is the same for all of us."

Red Legs looked off to the east. "What about that white man. Does he have a spirit?"

Spotted Calf's dark eyes sparkled, but he replied solemnly. "Yes. I think the white man has a spirit."

The boy poked at the fire. "Grandfather High Hawk and his family are sad. They cry."

"Death brings sadness," the old warrior told him. "It is sad when someone or something we care about leaves us. To show our sadness, we cry."

"Is it right to cry?"

"Yes. At times like this, it is."

"Is death a bad thing?"

"No. Sometimes it is difficult to understand why someone must die. Like now. The way that old grandmother died makes me angry, but death does not make me angry. Death is a part of life. It will come to all of us. Perhaps on the hunt, or in battle. Or some of us will live so long that we will wear out our bodies. Then we will die." Spotted Calf paused for a moment then pointed to the circle of stones around the fire. "See that circle?" he asked. "That circle is life. It begins with birth and ends with death. That is how things are."

Red Legs stared long into the fire. He finally glanced up at the old man. "I am afraid to die," he said.

The old warrior nodded. "Yes. Many are. But as you grow older and gain wisdom, you will learn that death is not to be feared. You will grow to be a fine hunter and warrior.

Someday you will come face-to-face with death. It may come to you in the form of a great bear or an enemy warrior. And you will fight. But you will not fight against death. You will fight for life. But no matter what, death will come sooner or later. If you understand that, your fear will go away."

The boy looked off to the north. "Will my uncle, Whirlwind, and my cousin, Walks High, come face-to-face with death?"

"Yes, they will."

"What will they do?"

"They are warriors, they will fight . . . for their lives, for our lives. And if death should come, they will meet it as bravely as they can."

"Did the grandmother who was killed meet death bravely?"

"Yes, she did."

"But she was not a warrior."

Spotted Calf smiled. "Bravery does not belong only to warriors. She who was killed lived a good, long life. She has helped to raise many warriors. She understood, better than some warriors, what it means to be brave."

Red Legs looked yet again toward the High Hawk lodge. "Will she be buried in the sky, Grandfather?"

The old warrior nodded. "Yes. We will bury her in the sky on a bed of sage. Some young men have already put up the four poles that will hold up her burial scaffold. Even now her spirit begins the journey. As your grandfather, Stone, prepares her body for burial, he sings for her spirit. He sings to send her on her way. Tonight, we will sit with her family and mourn with them, but we will also remember her life and all that she was to each of us. Then tomorrow we will carry her to her burial scaffold . . . and bury her in the sky."

Whirlwind reined his horse to a stop. They were heading northward up a long, gradual slope. In the distance, the back of an undulating east-west ridge was visible. Beyond that ridge lay the valley of the two rivers, where the Smoking Earth River flowed into the White Earth River. The tracks they were following were heading toward that valley.

Whirlwind could see that the horse which made the tracks was tired. There were clear signs of it stumbling. It was carrying two and had been ridden hard. Those signs told the war leader that he and his warriors were on the trail of the one who had killed a revered old woman and stolen the girl promised in marriage to his son.

He motioned for a halt and dismounted to study the signs. But there was another reason to stop. He had noticed a movement to the south at about three hundred paces. Whirlwind knew that the killer could not have doubled back and guessed that someone from the camp was following them.

Whirlwind led his horses back down the slope. "We are being followed," he said. The younger warriors nodded and moved off to either side of the trail. Each found a low spot behind soapweeds and slight rises. Dismounting, they tapped their horses, one after the other, behind the right knee and pulled down on their jaw ropes. The horses responded to the cues and dropped down out of sight. Then each warrior crouched between his horses, with a bow strung and an arrow nocked.

A long stone's throw down the trail, a man on a bay gelding looked up the slope. He pulled his horse to a halt and shifted his hips to ease the pain in his side as he studied the trail. Several sets of tracks confirmed what he already surmised—that Whirlwind's group was still pushing hard. He had been able to catch only a momentary glimpse of them further up on the slope. But as he looked up the slope again, his eyes widened in surprise. The four warriors he had been following had suddenly vanished.

Six

Her Good Trail stared apprehensively at the long, encased weapon tied to a lodgepole. She remembered well the day her husband had brought it home, along with a story that chilled her heart. A story of how he had had to kill a white man who tried to kill Whirlwind with this weapon—this weapon in her lodge. Like a bow sent an arrow, it had sent something that had torn through the side of her husband's shirt. Something that could have made her a widow if it had been a hand's width or two toward the shooter's left.

Like the wife of every hunter-warrior in the Wolf Tail encampment, and among all the Lakota, she spent much of her time waiting. Waiting for her husband to return from a hunt or from the warpath. A hunt was not so dangerous, though accidents did happen and enemy war parties did not hesitate to attack lone Lakota hunters. It was more difficult to wait at times like this when Whirlwind faced the perils of the warpath. And now not only did she feel the added weight of having a son riding that same path but the burden of knowledge that Whirlwind, as war leader, would put himself in harm's way before he would ask any other warrior to do the same. Many times, as now, she wondered if her husband would return at all. There were other moments when Her Good Trail wished that she could ride out with her husband and face the dangers with him. Although women warriors were not unknown among the Lakota, in spite of all her worry she knew that her way was to wait. As Whirlwind had told her many times, it took no less courage to wait. Besides, each time he rode away, he promised to return. And she always promised to wait.

She glared at the holy iron. Whirlwind had chosen not to use it, even to the point of hiding it. She knew he did not fear it, because he was not afraid of his own dying. Only once since he had brought it home had he expressed his real feelings about the weapon. "I believe it has a power that cannot be seen," he had said. "I think it can do something to the mind and the heart of he who carries it. It can kill the thinking which should guide a person to do what is right and turn him off onto the wrong path."

She agreed with her husband. The weapon was strange and mysterious. It did not seem to be of this world. Whirlwind's description of its power was almost beyond belief. It had to be the most fearful thing ever seen by the Wolf Tail people. Over the winters of her life with Whirlwind, she had never seen him as troubled by any one thing as he was by the holy iron. That in itself was worrisome. Though many people saw him as a fearless warrior, she knew him to be a profound thinker. Many evenings in their lodge passed with him staring into the fire, absorbed in quiet thoughts. Even in his younger days, before he became her husband, he had been much quieter than other young men. It was that quietness which found a place in her heart, because he did not strut or talk of his exploits on the warpath. In fact, one of the first things he had said to her, as they stood for the first time under his courting robe, was about the stars. "I wonder how far away they are," he had said. To her, only someone who could think deeply would have such a thought. Now, she knew that the holy iron was much on his mind. She knew that others looked to him because he considered things carefully. It was the reason the old men had asked him to be war leader. And it was the reason her father had accepted the bride offering of twelve horses from Whirlwind's family, even though Noisy Hawk's family had offered twice as many. "Better to walk with a man who takes a careful step," her father Hollow Horn had said, "and stoops to look at a blade of grass, rather than one who tramples everything in his way because he thinks his own going is the most important thing." Her father had been right. She had not once regretted the path she had taken with Whirlwind, even though some of the things which had appeared along their path sometimes had been bothersome. Like the holy iron.

At first, Whirlwind had patiently and politely allowed some of the warriors to look at the weapon, but he always declined when asked to shoot it. So Her Good Trail had never seen the weapon used. It was just as well. This weapon of the white man had nearly killed her husband. She hated it. But as time passed since that day nearly four winters ago, she had thought about it less and less. Until Whirlwind brought home the wounded white man.

"De la Verendrye" he called himself—a strange name, seemingly without meaning. She thought of him as The Beard. The Beard had nearly died after being shot with his own holy iron, by another white man, he had said. Now Her Good Trail could not get the strange, fearful weapon out of her mind. Especially now. Her husband and son were in pursuit of someone with a holy iron, someone who had killed one of the kindest and wisest old women in the Wolf Tail camp and had also tried to kill The Beard.

She glared at the outline of the weapon hanging in her lodge. Whatever it was, to her it was a mystery—like the white man her husband had saved.

De la Verendrye was certain he was about to die. Four warriors had suddenly risen out of the earth. Snorting in confusion and fear, his horse first jumped sideways then spun, hooves thudding the ground like erratic drumbeats.

Three of the warriors were poised with drawn bows. In their dark eyes was the same look de la Verendrye had seen in a puma he had encountered near the Great Muddy. The puma had been deadly calm, certain of its own strength and ability to kill. She had measured him and sensed that, of the two of them, she was the stronger. As he had watched the great cat lazily switch her tail and flex her claws, de la Verendrye sensed that the puma knew that she could snuff out the two-legged at any moment she chose. These Wolf Warriors knew exactly the same thing.

Like the puma, the warriors let him live.

Whirlwind approached. De la Verendrye brought the nervous bay under control. The other warriors lowered their weapons and cued their horses to stand back up.

De la Verendrye was astonished. Where there had been nothing, there now stood eight horses—four riding horses laden with equipment and four war horses with loose halters and neck ropes.

Whirlwind grabbed the bay's reins and looked hard into the Frenchman's eyes. "Why do you come?" he asked.

"I want to help."

"Help? With what?" The warrior's hard stare was relentless.

The white man glanced toward the other warriors. They were calmly waiting. "Bruneaux," he said. "I want to help catch Bruneaux."

Whirlwind seemed amused by the reply. "Why? Is it because you think we cannot?"

"No! No." De la Verendrye held up a hand. "No, I know you can catch him. I know you will catch him. But . . . he tried to kill me . . ."

Whirlwind's eyes turned blacker. "He killed one of our people. He took a young woman. One who is promised in marriage to my son. Do you think your claim comes before ours?"

De la Verendrye fought to control his fear. He knew that Whirlwind was a reasonable man, unlike Bear Heart. But he also realized that Whirlwind could not be bluffed.

The Frenchman carefully fashioned his answer. "Friend," he said, "that is not what I meant. I know what Bruneaux has done. But I also know about his weapon. The holy iron. It is *my* weapon. I know what it can do." He paused to look up the slope to the distant ridge. "If he is on that ridge, he could kill any one of us from there—if his aim is good."

Whirlwind looked toward the ridge and motioned the younger warriors toward the cover of a low bank to the left of the trail.

De la Verendrye pressed his momentary advantage. "I know about the weapon Bruneaux has. With that knowledge, I can help you."

Whirlwind motioned for the Frenchman to dismount. "Perhaps we should talk," he said.

A few clouds rode the high breezes. Now and then one briefly blocked the sun, bringing a grayness to the land. The sun itself was relentlessly stalking the western rim of the Earth.

Whirlwind and the young warriors had ridden a fast pace after picking up the killer's trail. A short rest would be good for the horses. They led them down the slope until they were completely out of sight of the ridge top.

The war leader of the Wolf Tail people knew this country well. There were many good hiding places along the wide ridge above them where an enemy could wait to attack. The last thing he wanted was to be ambushed and shot by a man with a holy iron, as he had almost been four winters ago near where they were now—the valley of the two rivers. It was there that he had happened upon a canoe loaded with furs—a canoe belonging to a white man with a holy iron.

Whirlwind had hidden near the canoe and waited until the white man had later appeared with a load of furs, which he had added to the several already in the canoe. It was the first white man Whirlwind had ever seen, but after his initial surprise, he realized that except for the color of his skin, his clothes, and his beard, the white man looked like any other man. The warrior remembered wondering if the White Earth River was deep enough to float a canoe loaded with furs and the weight of a man.

After tying down the furs in the canoe, the white man had built a fire and made a night camp. He had not been very watchful and had seemed deep in thought most of the time. Whirlwind had watched the man cook some kind of a meal in a strange black object hanging over the fire. After the man had finished his meal, Whirlwind had decided that it was a good time to learn more about this strange person wandering alone and far into Lakota territory. Just before he had left his hiding place, the warrior had decided to keep his bow unstrung and in its case since a weapon at the ready was not a sign of friendship. He had been a short stone's throw from the camp before the white man noticed him. After that, things happened swiftly.

With a cry, the white man grabbed and lifted a long, lance-like pole and pointed it at the approaching warrior. In the next instant, a small puff of white smoke billowed from near the man's right hand as he held the pole to his shoulder. Less than a heartbeat after that, more smoke billowed from the end pointing toward Whirlwind. Then, thunder crashed through the air!

Whirlwind had jumped back. Something had tugged at his shirt. Looking down at his left side, he could see the hole in the material just above his left hip. Stories of the Ojibway leaped from his memory. The Ojibway had used such weapons against Whirlwind's people, long ago.

The white man had knelt and was going through some

strange motions with parts of his weapon. Whirlwind did not hesitate after that. Even as the thunderous voice of the white man's weapon was still echoing through the river bottom, he reached around and slid his encased bow and quiver of arrows to the front. In a heartbeat, the bow was out. In another, it was strung.

Whirlwind's hands had moved faster than a striking rattlesnake. He pulled out two arrows. The first was on his bowstring even as the white man was still struggling with his own weapon. With motions so swift they were hard for the eye to follow, the warrior had lifted the bow, pulled back on the string, and released the arrow.

The arrow flicked out, faster than a darting swallow. It pierced the white man's chest and buried itself until only the back half of the feathers could be seen. The white man had fallen backwards, clutching at the arrow spilling his lifeblood onto the sands of the river's edge. A second arrow was already on the string of Whirlwind's bow, but there was no need for it. By the time Whirlwind had stepped carefully to within six paces of him, the white man was dead. He died like any man would, the warrior remembered thinking.

Whirlwind let the hard memory of that encounter fade back into the shadowy valleys of his mind. But he knew that the dead trapper's weapon was very likely the same as the one the wounded white man had been shot with. He also knew, as the old men reminded everyone, that knowledge was a warrior's best weapon. It was time to arm themselves further against the one who had killed the mother of High Hawk.

"Tell us about your weapon," the war leader said to de la Verendrye.

"The ball it sends is a little bigger than this," de la Verendrye began, pointing to the tip of his little finger. "It flies faster than you can see." He motioned toward the ridge.

"If Bruneaux is up there, the ball would reach us before you would finish counting one-two."

The three younger warriors exchanged doubtful glances.

"You should believe him, just to be safe," Whirlwind advised quietly. "There is no honor in dying stupidly."

The warriors nodded, remembering their leader's encounter with the white man near the White Earth River.

"But," the Frenchman continued, "the holy iron cannot shoot the balls as fast as you can shoot arrows. After it shoots, it takes to the count of thirty-five before it is ready to shoot again. That is important to know. Still, do not forget it can reach far, far beyond your arrows."

Whirlwind allowed a moment for the younger warriors to consider the white man's words. Then he looked up the slope. "We need to know if the man is on the ridge. We can carefully scout the whole ridge, on both sides, up and down every gully and ravine, but darkness would come before we could finish. That would give him an advantage."

"There is a faster way, a decoy," Whirlwind went on. The war leader paused to pick three blades of grass, then held them between his palms to the younger warriors. They each picked one. "If he is up there, perhaps a decoy can trick him into shooting, and give away his location."

"That would be dangerous," pointed out Walks High.

Whirlwind looked to de la Verendrye. "How far can I ride from the ridge top and still stay beyond the reach of the holy iron?"

De la Verendrye glanced up the ridge. "We are about three hundred paces from the top," he estimated. "It would not be easy to hit something the size of a man from that distance. But it could be done, if the man was a very good shot. To be safe, do not move closer than that."

Lone Elk held up his blade of grass. "Uncle," he said, "if you are going to be the decoy, why did you have us draw these?"

Whirlwind smiled. "Whoever has drawn the shortest will guard the horses."

Red Lance sighed and tossed aside his short stem.

"I will ride along the bottom of this slope," Whirlwind continued. "The two of you," he said to Walks High and Lone Elk, "will work your way up the slope. Stay hidden. If the man is up there, and if he shoots, he will give away his location. I will ride up the slope toward him—until the count of thirty. After that, we all will stay out of sight and close in, until one of us gets a clear shot." He glanced at de la Verendrye. "It would be good if you could hold the horses, while my nephew stands guard."

The Frenchman nodded. "Remember," he said, "when the holy iron shoots, there will be a cloud of white smoke."

On the lip of a cutbank, a man in dirty buckskins lay flat and looked south. The four riders had turned and moved back down the slope and out of sight. Bruneaux knew that he was at the edge of the flintlock's range. But when the riders moved up the slope again, they would inevitably come within his killing range.

These Lakota were sure to be like some of the people living near the Great Muddy River. They would be in awe of the gun. One shot and they would turn and run, especially if it was a hit. After that, he could travel slowly and enjoy his prize. Perhaps, even though he had not planned it, he had acquired a prize just as valuable as de la Verendrye's gold.

He savored the sudden images running through his imagination as his probing gaze lingered on the girl. It had been far too long since he had bedded a woman. She was good for that. And there were men who would pay much for a girl such as this, for the same purpose he would use her. With an effort, he turned his attention back down the slope.

A curse slid from his mouth. A lone rider was moving east at a lope, just within range.

Sun Rise Woman pushed herself against the bank, holding tightly to the dirt in her hands. They were nearby! She knew from the white man's reactions that he had seen someone. Whirlwind and Walks High, for certain! Others, too, more than likely. This would be over soon.

Bruneaux reached for the gun, snugged the stock against his right shoulder, estimated the distance, and cocked back the hammer. He cursed again, suddenly realizing that the lone horseman was a decoy, trying to draw a shot that would give away his location.

"The savages can think after all," he muttered, slowly uncocking the hammer. His eyes darted over the landscape. Another realization sent a shiver through him. Though he had not taken a shot, he had been watching the decoy and had momentarily forgotten about the other three riders.

Bruneaux's breath quickened. They were moving toward him he was certain. Perhaps working around behind him. Indecision crowded him. Down the slope, the lone horse and rider were still moving. Then, to Bruneaux's amazement, the man reined his horse to a stop.

Bruneaux pulled back the hammer again. If he could kill the decoy, he was certain the others would run. It was the easiest way out of this situation. He sucked in a breath and aimed carefully. "Hold still, you heathen," he whispered, and pulled the trigger.

Whirlwind saw a small eruption of dirt near a soapweed about ten paces upslope, followed by the unmistakable boom of the holy iron. The ruse had worked.

A white cloud of smoke hung just above the ridge. Whirlwind urged his war horse into a gallop and rode toward it. Counting as he rode, the warrior turned aside into a gully at the count of twenty. By the count of thirty he was safely out of sight.

The warrior dismounted and ground-tied his horse. He quickly estimated the distance to the ridge top to be about a hundred paces, perhaps less. After the shot from the holy iron, he had ridden about two hundred paces up a hard slope.

Whirlwind gazed appreciatively at his favorite war horse. The animal was barely winded. "You can rest here, my friend," he told the horse. "From here on, it is my fight." The gray roan brought his ears forward at the sound of the warrior's voice. Several summers and autumns of patient and careful training had turned the horse into the finest war horse he had ever ridden. But the gray had been born with the heart to be a warrior. He had a gift for remaining calm amidst confusion and noise, an ability that could not be taught. Now he stood patiently and intently watched his rider. With a nod at the roan, Whirlwind turned his attention up the slope.

From behind the bristly, sheltering leaves of a soap-weed, he studied the skyline. Meanwhile, he uncased his bow and strung it. A hand felt for the war club at his belt. Such movements came instinctively, as if his hands had eyes of their own. Preparations completed, Whirlwind moved to the bottom of the gully and began to follow it toward the top of the ridge.

The boom of the holy iron echoed down the slope. A stone's throw apart, Walks High and Lone Elk peeked cautiously from cover. A small cloud of white smoke hung just above the ridge, northeast of their positions and just within bow range. Lone Elk was ahead of his friend and closer to the cloud of smoke. For that, he was glad. He was well aware of his friend Walks High's tendency for reckless-ness in battle. And he feared that, now, with the good chance that Sun Rise Woman was the captive of the shooter of the holy iron, Walks High might become especially reckless. Walks High needed to be watched closely.

Lone Elk observed as Walks High belly-crawled to a slight rise. He waved and caught the big warrior's attention then motioned that he would move further to the north. Walks High motioned his acknowledgment.

Bruneaux gasped. His shot had been short, and the rider was galloping up the slope. He lost precious moments to indecision. Dropping from the bank, he fumbled for the powder horn and shot bag. His hands trembled as he pulled at the drawstring on the bag, spilling lead balls in his panic. He whimpered and bent to scoop them from the dirt.

Sun Rise Woman seized the opportunity to attempt escape. Though her wrists and ankles were bound tightly, she managed to push herself along the bank by digging her heels into the ground. When she realized that the white man's attention was totally focused elsewhere, she stopped and pulled at the wrist bindings with her teeth.

Whirlwind stayed low, now and then crawling on elbows and knees, but careful to move slowly to avoid raising dust. The gully narrowed until he could no longer hide in it. Level ground was just ahead. Without raising up, the warrior knew he was close to the killer's location.

Bruneaux finished reloading and cocked his weapon. Fear was rising in him, nearly out of control. His pursuers had not fled at the boom of the flintlock as he had expected.

Henri Bruneaux was a bully. He had often pushed others around and gotten his way with blustering and threats. Like the time the trader in Saint Louis had said that two beaver pelts were not worth six horns of powder but had been pushed to change his mind after Bruneaux had broken nearly every chair and table in his place. Many, many times all Bruneaux needed to do to gain the upper hand was bellow in rage, flail his arms, and flash his angry, gray eyes. He knew it was a sight to chill the heart of even the most stouthearted man. Until now. There was no way to bluff his way through this. In fact, he could see only one way to get out alive—run.

Bruneaux's eyes darted erratically. He needed a diversion. He uncocked the flintlock and drew his knife. The girl. He would use the girl.

Sun Rise Woman gasped at the sight of the white man's knife. He crouched over her an instant before he sliced the thongs holding her ankles. Before she could react, he grabbed her arm and hauled her up onto the edge of the bank, pushing her up until she stood. Then Bruneaux jumped away from the girl.

Lone Elk saw Sun Rise Woman immediately. The snake of a white man was going to shoot her, he was certain. With a shout, he leaped from his cover and ran for the girl.

Walks High heard the shout and came out of his cover in time to see Lone Elk jerk in midstride and fall face down. Then the awesome boom of the holy iron filled the air.

Walks High reacted in a heartbeat. His bow hand flicked the feathered end of an arrow onto the string, and his right hand drew the powerful bow. In less than another heartbeat, the shaft hissed toward the figure in dark buckskins just beneath a white cloud of smoke.

Whirlwind knelt and drew his bow. Sun Rise Woman had suddenly appeared on the skyline, just before he saw Lone Elk jump to his feet. His worst fear came to pass as Whirlwind saw the body of the slender warrior spin and fall to the earth. An instant later the girl turned and threw herself to the ground. Now Whirlwind had a clear view of the man in dark buckskins, and he loosed his arrow.

Bruneaux leaned against the cutbank as he pulled the trigger, grunting in satisfaction as the warrior fell. In the next heavy heartbeat a sudden hiss caught his ear. Pain seared his left cheek. A flint-tipped arrow had sliced a path just under the cheekbone. As Bruneaux instinctively reached for his face, he heard another hiss, and the second arrow, from another direction, embedded itself in the bank, protruding just below his crotch. Bruneaux stared in terror at the quivering shaft before rushing blindly toward his horse.

Whirlwind shot another arrow at the dark figure merci-lessly whipping the bay horse into a gallop. It passed just over the rider's head. The warrior carefully observed the direction in which the fleeing horse and rider were headed. In a heartbeat he decided that the killer could be tracked after he had attended to Sun Rise Woman and Lone Elk.

It was past sunset. A fire burned on the sandy bed of an old watercourse. Lone Elk reclined against the slope of its dry bank. Though his face was a mask of pain, he did not give voice to it. Inside the fire's glow, four people sat with the wounded warrior: Walks High, Sun Rise Woman, de la Verendrye, and Whirlwind. Red Lance was just outside of the reach of the firelight, wrapped in a deer-hide robe. He sat among the picketed horses, weapons at the ready. He had the first watch. All of them wore the story of this day on their faces, especially Sun Rise Woman.

Her only outward injuries were the bruises around her ankles, wrists, and the side of her mouth. But there were other injuries which could not be seen.

Sun Rise Woman had been silent since Walks High had told her that her grandmother was dead. Her grandmother's face floated in her mind, like a wispy cloud being carried toward the horizon by a relentless wind. What good was it to be alive when Grandmother Walks Far was not? Walks High's offering of food sat untouched at her feet. Her eyes were swollen from her crying, and she seemed not to notice when Walks High gently placed a robe around her shoulders.

The young warrior looked helplessly toward his father. Whirlwind motioned for his son to follow him to the other side of the fire, well out of earshot of the others.

Walks High was confused by Sun Rise Woman's silence and angrily blamed himself for Lone Elk's pain. He forced himself to listen as his father unfolded a plan.

"Tomorrow, at dawn, I will start after the killer," Whirlwind said in a low voice.

"I do not think you should go alone," said Walks High.

"It is the only way," Whirlwind replied evenly. "Lone Elk is wounded, and the white man is of no use. The killer's trail is getting cold, even now. It would be better if a small war party could go after him, but if we all go back to the village tomorrow, it would be two days before anyone could continue pursuing the killer. No, it is better that I take up his trail while it is fresh."

"Still . . ." Walks High protested.

Whirlwind held up a hand. "I will capture the man and bring him back to the village. The old men will decide what is to be done with him. In the meantime, you and Red Lance also have a duty—to make certain that everyone else returns home safely. My friend High Hawk will be anxious for news of his daughter."

Walks High nodded. "We will see to it."

"Good." The war leader glanced toward the girl and leaned closer to his son. "And be patient with my future daughter-in-law," he advised. "Stay close to her. She is not angry with you. She blames herself for her grandmother's death, just as you blame yourself for Lone Elk's pain. Much has happened this day. It is best to let it pass. There will be time enough to look back on it. Then you can decide if it is better to be angry or to pity yourself . . . or just accept what has happened."

Walks High glanced at Sun Rise Woman and nodded to his father.

Whirlwind stood and crossed over to Lone Elk. He touched the wounded warrior lightly on a shoulder. "Nephew, are you still with us?" he asked.

Lone Elk opened his eyes and replied with an embarrassed smile. The ball from the holy iron had hit him just above the left hip, going clear through.

The war leader returned the smile. "I would be honored to give you a red-painted eagle feather," he said, "and to tell the Wolf Warrior Society of your courage. But first I must capture the one who has brought so much grief to our people and gave you the wound."

"Thank you, Uncle," Lone Elk replied. "A red-painted eagle feather from you would be the honor of a lifetime."

Beyond the firelight, one of the horses nickered softly. A nearby screech owl warned of a chilly night with his wavering cry. From the distant hills inside the strong folds of darkness, a coyote yelped and lifted a thin howl. But as it died away, a deeper and stronger voice could be heard. The howl began on a sharp, clear note and rose higher and higher until, at last, it faded away. It was the unmistakable song of a wolf.

Whirlwind touched the small bag hanging on his chest. Inside was a fang, a connection to his guiding spirit. He smiled as the wolf lifted his voice again and filled the darkness.

Seven

Walks High emerged from the lodge of Lone Elk's grandmother and looked toward the sunset. A thick red and gold haze swirled above the horizon, seeming to reflect his confusion and worry.

Lone Elk was recovering. He was already walking without help, after four days of his grandmother's skillful care. The old woman knew much about healing plants.

At the moment his wounded friend was not the main source of Walks High's worry. It was his father and Sun Rise Woman. He expected his father to have returned, certainly by the end of this day. And Sun Rise Woman was more stricken by her grandmother's death than he had realized. She had asked that they postpone their marriage ceremony for thirteen moons—one winter from now. Walks High had agreed to the request, though he did not want to and did not feel like it. He had a feeling that a refusal on his part would have made no difference and very possibly could have ended everything for him and Sun Rise Woman. It all was very confusing.

Thirteen moons. It was a very long time to wait. Much could happen in thirteen moons. In that amount of time, he remembered, a thin, shy girl had turned into a beautiful, slender young woman—one whose smile made his feet stumble over things that were not there.

He had not known what to do about his feelings for Sun Rise Woman until his grandfather Spotted Calf had brought him an elk-hide courting robe. Light brown hair was on the outside, and it was softly tanned on the inside, with pairs of four-leggeds painted on it: Male and female wolves, deer, otters, elk, and others. But the bull elk and his mate were at the center of this robe, for he was considered to be the most powerful when it came to matters of courtship. "Sees at Night, the Elk Dreamer, the one who knows about the power of the elk during the courtship, painted this robe for me. I used it to court your grandmother, and she did not ever look at another man," he had told Walks High. "I loaned it to your father. So you can see its power is good, because you are here."

It had been a long while before Walks High took his place among the long line of hopeful young men who gathered nearly every summer evening outside the lodge of High Hawk. To everyone's surprise, including his own, the only one invited to the door had been Walks High. "What has taken you so long?" Grandmother Walks Far had asked. Once beneath the courting robe, as he wrapped it around them while he and Sun Rise Woman stood in the doorway of her mother and father's lodge, he could not think of another young woman. And it was only then that he understood the long, lingering looks that often passed between his own mother and father.

Now that same young woman who once could not take her eyes from him acted as though he were nothing. Thirteen moons was a very long time.

Walks High looked around at the encampment as he walked slowly toward the home of Red Lance. Only a few cooking fires were outside now. Evenings were turning crisp; winter was close. Women cooking inside the lodges was one certain sign of winter.

A horse, sometimes two, was picketed outside of nearly every lodge. Children were still out playing. Walks High could hear some older boys noisily playing the knocking-them-off-their-horses game, somewhere on the western edge of the camp. It was a loud, dangerous, and purposeful game in which they imitated warriors fighting in battle. The bruises, bloody noses, and black eyes they gave each other now with their wooden-headed war clubs and blunt lances would help them win eagle feathers in the real battles yet to come. In a few winters, those boys would be warriors.

A dog brushed by his leg as Walks High arrived at the lodge of Red Lance and his family. He scratched lightly on the side of the door. "Come in," said a man's voice. Walks High pulled the buffalo-hide covering aside and entered. Red Lance sat to the left of the fire, making arrows. His father, No Two Horns, sat at the back watching his son. Sings on the Hill, Red Lance's mother, was busy tending to the deer ribs roasting over the fire. A delicious aroma filled the cozy home. His friend's parents smiled as Walks High took a seat next to Red Lance.

"It is good you came," the woman said. "Stay long enough to eat with us."

Walks High said his thanks and nodded. Though he had just had a bowl of elk stew at Lone Elk's lodge, he was too polite to refuse.

"Is there news of your father?" No Two Horns asked.

Walks High shook his head. "No. That is why I have come to see my friend," he replied, taking an arrow that Red Lance held out to him. He inspected the arrow closely. "If he has not returned by midday tomorrow, I will ride out to find his trail and follow him." He looked at his friend. "I could be talked into trading one of my new colts for twenty of these," he said, handing the arrow back.

Red Lance smiled. "Then, let's talk. And, if you are riding out tomorrow, I will ride with you."

No Two Horns agreed. Unfettered pride sparkled in his eyes as he spoke to the two young warriors. "It is a good idea," he told them. "My nephew—our war leader—has taken on a difficult task. Though I do not doubt his ability, I am afraid of the white man's treachery. It would be good if you would ride out in search of him. There is nothing wrong in making sure that things turn out right. Stone has asked the old men to gather for a meeting this evening. I will tell them of your plan."

Walks High nodded, as Sings on the Hill placed a plate of ribs and a bowl of wild peppermint tea in front of each of the young men. "You will be careful," she implored. "There has been enough sadness lately."

"Mother," Walks High said, using the title of respect to his friend's mother, "we will be careful. There is much to live for. Like your cooking, and your kindness."

As Whirlwind had hoped, the killer's trail was easy to follow. The white man had ridden only a short distance to the north, from the ridge where he had wounded Lone Elk, before he turned west. He was staying close to the White Earth River.

Low, dark clouds covered nearly all of the western half of the sky as the warrior stopped at a high point overlooking the river. Below him, to the north, across the river was a fairly thick stand of cottonwood, buffaloberry, and willow trees. Ahead of him was a high shale bank which angled steeply down to the river. All the signs indicated that the killer had ridden on the dim deer trail along the edge of the bank.

Whirlwind patted the roan's neck and urged him into a walk. He had sent the buckskin mare back with Walks High for Sun Rise Woman to ride. Besides, he could move faster with one horse, and the gray war horse was always eager for the trail.

They moved along the edge of the bank. Whirlwind carefully looked into the stand of trees below him, but he was certain the white man was somewhere ahead. Then suddenly the roan reared and let out a squeal of pain and surprise. Whirlwind felt the horse's body grow limp as they fell over the edge of the bank. Then he heard the distant boom of a holy iron!

The horse's body hit the earth hard, crushing the warrior's left knee. But there was no time to react to pain. Whirlwind lifted his forearm to shield his face as the roan's body rolled. The crushing weight shifted over and carried the warrior into the cold waters of the river with his horse. They hit with a loud, furious splash, sending a spray of white water nearly to the opposite bank.

Although Whirlwind was pinned beneath his horse as it lay in the water on its right side, he could pull his head up above the water. The pain in his left knee, as much as the icy water, nearly took his breath away. He gasped for air, wiped the freezing water from his eyes, and looked west. The sound of the holy iron had come from that direction.

Even as he looked for his enemy, he began to mourn for the horse. Even as he struggled to pull his leg from beneath its crushing weight, memories of the battles they had fought together and the long trails they had ridden flashed in his mind like silent lightning. Whirlwind pulled his right leg loose from beneath the horse, but he stayed in the water, shivering behind the roan's body. The killer, who was somewhere ahead, had seen them fall into the water and would be watching. In the sky low clouds hid the sun, but Whirlwind knew it was past midafternoon. Although he had to stay in the icy water to let the killer think both horse and rider were dead, he knew that he could not stay in the water long before his shivering became uncontrollable. Once that happened death would be a certainty.

He waited. He could hear his own heart pounding heavily. A thin line of red laced the river's chalky water—blood from his war horse.

Rising up slightly from behind the horse's shoulder, he scanned the skyline along the high bank and then studied the bottomland across the river to the west. He could see nothing moving. Ducking back down, he pressed himself against the roan. There was nothing but cold flesh.

Whirlwind recalled how the roan's warmth had saved his life during a sudden blizzard last spring, after Pawnee raiders had been chased away from the Wolf Tail encampment and he had followed three fleeing warriors for two days. On the way home, he had gotten caught in the unexpected blizzard and had spent the night wedged between a high cutbank and the gray roan. The war horse's body heat had kept him warm all through the night.

Now beside the roan's cold body Whirlwind continued to wait in the icy waters of the White Earth River. Eventually, a movement on the skyline along the high bank caught Whirlwind's eye. He stayed motionless until he saw that the dark shadow against the sky was a young black-tailed buck. He stood gazing down into the little valley and then turned leisurely to the south, browsing a little as he went. It was all the sign the warrior needed. If the buck felt safe enough to graze, the man with the holy iron could not be close by.

Whirlwind immediately crawled out of the water to the dry bank. Only now did he begin to feel pain in places other than his knee. His right shoulder was throbbing, and a few ribs on his left side were very tender. He looked up at the bank as he hurried to shed his wet shirt and leggings. With his hands he quickly rubbed himself as dry as he could, squeezing the water from his hair.

He continued to watch the skyline for any sign of danger. Reluctantly, he waded back into the water toward the horse. He untied the neck and jaw ropes. His encased bow and quiver of arrows had been caught under the body of the roan, along with his lance, which was broken. His rawhide clothes bag and deer-hide robe were still tied to the neck rope. But everything was wet, or broken. For the time being, he bundled everything in the robe and tied it with the neck rope.

After he had taken all of his things, he knelt in the water beside the roan. Anger and grief rose up in him with equal swiftness. "My friend," he said, "I will never forget you. If I could have half your courage, I would be the greatest warrior to walk the land."

He left the water, grabbed his wet bundle, and started moving cautiously alongside the water. Night was coming. He needed shelter—a place to rest and think.

His knee was too painful for him to travel fast, but he managed to climb back up the low end of the ridge and go down the other side. Before he did, he paused for one last look at his horse.

A long arrow's cast from the ridge, he found a deep, narrow gully. Before he settled in, he picked several handfuls of grass and rubbed himself dry. By the time he finished squeezing most of the water from his clothing, it was dark. But he had not the means to make a fire. The best he could do to improve his shelter was lay the wet deer-hide robe across the top of the gully. Sitting beneath that, he spent the night shivering and dozing. And the night was cold, so very cold.

With dawn's first light, he could see his own breath and wondered how he had lived through the night. He was shivering hard. The hide across the top of the gully was cold and stiff and so were his clothes. Reaching for strength deep within, he forced himself to leave the shelter. After gathering his things as best he could, he began to walk, for the sole reason that movement would help warm him.

By midday he came to a plum thicket and crawled into it. He was both tired and hungry, but fatigue won the battle and he fell asleep.

The piercing cry of a hunting hawk woke him. As he gathered his wits, he realized it was late in the day and a cold night was approaching. He knew that the plum thicket was the best shelter he could have found—except for his own lodge. Ignoring the drumming pain in his left knee, Whirlwind worked quickly. With his knife, he fashioned a fire starter, which looked exactly like a small bow, no longer than three hand widths, with a loose string. The drill, a twig the thickness of his thumb and twice as long, with one end rounded and the other sharpened, was twisted into the string. He held it in place with a palm-sized piece of wood over the rounded end. The pointed end fit into the groove he carved into the wrist-sized piece of deadfall, which was the base. He picked dry grass and dead twigs for kindling and arranged them next to the base. Then he spun the drill by pulling the bow back and forth, working it faster and faster until smoke rose from the base and tiny, hot embers fell among the kindling. He leaned over and blew gently until the kindling caught fire from the hot embers.

Now he had fire. Something that was far from his reality only the night before. He looked more closely at his shelter. It was a good hiding place. It hid the small fire and provided protection from the cold. He wove dry brush in and out of the plum stalks, creating additional windbreaks and heat reflectors. All the while he improved his shelter he could see the gray roan galloping across the prairies, and up into the sky. He could also see Her Good Trail laying in wood for the night fire, and then covering herself with the thick, warm buffalo-hide sleeping robe. He smiled for the first time in several days. Then he decided to think seriously about his situation.

He had spent the previous night in the bottom of a gully, without the comfort and warmth of a fire, not far from where his war horse had been killed. His situation this coming night was considerably better. He had shelter and warmth—even a little dried meat, which he had managed to recover. A man could survive on so little, he thought.

Whirlwind untied and unrolled the deer robe, in which he had been carrying the bits and pieces of weapons he had managed to salvage. He put the robe over his shoulders, and by the light of the fire, he took stock of his meager arsenal. It was better than nothing at all, he decided: Twelve arrowheads, three arrows, a flint lance head with only a short length of the shaft, a war club, six spare goose feathers already cut and split for fletching, a spare bowstring, a bundle of sinew, an arrow straightener and sizer, the arrow quiver and bow case (both empty), some leather cordage, and his flint knife.

The only things not broken or damaged in the long fall down the river embankment were the three arrows, his knife, and the quiver and bow case. He had also recovered his rawhide case—with spare clothing and food in it—as well as the war horse's neck and jaw ropes. Over thirty arrows were broken or ruined, and his lance was shattered in three places. The arrow quiver and bow case were still damp from their dunking in the river, even after two days.

The severest losses were the horse and the bow. A warrior without both would face a most difficult test. The bow had been a gift from his father, one of Spotted Calf's finest efforts. But as fine as it was, it could be replaced with any one of three others hanging in his lodge. Or he would find the materials to make one, if he decided to continue pursuing the white man. The horse was another matter. Whirlwind had raised the gray roan. Even as a colt, he had been fearless and aloof. Now he lay dead in an icy river—killed by a white man's holy iron.

Whirlwind added a handful of small broken branches to the fire and leaned back. He was two days' travel, by horse, from the Wolf Tail encampment on the Smoking Earth River. The white man was now two days ahead of him, heading west. To pursue him without effective weapons would be foolish. Even with adequate weapons, Whirlwind could, at best, only hobble along until the injured knee healed.

To the west, through the tangle of plum tree branches, he could see the last dim light of day. He sank further into his makeshift backrest, yielding to fatigue and pain. He needed rest and time to think. Perhaps the morning would help bring some idea of which way to go. He stared at the life-giving flames and yearned for home. The warmth and safety of his own lodge and Her Good Trail's soothing touch seemed like an unreachable dream. So, too, the wisdom of the old ones. Whirlwind felt truly alone—for the first time in his life.

White Crane, perhaps the oldest of the Wolf Tail people, continued to speak. "Since my days as a young man, I have heard of the white men," he said. "I have heard more bad than good. My grandfather was a boy when our enemies, the Ojibway, drove our people from the lake country. They traded furs to the white men for holy irons. The holy irons took away their sense of honor. They killed because the holy iron made killing easier." He paused to catch a breath and clear his throat. "Knowing that, I am glad that my nephew kept his captured holy iron hidden away in his lodge. Our curiosity about the thing died away, until he brought the wounded white man back to our village. Now look at us. We are gathered again, talking about white men and holy irons. White men and holy irons may not be the best things about this world. But they are part of our world now. We must be careful how we handle both."

Sounds of affirmation for White Crane's words coursed through the council lodge. White men and holy irons had been on many minds. However, the wounded one's ability to speak Lakota had eased some worry—until the mother of High Hawk had been killed and his daughter stolen.

"We must be careful," White Crane continued, "beginning with the white man who is still among us. He himself seems to be a good person, but I have seen that death and difficulty have come to us because of him. We should talk of what to do about him. Perhaps he should be asked to leave. Or made to leave. I want to know your thoughts."

Circling Bear held up a hand and glanced briefly around at the other seventeen men who sat in two circles around the fire. "My relatives," he said, "I do not want to blame anyone for what has happened to our people in the last few days. Life is a mystery. We cannot know what tomorrow will bring, and blaming someone for what happened yesterday does not soften pain and grief. Still, we can do things to avoid trouble later. Perhaps one of those things we can do is to send the white man away."

Murmurs of agreement flowed through the council lodge. No Two Horns waited for them to subside. "There is always an answer to every difficulty," he began. "Sometimes such an answer is right, sometimes it is wrong. Sending the white man away is something we can do, but I am afraid there are more like him. Perhaps they will not all cross our paths, but what they do, what they think, and what they are will be part of our world from now on.

"We should remember that we spoke of learning from this particular white man, about his kind. If we do that, perhaps we can stop some of the trouble that may come our way, because of his kind. Besides, my son told me how the bearded one described the way the holy iron shoots. That is something useful. He and the son of our war leader will need that knowledge, since they will ride out tomorrow if our war leader does not return by midday."

The council of old men did not meet to tell others what to do. They met to talk. Sometimes they talked through the entire day, or an entire night. They talked until they were certain they had approached a thing from every possible direction—until all who wished had added their voices. To do otherwise would leave them short of their purpose and responsibility: To advise, to offer guidance. They did not often come away agreeing on one thing or with the same opinion. There were always many viewpoints, sometimes as many as there were old men in the council lodge. That was the purpose. Many opinions, given with the weight of experience and wisdom offered many choices.

No Two Horns, Stone, White Crane, and the others did not speak with the power of authority behind their words. They spoke with the power of wisdom. A wisdom which understood that individual choice was the ultimate right, with the further knowledge that wisdom came from making wrong choices as well as right choices.

Bear Heart was not one of the council of old men, though his status among the people and in the Wolf Warrior Society entitled him to sit in the council lodge. He had been politely enduring this night's discussions, until he heard the words of No Two Horns. He came to his feet.

"Grandfather," he said to the medicine man, Stone. "I would speak." After the medicine man's nod of assent, the warrior threw back his shoulders, letting the silence in the lodge gather attention toward him. "Grandfathers," he said, "you know my feelings about the white man among us. I would not have brought him here. But he is here, and while he is here he can be useful." He paused, pulling the war club from his belt to hold it up. "Things change," he went on. "There was a time when this was all the weapon we needed. Then we made slings, then lances. My grandfather told me stories of how some people used a sending-stick to throw a large arrow. Then the bow came along. The arrows became smaller and faster and could reach farther than the arrow from the sending-stick. Now the white man has a weapon better than our bows and arrows—the holy iron. As I said, things change. We would be foolish to turn our backs on holy irons just because we do not like them, or understand how they work. Grandfather White Crane has reminded us of how the Ojibway used holy irons against our people long ago. I am sure that others of our enemies will use the holy iron against us. The way I see it, we have no choice. We have to change. And the white man who is here now can help us."

"In what ways can the bearded one help us?" Stone wanted to know.

Bear Heart smiled. "First, by showing us how to use the holy iron. Then by helping us get more of them."

Stone cleared his throat. "If it was man who made the holy iron, then other men can learn how it works. And we know that white men are somewhere to the east of us, perhaps waiting across the Grandfather River. Waiting like a flood to break across. We know they have holy irons. We can take some or trade for them. In my mind, knowing how to use a holy iron or having many of them is not the worrisome thing." The medicine man paused and glanced slowly around at the circle of faces. "A holy iron is like other weapons. It can be used to protect the people. It can be used in the hunt. But, in another way, it is different. It has a power that is more than we can see and hear. That is what our war leader has tried to tell us, and we should not forget that. The holy iron, I fear, can do something to the spirit of a man. Something bad. If that were not so, then why have so many of our warriors asked my nephew Whirlwind to see the weapon—if only to touch it? I know that some of our warriors have asked him to shoot it. Why? I think that some of our warriors are drawn to a power they cannot name. And I am afraid it is a kind of power that can cloud their minds."

Stone bowed his head and leaned back against his willow backrest. Silence flowed through the lodge. Bear Heart started to speak but was silenced with a wave of hand by White Crane. The warrior stood and took his anger out of the council lodge and into the night.

Walks High looked at the white man in his mother's lodge and put wood on the fire. He deliberately ignored the man for a long moment. When the white man could no longer hide his nervousness, the young warrior finally spoke.

"Why do you ask my mother for my father's holy iron?"

De la Verendrye cleared his throat. "I have a matter to settle with Bruneaux. He has much to answer for—killing High Hawk's mother and abducting Sun Rise Woman. But without the holy iron, I can do nothing. If your mother would allow me to take your father's holy iron, I would be borrowing it only until this matter is settled."

"You want to kill the other white man yourself?"

Like his father, Walks High had a relentless stare, and de la Verendrye knew to be cautious with the son as well. "I would like to," he replied honestly. "He deserves to die for the things he has done. But I think he should answer to you people. So I want to help find him and capture him. With your father's holy iron, I can do that."

The young warrior turned his attention briefly to a handful of arrows beside his knee while he considered the white man's words. "It is for my mother to say," he decided. "You helped us near the valley of the two rivers, so I will believe you. My friend Red Lance and I will ride out at midday tomorrow if my father does not return by then. With or without a holy iron, you may come with us, if you wish. But I want you to know this. I am sad that you need the holy iron to be strong. My father is right. I think for some it is the holy iron which makes the man."

It was hard for de la Verendrye to ignore the weapon hanging from a lodgepole at the back. He glanced at it and then briefly at Her Good Trail. Her face gave no indication of any answer. The man sighed and rose to a knee, preparing to leave. "Thank you," he said to the young warrior and his mother. "Thank you for listening to me."

Her Good Trail nodded and smiled, then watched the man move stiffly out the door. She was quiet for a time after the visitor finished putting the door covering back into place. Walks High picked up the arrows, an arrow cup, and a coyote-hide quiver. He, too, sighed as he began to load the arrows in the cup. For Her Good Trail, her son's sigh was like a blast of wind inside the silent lodge. She knew that they were both hiding worries and fears. The empty place at the back of the lodge seemed to take up more space tonight.

"My son," she finally said. "Would you be angry if I let the bearded one use your father's holy iron?" She glanced sideways at the thing hidden in its elk-hide case. It would be good to have it out of her home.

Walks High finished putting all the arrows in the cup and then slid them all into the quiver. He shook his head. "No, Mother. I would not be angry." He glanced at the empty spot at the rear of the lodge. "My father would understand. The white man did help us with his knowledge of such a weapon. Perhaps, if he had not . . ."

Her Good Trail nodded and laid a tender hand on her son's shoulder. There had been pain in his eyes for some days now, ever since he and Red Lance had returned with Sun Rise Woman and the white man. She knew what it was, but she also knew that her son, like his father, preferred to keep many things to himself. It was the way Lakota men showed strength. Nevertheless, she wished her son would talk to her about Sun Rise Woman.

Even as a small boy, Walks High had been much like his father. She remembered when he had fallen from a tree in Spring Creek Valley and hurt his arm badly. Even though he was only four winters old, he didn't cry. Another time, when he was seven winters old, he had been bitten by a badger. He did not tell anyone of that injury until Her Good Trail saw him washing the wound on the back of his leg, one day when she had gone to fetch water at a secluded spot along the river. Still, even the bravest of warriors could not hide a broken heart. And even the strongest of mothers could not mend such a wound.

Her Good Trail looked at the forceful, busy hands of her son. She squeezed his shoulder for a heartbeat and then moved toward the meat cases. Deer stew would be good on a night like this. "Do you suppose the white man's name has a meaning?" she asked suddenly.

Walks High shook his head. "I do not know. Perhaps we should ask him."

She shrugged. "He is like most men. But he is different, too. And it is more than his white skin."

"I think . . . I think he is a good man," said the young warrior. "But perhaps he is good at fooling everyone."

"Time will tell," replied Her Good Trail, stirring the hot coals in the firepit. "But I do have a name for him."

Walks High looked expectantly toward his mother.

"Beard," she said, stroking her chin.

The young man smiled. "Beard," he said.

On the opposite side of the camp circle from the lodge of Whirlwind, a warrior inside a cozy lodge stared hard into the fire without seeing the dancing flames. A young woman turned the meat roasting over the fire and cast a soft glance toward her husband. The warrior sat against a backrest covered with the hide of a black bear. Over the dew liner behind him hung another very large bear hide, one that was tanned and elaborately and skillfully painted. Bear Heart had killed the large bear when he was fifteen winters old, with three fast arrows through the great animal's heart. It had suddenly appeared and challenged him for possession of the fat doe the young hunter had tracked and killed. Little Tree, as he was known then, had put the first arrow into the great bear's heart while the animal was busy roaring his challenge. When the animal paused in surprise at the pain caused by his puny adversary, the young hunter sent two more arrows into its heart. He had to climb a tree to avoid being torn apart by the charging animal. But on that day he had earned his warrior name, and he had learned that no one had a right to take what was rightfully his.

Nearby were all the objects which showed Bear Heart as a warrior: Two shields, four lances, four bows with quivers of arrows, war clubs, knives, ropes, and tools for making weapons. Yet, as he stared into the fire, what he saw was something which was not there.

Light Haired Woman softly cleared her throat. "The meat is cooked," she said. "Eat."

Bear Heart's dark, blank eyes lingered for a moment longer on the image in his mind, a long, shiny weapon made of wood and iron, before he looked at his wife. She slid a piece of deer meat off the roasting stick and onto a shallow wooden plate. He smiled as he took the food. After a few bites, he was aware again as he had been earlier that there was something different about her. There had been for some time now, and he had been meaning to ask her about it. "My wife," he said, "do you not feel well?"

Light Haired Woman dropped her gaze as a flush spread across her face. "I am well," she said, barely above a whisper.

"Then, is there something which troubles you?"

She shook her head. "There is nothing that troubles me. But . . . "

"Is there something that you should tell me?"

Light Haired Woman nodded. "I am . . . with child."

Bear Heart stared at his young wife. Her words brought both joy and sadness. Images of a boy, eight winters old, and his mother lost in a flood came rushing back to him like the torrent which had taken them. Since then he had been alone and had filled the emptiness in his life with anger—until two winters ago when the daughter of Comes Flying had caught his eye. Even Light Haired Woman, though, had not been able to push aside all of the anger. During the many lonely winters of his life he had sought the warpath more often than any other warrior in the Wolf Tail band. He became known for his courage as well as his recklessness. Although he did kill many enemies, he also found that fewer and fewer warriors followed him onto the warpath. But that did not matter, because a hard heart was the best thing a warrior could have. He would rather fight alone than rely on all the softhearted warriors he could find. Bear Heart let go of the memories, took Light Haired Woman's hand in his, and whispered, "My heart is glad to hear your words."

The young woman's lips quivered as a soft smile bent the corners of her mouth. But she did not let any tears come because she knew that her husband favored strength most of all. "It is my prayer that this son grow to be like his father."

"To be more than his father," the warrior replied. "Because our world is changing. He will need to be strong and not afraid of new and different things."

Bear Heart returned his gaze to the fire. Again, he was seeing something beyond the flames. "I must travel tomorrow," he said after a moment. "The sons of Whirlwind and No Two Horns are riding out to pick up Whirlwind's trail. And Whirlwind is chasing a man with a holy iron. I must ride, too."

Light Haired Woman nodded and for only a heartbeat or two placed a hand over her waist.

Dawn came with a strong red glow. Whirlwind could hear a large flock of geese take to wing. Their sharp trumpeting filled the cold air of the new day. It was late in the season for geese to be flying south, Whirlwind thought. But he knew that those geese would endeavor to fulfill their purpose, to follow the cycle of their lives—no matter the odds.

He banked his fire and thought about the dream which had eventually stirred him to wakefulness sometime in the night. In it he had watched a wolf defend his den and his family against a pack of gray dogs. The dogs were few at first. But as the wolf chased away the first ones, others came. The harder the wolf fought, the faster the dogs grew in number.

There had been no ending to the dream because Whirlwind had awakened angrily. Nevertheless, it served to remind him of his own chosen path: That of the warrior, who was committed to defending his people, no matter how threatening the enemy.

He had slept comfortably inside the plum thicket and felt rested. Even the injured knee was not as painful since the swelling had gone down a little. To the east the day became brighter and brighter as the sun shed the dark robe of the horizon, piercing a low cloud bank with straight, red shafts of light.

Whirlwind maneuvered himself out of the sheltering thicket and stood east of it to face the sun. As the renewing rays bathed him with their warmth, he lifted his face and his voice to the sky: "Grandfather, thank you for my family, and for keeping them safe . . . thank you for making me what I am . . . thank you most of all for the difficult things which will help me to grow stronger and wiser . . ."

Eight

The crashing boom of the gun echoed down the narrow valley of a creek which flowed into the White Earth River. As the echo faded, a young white-tailed buck jerked and was still. His life slipped out, soaking red onto the bed of fallen leaves. Sixty paces up a slope, a sun-darkened, bearded face broke out into a smile, below the white smoke hanging in the air. Noisily, the man came to his feet and walked down the slope toward the dead deer.

Heavy footfalls scattered dry leaves and filled the narrow valley with harsh sounds. All around—in a gully, inside a thicket, at the edge of a meadow, on the flats, or on the branches of trees—those who traveled on four legs or flew through the air heard the raucous intruder. And the breezes carried a strange, heavy odor, as unwelcome as the noise. All who smelled it or heard the crashing footfalls fled or scurried deep into a burrow, or wove themselves into a thicket, or climbed into the safe reaches of the sky.

Here was a new and different two-legged. One who moved outside the flow, and not with it. One who did not understand, or care, that there was a harmony to the way things were on the land. A stranger who did not see the beauty and vitality in the animal he had just killed. One who cared only that now he had something to eat.

Henri Bruneaux cast a quick, cautious glance toward the eastern horizon. The man on the gray horse should be dead.

Both horse and rider had fallen into the river, and neither one had moved from that spot. He scanned the skyline carelessly. He was not a patient man. But he was lucky, sometimes. It was while waiting for a clear shot at a fat doe that he had seen the Indian on the gray horse. He knew that horse. It had been ridden by one of those heathens back on that ridge. He could still see the warrior and his horse rolling down that long embankment. A smile came and vanished, as he lifted a finger to touch the long, dried blood scab on his cheek. An arrow had come that close! But his flintlock had been better. His attempt to kill the Indian on the gray horse had been a long shot but a good one.

Bruneaux reached the dead deer and looked around. An utter silence lay like a heavy robe. The land was wide open, and free for the taking. But sometimes it was too quiet. He reached for his knife and then decided to reload the flintlock instead. As he did, he looked east, nervously checking every tree, clump of soapweeds, and knob that stood on the horizon. There was nothing. At least not a warrior on a gray horse.

He finished reloading and nonchalantly leaned the flintlock against the trunk of a small oak. Drawing his knife, he yanked at one of the dead deer's forelegs, flopped the carcass over, and began slashing at the flank. With ragged strokes, he hacked off a hindquarter without skinning it. It was all he wanted.

Tossing his booty over a shoulder, he grabbed his weapon and walked south toward a narrow, shadowy gully filled with scrub oaks. Not once did he look back at the bleeding carcass he left behind.

Walks High offered the halter rope of a sturdy dun mare to de la Verendrye. The Frenchman hesitated. His own bay was already packed and ready for travel.

"This mare is the first horse I raised from a colt. And the first one I trained by myself," Walks High added, patting the mare.

"In that case," de la Verendrye returned, "I cannot take her from you."

The tall, young warrior smiled. "I am only lending her to you. She is gentle, with an easy stride. I have noticed that your bay has a jarring step that would be hard on your injury."

The Frenchman nodded emphatically to hide his embarrassment. "Yes, I understand. Thank you."

De la Verendrye took the mare's lead rope. Working quickly, he removed the bay's bridle with its iron bit and fashioned a halter from a long, braided buffalo-hair rope. He decided to follow the warriors' example, to ride one horse and lead another. In that way, one horse was always fresher.

Most of the Lakota warriors, he had heard, had special horses for warfare and for buffalo hunting. The war horse was sometimes ridden on the warpath, though it was most often ridden into battle. Likewise, the buffalo horse was not ridden until the hunter had spotted the buffalo. The war horse was not often ridden for pleasure nor to chase the buffalo. Nor was the buffalo horse intended for use as a war horse. Each was specially selected and trained for a particular calling.

Walks High slipped a jaw rope on the mare and stared with curiosity at the bridle the white man had removed from the bay.

Noticing the warrior's quizzical look, de la Verendrye held up the bridle. "It is a white man's way of controlling the horse, although it is hard on the mouth." He pointed to the bit. "This part is made of iron."

Red Lance walked up behind his friend, and both young warriors stared at the leather bridle with its strange iron bit. Walks High shrugged. "Different people do the same things in different ways," he decided. "We start training our horses when they are still small colts. They are easier to handle, and they grow up knowing us, and trusting us. Perhaps your way, with the iron mouthpiece, is a good way for a horse that is mean."

"Yes," the Frenchman agreed, "but I think your jaw rope and your ways of teaching them are better—and easier on the horse."

Remembering the journey ahead, the warriors lost interest in the curious apparatus and turned away to finish preparations.

De la Verendrye decided to keep his small bundle on the bay. All he had was a bag of food, a pair of spare moccasins, a bow drill fire starter, and a small deer hide that had been given to him by Whirlwind's father. He would make gloves and winter moccasins from that hide. His only weapon was the flint knife at his belt. Her Good Trail did not seem inclined to let him use her husband's flintlock.

The Frenchman was ready for travel. He waited and watched the two young Lakota warriors. Both of them would ride dark bay geldings, though Walks High's was slightly larger. Red Lance's war horse was a black-and-white paint gelding while Walks High's was a coal black mare. Each war horse had a braided buffalo-hair rope double-looped around the neck and tied into the mane at the withers. To that neck rope, a war lance adorned with streamers and eagle feathers was tied on the right side, with its glistening stone point toward the sky. On the left hung a buffalo-hide shield inside its painted, soft hide case.

Each warrior carried his bow and arrows on his back. A long, doubled carry strap connected the long, narrow bow case and arrow quiver. The bow case, with bow inside, hung just above the quiver full of forty or so arrows. With the carry strap slung over the points of the shoulders, the bow and arrows hung horizontally just at the small of the back. The feathered end of the arrows and the tip of the encased bow pointed to the warrior's left. To keep the load from bouncing, especially at a trot or a lope, a long, thin cord attached to the quiver's ridge stick was tied around the waist.

On the warpath, the warrior always carried his bow and arrows. When the moment came to change horses, he had all the equipment he would need, since the lance and shield were already tied to the war horse.

De la Verendrye had heard about the Lakota, these warriors who hunted buffalo, from their more sedentary Dakota relatives living east of the Great Muddy River. Everything he had heard was true. Five days ago, he had watched Whirlwind, Walks High, and Lone Elk stalk a hidden enemy. They had all moved up that slope with the grace of a puma and the tenacity of a wolf. He was glad he was not Bruneaux.

A shiver went through him as he suddenly remembered his last conversation with Bear Heart. In a way, he was relieved that Her Good Trail had not given him the flintlock. Bear Heart, no doubt, would be angry, and de la Verendrye did not want to incur that warrior's wrath.

He led the borrowed mare and his own bay toward the northern edge of the encampment, to wait for Walks High and Red Lance. He wondered why the activity in camp seemed to have a different rhythm and purpose this day. Then de la Verendrye remembered that tomorrow the people would move south to the winter encampment. Today was a day of preparation.

"Beard." A soft voice came from the other side of the bay horse.

The white man looked back and saw Her Good Trail walking toward him with the flintlock in her arms. He stopped.

She handed him the elk-hide encased weapon. "You say you will use this to help my husband and my son. I will believe you, because my husband and my son are the most precious things I have in this life. But you will have to answer any questions my husband may have."

De la Verendrye cradled the weapon for a moment. It felt strangely heavy. He looked at the woman. "I will do what

I can to help," he assured her. "This . . . holy iron . . . can be used to do something good. I hope I can prove that to you and to your husband."

Doubt flickered in her eyes for a heartbeat. "I do not know about that," she admitted. "My husband does not like that thing. I do not like it either. I do not know if it can be made to do anything good."

For a little while, all he could do was blink his eyes rapidly and look at the ground. He could not find an answer to her words. He wondered if she somehow knew about his dark thoughts of revenge, thoughts he did not want to share with anyone. He looked up to catch her intently studying his face.

Her Good Trail looked away but smiled demurely. "My son and I talked last night," she said. "We have a name for you."

The Frenchman looked nervously around at the gathering crowd, half expecting Bear Heart to appear and contest him for possession of the weapon. He suddenly realized what Her Good Trail had said. "A name?" he asked. "What name?"

"Beard," she replied. "It is suited to you and no one else."

The white man's hand went to his chin and scratched the thick, reddish brown swath. "Beard," he muttered, thoughtfully.

"Yes," Her Good Trail reaffirmed. "Beard."

Walks High was right. The dun mare moved very smoothly. They had been riding since midday, heading for the ridge where they had last seen the killer of High Hawk's mother. They stayed west of the Smoking Earth River, using the trees for cover. Though they sometimes held the horses to a trot for long distances, the mare's gait was smooth. In addition, she had easily maintained the pace set by Walks High's tall bay.

Walks High signaled for a rest and led them into a low spot filled with willow and buffaloberry trees. As they all dismounted, Red Lance glanced toward de la Verendrye. "We hid in this spot one time last fall," he said, motioning toward the other warrior. "We were following eight Arikara warriors. They doubled back on us. We came in here and laid the horses down, covering them with branches and leaves." He looked toward his friend. "Remember that?"

Walks High smiled as he sat down in front of his horses' forelegs. "All the time," he replied.

Red Lance pointed to the east edge of the tiny grove. "They rode all around us," he said. "One of them stopped there. I could have reached out and touched his foot. Good thing it was just after sundown. Otherwise they would have seen us in here."

"Good thing you did not reach out for his foot," Walks High reminded his friend. "He would have relieved himself all over your hand. Remember that?"

Red Lance chuckled. "All the time," he said. "He almost got me as it was."

The Frenchman looked amused for a moment then glanced back and forth at the two warriors. "They were Arikara, you said?"

Red Lance nodded. "A war party, I think."

"Where are they from?"

"North," said Red Lance. "Beyond the Knife River. Maybe fifteen days' ride. Some of our people live south of the Knife River. We see Arikara more than they do. Now and then, small war parties and hunting parties of Arikara wander down into our country."

"What are they like? Can you understand their language?" de la Verendrye asked.

"They hunt buffalo like we do. But I think their numbers are smaller. They are good warriors. Their language is different. My father said that one of the Lakota villages to the north had two Arikara girls they took as captives. One of them was taken as a wife, and the other stayed, too. They were sisters. They . . ." Red Lance looked toward the other warrior.

Walks High was holding up a silencing hand and pointing to the dun mare. She had her ears forward and was staring intently to the south, nostrils flaring.

"Someone is coming," whispered Walks High.

Without another word both warriors reacted. With smooth, rapid movements, they each moved bow case and quiver to the front, uncased the bow, strung it, and pulled out a handful of arrows.

De la Verendrye thought about grabbing the flintlock but made no move. He was not certain if it was in firing condition after being kept inside an elk-hide case for four years. He looked away from Walks High's questioning glance.

Both warriors were kneeling now, and each had an arrow on the string. Soon, the sound of walking horses reached them. A long stone's throw to the south, a rider appeared among the trees. The young warriors relaxed.

Red Lance looked aside at the white man. "Bear Heart," he said.

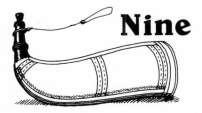

Nine

Spotted Calf looked gently at the young woman. If things had been happening according to plan, it would be only days before she would become his grandson's wife. But Walks Far's death was hardest on her granddaughters. The wedding of Sun Rise Woman and Walks High was to have taken place at the winter camp. Now, instead, her hair was cut short, and the mourning gashes on her forearms were fresh scars. She, with her family, would mourn until the next Moon of Falling Leaves. Over the course of those thirteen moons they would not participate in the dances and feasts. Only thereafter would she be free to wed her betrothed warrior.

Her face was haggard. Gone was the usual sparkle from her eyes as she came to the old man's fire.

Sun Rise Woman avoided looking at the old man as she spoke. "I wanted to talk with him before he left yesterday," she said. But I did not know he was going. He did not tell me. Maybe . . . I think . . . he is angry with me. When I last spoke with him, I was not thinking clearly, and I am afraid that I made him feel that I no longer wanted to be his wife. I asked him to put off our wedding and told him that my grandmother was the most important person in my life. I did not mean it the way it sounded, but he walked away from me before I could explain. Because I mourn my grandmother my heart is heavy with sadness, but the feelings I have for your grandson are still strong. I wish he were here now."

Spotted Calf had noticed that Walks High had been unusually quiet for several days before he and Red Lance had ridden out after Whirlwind. He thought he knew why, but he decided to let the girl explain.

"Why do you think my grandson is angry with you?"

Moisture filled the girl's eyes. She pulled the elk-hide robe tighter around her shoulders and stared for a long moment into Spotted Calf's outside fire. Only a few people were moving around outside their lodges, since it was just after dawn and the air was crisp. "Because I asked him to wait thirteen moons for us to get married," she told the old man.

The old man waited, but the girl said no more. Her eyes looked into the flames, yet she did not see them.

"We do have our ways," he reminded her. "When we lose someone to death, we mourn. We all know these things. I know that my grandson knows it."

"My grandmother, she . . . ." A tear slid down the girl's face. She struggled to keep herself together.

"Your grandmother was good, strong, and wise. I know that losing her is the hardest thing you have ever endured. I also know that it was difficult things which made her wise and strong. We are not born with such goodness, strength, and wisdom. She was an Only One. She did not take another husband even after your grandfather was killed when your father was still a boy. This so impressed your mother that she vowed to be an Only One if anything ever happened to your father. Her blood is in you, and you can learn to be strong. You, too, can turn a bad thing into something good."

Sun Rise Woman pulled her eyes away from the fire and looked up, but not directly into the old man's face. "What do you mean?" she asked.

"Even bad things have a purpose. If you do not allow something bad to defeat you, it can serve a purpose by making you stronger." Spotted Calf spoke softly, knowing that she was on the edge of falling apart. "Mourn for your grandmother. Many of us are mourning with you and your family. Your family has honored all of our customs, which must be remembered and followed at times like this. Your family cooked and offered food to the people. That is a way of asking others to share your grief with you. When we came to eat the food you had prepared, it was our way of saying that we share your grief. Then you all gave away your finest things, until you had nothing left to wear and no robes to keep you warm at night. Then some of the people turned around and gave *you* clothing and robes. That is their way of telling you that life goes on. No one would have left you naked and cold. Whatever happens to any of us, there is still dignity. There is still life, and it goes on."

Sun Rise Woman wiped away her tears. After a moment, she held her hands over the fire to warm them. "I think I will talk with my mother and father. If they agree, maybe Walks High and I can marry in the summer."

Even as the woman he loved wrapped her thoughts around him, Walks High gazed down a long embankment. Below, at the river's edge, were bones—the bones of a large animal. The warrior turned to his friend. "My father's trail leads here," he said, pointing to a spot on the narrow animal trail running along the edge of the embankment. "Then it ends." He shrugged and threw up his hands. "We have backtracked two times. I am confused."

Red Lance took a long look at the bones below them, until a low whistle downslope caught his attention. Both he and Walks High grabbed their bows. It was the white man. They had left him with the horses, and now he was pointing off to the west. The warriors instinctively ducked below the skyline and looked west.

Bear Heart appeared just below the crest of a long hill, loping his horse toward them.

The three warriors met in the shallow draw where de la Verendrye was waiting with the horses. Bear Heart dismounted and motioned for the others to join him.

The four men crouched down behind a sparse chokecherry thicket. In the morning half of the sky, the sun was a low, dim glow behind the thick clouds. There was a bite to the air this morning, and each man had a robe tied around his shoulder.

Bear Heart rubbed his hands as he spoke: "I found the white man's trail further west. But it came back to the east along the river, to some thick willows. There the man left his horse and walked further east. He backtracked up the slope from the river, to the edge of the high bank. It looks like he might have stayed there for a time. The grass was flat where he was lying. Then he came east again, but after he stepped onto the loose shale, his tracks are hard to follow. Did you find anything?"

Walks High stared at the older warrior. He had never liked the man. Bear Heart was a hard man, always ready with criticism, especially for Whirlwind. Everyone knew he was hard on anyone who rode the warpath with him. Like the time he ridiculed Spotted Horse just because Spotted Horse's roan stepped into a prairie dog hole. But Bear Heart was not the leader here. Moreover, Walks High knew that Bear Heart did not care about Whirlwind's well-being. Though his father had never told him, Walks High had learned from others that Bear Heart's intense dislike of Whirlwind came from the fact that High Hawk had passed the lance of the war leader to Whirlwind instead of him. At the moment, Bear Heart's reason for joining the two younger warriors was not clear. He had not revealed it to

Walks High or Red Lance. But, because of the white man's guarded behavior, Walks High had his suspicions. Walks High knew he would have to watch the older warrior very closely. But in a strange way, Bear Heart would be useful since he was the best tracker among the Wolf Warriors.

"The tracks of my father's horse end at the edge of the bank above the river. He did not turn in any direction from the spot where they stop."

Bear Heart frowned. "Perhaps you should show me that spot." The younger warriors nodded and stood. "And you should come, too," Bear Heart said to de la Verendrye.

The signs were old but plain. A horse had come at a fast walk along the narrow animal trail, and then there were no more tracks. Bear Heart looked west along the edge of the shale bank. Although it was longer than it was high, the top of it was still far above the river. Bear Heart pointed to a slight dip near where the loose dirt and shale ended on the west edge of the inward curving bank. "That is where the white man hid," he said. He motioned for de la Verendrye. "From where we stand, I would say it is less than one hundred paces to where the other white man lay in hiding," he said to de la Verendrye. "Is that within the killing range of the holy iron?"

De la Verendrye cautiously approached the warriors, keeping the two younger ones between himself and Bear Heart. He looked toward the dip at the top edge of the west end of the shale bank. He nodded once. "Yes," he said, "that is an easy shot."

All three warriors looked hard at the white man. Walks High turned a worried face to Red Lance. Their eyes locked, then they both looked down toward the river. Toward the bones on the water's edge.

They rode across the river twice to reach the bones. Crossing once at the bottom of the long slope some distance downstream, they followed the north bank upstream until they were directly across from the bones. Then, leaving de la Verendrye with the war horses, they rode across for the second time—this time much more cautiously.

"It's a horse," Bear Heart said.

Part of the carcass was on the bank, the hindquarters. The shoulders, neck, and head were underwater. It was fresh, and they could see that coyotes had cleaned the exposed parts, leaving some flesh on the underside of the neck and head.

Walks High slid the tip of his war lance under the head and levered it up out of the water. His mouth grew tight. This had been his father's war horse. A broken eagle feather was still tied into its mane behind the right ear.

By the middle of the afternoon they had finished searching both sides of the river, both upstream and down. They had found a set of fresh bear tracks as well as many coyote signs—but no sign of Whirlwind. The sun was now an even fainter glow behind the clouds, which had grown darker. Large snowflakes began to fall. The three Wolf Warriors rejoined the white man where they had left him and their horses hidden in a buffaloberry stand. He was working with the holy iron when they returned.

Bear Heart gave de la Verendrye a long, hard stare but said nothing.

Red Lance, however, was curious. "Will it work?" he asked.

De la Verendrye nodded. "I think so. I could find nothing wrong with it. It just needed to be cleaned and . . . it needs to be rubbed with some grease." He glanced toward the grim-faced Walks High. "Did you find anything?"

"The body of my father's horse—nothing more," replied Walks High.

"But that is good," Red Lance pointed out. "I think my uncle is alive. Otherwise we would have found . . . something."

Bear Heart untied two large rabbits and brought them to the fire de la Verendrye had going. "I think so, too," he said. "Our war leader is alive." He tossed the dead rabbits at the white man's feet. "Can you cook?"

De la Verendrye nodded without looking up at Bear Heart. Then he glanced toward Walks High as he pulled his knife and reached for the carcasses. "What do you think happened? Did the horse fall?"

Bear Heart answered. "Yes. The horse fell—after it was shot with the holy iron." He pointed toward the long, high shale embankment. "On the west end, the white man hid and laid in wait. When he shot, his aim was low and he hit the horse. The horse fell and slid down the embankment. Either our war leader jumped off, or he could not. But I know he is alive."

De la Verendrye cleared his throat and spoke to Bear Heart for the first time since the warrior had joined them. "How do you know?"

Bear Heart looked down on the white man and watched him gut and skin the rabbits. "The dead horse," he said. "The neck and jaw ropes are gone. There are no weapons anywhere—no lance, no bow, no arrows. The white man would not have come for those things. Just as we do not know how to use your holy iron, you white men do not know how to use our weapons. The white man did not take Whirlwind's weapons. Whirlwind gathered up his own weapons. He is alive. Besides, after the white man shot he walked back to his horse in the willows. There are two sets of tracks, one from the willows to his hiding place and one back. If he had gone to where the dead horse is, his second set of tracks would have returned to the willows from a different place." The warrior paused, a mixture of contempt and amusement dancing in his dark eyes.

De la Verendrye finished skinning the last rabbit. Then he grabbed one in each hand and stood up.

"Where are you going?" Bear Heart asked.

"To the river." He held up the rabbits. "To wash these and my hands."

Red Lance also stood up and followed de la Verendrye. Bear Heart watched them briefly and then sat down across the fire from Walks High.

"Your father is alive," he said to the younger warrior.

After a moment, Walks High nodded. "Yes. But where is he?"

Bear Heart glanced toward the west and then pointed with his thumb. "He is still after the white man," he said. "I know your father. I have known him longer than you have. I may not like him, but I know him. I would do many things differently than he does. Having the lance of the war leader does not mean that a man always does the right thing. But I do know this. He is like the animal in his vision—the wolf. Like the wolf, he will stay on the trail, follow the scent. Until he makes the kill."

Large snowflakes fell slowly to the Earth, seeming to not move at all. A hush fell with the snow over the valley of the White Earth River. A pair of dark, penetrating eyes looked out from beneath the brush covering a deep, narrow gully—looking for something that stood out in the sameness of white. Something that did not belong. An interloper who moved outside the flow of life.

Whirlwind added a handful of dry twigs to the low, smokeless fire. The rabbit roasting over the bed of coals began to smell good.

The shelter was ideal. He had covered over the south, upslope end of a narrow gully with dry brush. It was high enough inside for him to kneel but low enough to heat easily. A windbreak made of wrist-sized wood, between the doorway and the fire, also reflected heat inward. To the left of the fire, Whirlwind had stretched and pegged down the fresh hide of a rabbit. It and three more, with the hair left on, would make good coverings for his hands or moccasin liners to keep his feet warm. With the hair scraped or pulled off, and allowed to dry without further treatment, the rabbit hide would dry as rawhide and could then be soaked, cut into thin strips, and twisted into bowstring. He had not decided how he would use the rabbit hide, but he hoped the snares he had set earlier would catch three or four more.

The warrior flexed his injured knee. It was getting better each day. Wrapping it seemed to help since walking and putting weight on it was easier that way. Yesterday he had found a dead ash sapling and used it as a cane. Since it was as long as he was tall, he decided to make a lance out of it. He could still use it as a cane. With his knife he began to groove the notch for the stone lance point, pausing occasionally to fit the point.

Whirlwind looked out at the snow. Large flakes usually meant the snow would not fall for long. Already the flakes were thinning out, and he could see further into the valley. It did not matter that the snow would cover the white man's trail since Whirlwind knew that the killer was traveling west and following the valley of the White Earth River.

The rabbit was nearly done cooking, and Whirlwind looked forward to a good meal. He had traveled a long distance today, not as far as he would have riding a horse but far enough for a man walking with an injured knee. Along the way he had killed the rabbit with a sling he had made—his best weapon for the moment. Soon he would have a lance again, but it was the lack of a bow which worried him most.

Early this morning he had seen fresh bear tracks, big tracks. It was impossible to outrun a bear on foot, even without an injury. If he saw one, his only hope was to hide from it. If one came upon him by surprise, climbing a tree would be his only hope—if there was a tree close by and if he could move fast enough on his injured knee. With a bow, at least he would have a chance to defend himself.

Bears were not the only reason for having a good bow. A bow was his fang, his claw. It closed the distance between him and the wary white-tailed deer, so his family could have plenty of food and clothing. It brought down the most powerful animal that roamed these plains, the great buffalo. The bow added to his ability to defend his family and his people.

Still, Whirlwind reminded himself, the bow did not make the man and the warrior. It was the man, the hunter, the warrior who gave meaning to the weapon by using it to provide and protect. And he was not really without the bow, even now. Inside of him was the knowledge, and in his hands the skill, to make a bow.

Whirlwind put down the knife and inspected the notch of the lance. He smiled as the stone point slid tightly into the groove, as if it had always belonged there. It reminded him of something his father had said about making bows.

They had been traveling home in the snow. Returning with several good ash staves Spotted Calf had cut, just after the moon was new in the Moon of Frost in the Lodge. It was Whirlwind's seventeenth winter. They had to travel on snowshoes because the snow was deep that winter. At their night camp inside a cozy brush shelter, Spotted Calf pointed to one of the freshly cut staves. "It will take several winters to dry and season. When it is ready, I will carve away the outside to find the bow that is in it."

"There is a bow already inside?" Whirlwind could hear himself asking.

"Yes. There is. A man does not make a bow from such a piece of ash wood. He finds it. He carves away the parts that do not belong. He helps the bow to come out."

Whirlwind reluctantly let the memory fade away, but it had lent him strength, as it always did.

He looked out again. The snow had stopped. Silence lay over the valley like a comfortable robe. He was glad. Silence was a strong ally to the hunter and the warrior and at times like this a soothing presence.

He pulled the stone lance point from its notch. Next he would heat some water to soak his glue stick. Rubbing the softened glue inside the notch would help hold the point even tighter. Then he would wrap it with wet rawhide. After the rawhide and the glue dried, he would have a lance again.

Whirlwind moved the rabbit away from the coals. It was done cooking, and he was hungry. He pulled off a leg and took a bite, savoring the tender meat as he chewed. It was his first hot food in three days.

He continued to gaze out at the fading day. Tomorrow he would look for a thick chokecherry stalk or a young ash tree a little smaller than his wrist. If he could find one long enough, he knew a way to quickly make a bow. His father had taught him that many, many winters ago.

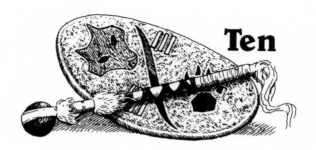

Ten

I n Whirlwind's absence Caught the Eagle, resplendent in a quilled war shirt, was the warrior leader for this journey to the winter encampment. Next to him rode Spotted Horse, carrying the eagle feather staff which signified Caught the Eagle's status as the ranking warrior leader among the Wolf Tail band. The remaining warriors rode on either side of the moving column of people.

In the column, some people walked, some rode horses, and some rode on drag poles pulled by horses. It was mostly the very old or the very young who rode on the drag poles, which were piled high with folded up lodges and household furnishings: Backrests, rawhide food and clothing cases, and containers with tools, utensils, weapons, and personal items. Only a few burial scaffolds had been left behind at the summer encampment site.

Beyond the mounted warriors on either side of the column, from the middle to the rear, the horses were being driven by older boys on horseback. Two smaller herds were easier to manage than one large one, since the total number of horses was nearly four hundred.

They had been traveling since midmorning. Snow had fallen for a short while in the afternoon, but it had stopped, although the sky was filled with thick, gray clouds. Everyone generally was in a good mood. The two-day journey was exciting, especially for the young, although the usual exuberance of such a move was tempered by the recent tragedy in the High Hawk family.

At the head of the column, just behind Caught the Eagle and the two scout warriors, rode three old men: Stone, White Crane, and Spotted Calf. At a bend in the Smoking Earth River, Stone sent one of the scout warriors back with word that they had reached the place for the overnight stop.

The three old men rode to the top of a small rise and reined in their horses to watch as the column dispersed itself along a high bench east of the river, a place where they had camped before.

The Wolf Tail people would set up the overnight encampment in a circular pattern, the same pattern they were in at both the summer and winter camps. The layout of their encampment was always the same; only the locations changed.

The horse herds were taken to the river for a drink. They were themselves a stream of colors: Brown, tan, reddish brown, white, black, gray. Roans, buckskins, paints. They filled the river from bank to bank as they lowered their heads and drank.

By the time the herd was finished watering, the lodges in the overnight camp were all set up. First, lodgepoles had been unpacked, arranged, and set up. Next, ridge poles, with the top of the lodges themselves attached, had been quickly raised—one with every heartbeat, it seemed. Soon the lodges were ready.

The three old men sitting on their horses up above the night camp were enthralled at the sight, though they had witnessed it many, many times. This was life. This was being Lakota. Only one other sight could compare to this: a buffalo hunt.

White Crane turned to his lifelong friend, the medicine man Stone. "Last night I had a dream," he said. "Our people were on the move, just like today. Suddenly, we came to different turns on the same road. Some of the people went in one direction, and some went in another. I did not know why."

Stone was quiet for a moment, thinking about his friend's words. "There are always things in our path that could divide us," he reminded the older man. "Perhaps your dream was about something in our path. In the path of the Wolf Tail people."

"Perhaps," replied White Crane, "but I do not want to envision our people as divided over anything. Do you suppose that is to come?"

Spotted Calf listened closely to his two old friends, even as he looked to the north and wondered where his son, grandson, and the others were.

After a long silence, the medicine man spoke again. "There is something in the middle of our road now," he said. "We have already talked about it in the council lodge."

"The white man?" asked White Crane. "Or the holy iron?"

"The holy iron. Yes," replied Stone. "But not the one white man who has come to be among us."

"His kind," offered Spotted Calf.

"Yes. His kind," Stone agreed.

"What can they do to divide us?" White Crane wanted to know.

Stone replied quickly. "With new things. New ways. Especially if they are a strong people."

"How can such a people be strong?" scoffed White Crane. "They do not live close to the Earth as we do."

"There are ways of being strong without being wise and without knowing the Earth. If they are like blades of grass, they may be numberless. Too many to count. Perhaps they are like ants, with their strength coming from their numbers." Stone paused to tighten the robe around his thin shoulders and to look up at a hawk circling just overhead. "I do not know the number of our people," he continued. "We are many. But we are not as many as the deer people, or the elk, and others. So our strength is not in numbers. Our strength is in knowing the Earth and our place on it. We are not swift like the antelope. We cannot fly like our relative the hawk up there. Our strength is in knowing that we can borrow something from each of our relatives to help make our lives better. We hunt like the wolf. When winter comes, we find a safe place like the bear does. Like the deer, we are always on the watch for enemies. In this way we know we are no more or no less than any being who is of the Earth. But do white men think this way?" The medicine man narrowed his eyes and looked down to the ground. "Last summer I threw a piece of meat to the ground," he went on. "First, only one ant came, and it could not move the meat. But in a while came another ant. Then another, until there were so many that they moved that piece of meat without difficulty. If white men have strength like that, perhaps they see no need to know the Earth. Perhaps they just take what they want."

The three friends fell silent. Stone and White Crane gazed at the night camp, where several fires were now burning outside while smoke was rising out of the smoke holes of many lodges.

Spotted Calf drew his elk-hide robe tighter around his shoulders and looked northward again. Images of his son and grandson swirled in his mind like a sudden snow squall. As a younger man he had followed the buffalo and elk many times, and he could not remember how many times he had set his feet on the warpath. Each time, he had done so because it was necessary, though he could see the pain in the eyes of Carries the Medicine, Whirlwind's mother. Only now did he understand the burden of those who waited.

In the nearly thirty winters of his life with Carries the Medicine, she had not once asked Spotted Calf to put aside his weapons and forsake the warpath. Like many Lakota women, she quietly and bravely waited for every war party to return. She had carried her burden. Spotted Calf soon learned what every Lakota warrior learned: Fathers might pass on to their sons the way of the warrior, but the sons learned their courage from their mothers. Warriors often reminded one another of this truth on the eve of battle, saying, "We cannot be defeated unless the hearts of our women are on the ground."

Spotted Calf sighed softly. The emptiness that had come when Carries the Medicine had left him and this life, nearly seven winters ago, was even greater than before they had married. The eagle feather bonnet hanging in his lodge was made from over sixty feathers, telling that he had ridden the warpath honorably and bravely. But he did not consider that the measure of his life. He felt that his life was as good as it could have been because he had won the love and loyalty of Carries the Medicine. And he saw her strength each time he looked into the face of their warrior son, the war leader of the Wolf Tail Lakota.

The old warrior understood that it was necessary for Whirlwind, Walks High, and Red Lance to put themselves in danger. It was the way of the warrior to protect the people, just as it was the way of the woman to care for the home and the family. Everyone had a purpose. Now it was his purpose, since he was one of the old ones, to use his knowledge and wisdom to help his people. He was still a skillful hunter. In fact, there was no one among the Wolf Tail people who could surpass his skill with the bow. And if necessary, he could take to the warpath again. But his place was no longer to be the first to ride the warpath or lead a heart-stopping gallop into a herd of buffalo. Now his place was to advise, to teach, and to guide. Spotted Calf reminded himself that the knowledge and skills that he had gained over the many, many winters of his life were now more valuable to others than they were to him. The best thing he could do now was to be strong and wise enough to accept this change.

He looked around at the secluded little valley where the people had made night camp. Many of the trees had given up their leaves. The ash, oak, chokecherry, buffaloberry, and plum had honored the cycle of change in their lives. They stood leafless but not lifeless. *I cannot be any different,* Spotted Calf thought. *Nothing lives forever, and nothing is the same forever.* Still, things changed in different ways. A tree could give up its leaves and then wait for new leaves. That kind of change was a known part of life. So was a man growing old. A wintry breeze did not belong in summer. When one came, as they now and then did, it was an unwelcome change. Perhaps that was what White Crane's dream was about. Unwelcome change. Yet that, too, had been part of Lakota life.

Spotted Calf glanced toward his companions. "My cousins," he said. "I think often of the stories my father told of his boyhood in the lake country to the north and east. It was a good life for our people. They were strong and had little to fear from enemies, until the Ojibway traded with the white men for holy irons. They became stronger and drove our people away. That was change we did not ask for. But when did change ever ask if it could visit itself upon us? And how many times has change not occurred because we said no to it? Still, not all change is bad. Many things have changed for our people since our fathers were born, some changes good, some bad. The coming of horses was a good change. They have spirits and a place in this world because they were born into it, as we are. It was not hard for us to find ways to travel this life together. But holy irons are different. They have no spirits and must depend on the wisdom of men to give them meaning. Some men will give them a good meaning. Some will give them a bad meaning. As I see it, that is one of the many things standing in our path."

White Crane nodded. His gaze traveled through time as well as space. Though he looked in the direction of a far

pine-covered hillside, Spotted Calf's words made him see the
days of his own boyhood. "Yes, that is true," he said. "I
remember my father's and grandfather's stories about the
buffalo runs, before the time of the horses. My grandfather
did learn to ride, and he saw how good it was to have horses.
Yet he still hunted the buffalo on foot." He paused. "Yes,
my friend. I think I understand your words."

"My father told me that his father's heart was sad until
his dying day because he had to leave the lake country,"
Stone said. "Many of those old ones felt the same. But, if
they had not left, the Ojibway might have killed them all.
They killed too many as it was. I can remember my grandfather's stories about the smoking waters, picking wild rice,
canoe races, and spear fishing. He liked to get up every day
before dawn to watch the mist grow over the lakes and listen
to the loons and the blackbirds. In his young manhood, he
made up a song from the sound of his paddle dipping into
the waters whenever he traveled in his canoe. It was his
life-song. His dying song. He said there were not enough
trees in this new prairie country to make one good canoe.
He was afraid of the Great Muddy River. If you remember,
my father and I took his body back to the lake country after
he died. He wanted to return to the Earth there, where he
was born."

"There are things in our path," Spotted Calf pointed out.
"There will always be. Things change. Our people left the
lake country and became prairie dwellers. The horse came to
us. It takes us two days to reach places that would have taken
six in the old days. We ride into the buffalo now to kill them,
instead of hiding in ambush or running them off a high place.
Now . . . now the thing that chased our people from the lake
country comes to us again, like a bad dream. The holy iron.

"Everything happens for a reason, Cousins. We made the
horse a part of our ways. We are stronger because we have
done so. Perhaps, then, we would be wise to take hold of the

holy iron. We can give it a good meaning, rather than turning away from it."

White Crane and Stone turned Spotted Calf's words over in their minds. They were all old hunter-warriors because they had carefully studied everything that lay in the paths they had traveled. Sometimes a being who passed by covered his trail by putting back the stone he had disturbed, thus hiding his trail. Old hunter-warriors knew that a lack of signs did not always mean there was no trail. By the same token, the heart of the being who left the trail could not be seen in his footprint. Therefore, he who studied the trail had to do so with more than his eyes. Old hunter-warriors knew this, too. That which could be seen with the eyes told only part of the story. In order to know the entire story, one also had to see with his heart and his mind.

Stone pointed to a young rider coming toward them as he spoke. "Your words are good and true, my friends. And two men come to my mind now: Whirlwind and Bear Heart. They look at the coming of the holy iron differently, as they look at many things differently. Many of us agree with Whirlwind when he says we must be careful of the holy iron. Some of us stand with Bear Heart when he says we are foolish for being too cautious." The medicine man paused and glanced at his old friend White Crane. "Whirlwind and Bear Heart came into my mind when you told of your dream. They are both strong men. Wherever each goes, people will follow. If they go in different directions, then . . ." Stone paused. "They are not friends, but they are also not enemies. As I see it, there is one thing which might turn them completely against each other. Perhaps it already has."

"The holy iron," said White Crane.

They fell silent as the rider came close. It was Red Legs.

"Grandfather," he said to Stone. "Caught the Eagle has sent me. He asks that you and the other grandfathers honor his family by eating in their lodge this evening."

The three old friends looked at one another. Stone turned with a smile to his grandson. "Tell our nephew that he and his family honors us to ask. We will come."

Red Legs spun his horse and urged it into a swift lope. "What will he see," wondered White Crane, "by the time he reaches the winter of his life? What place will the holy iron have among our people then?"

Stone and Spotted Calf nodded, but none of the three old warriors spoke further as they rode down into the encampment. Red Legs had already disappeared behind a row of lodges. A breeze from the north carried the distant song of a wolf, followed by a high, challenging whistle of a bull elk.

Eleven

Whirlwind looked at his back trail, mainly from habit but also to study the meandering path he had been following. He was certain it was the white man's trail. The size of the horse's hoofprints and the length of the stride was familiar to the warrior. According to the white man back in the Wolf Tail camp, the horse was a tall bay. The white man they had cornered on the ridge near the valley of the two rivers was riding a tall bay. If these were his tracks, then the rider was in no hurry. Whirlwind smiled inwardly. As far as the rider of the bay horse knew, his pursuer was dead, and that was an advantage for Whirlwind.

The warrior moved into a thin grove of oaks and sat down to rest. A gray-looking sun was in the lower half of the afternoon sky. Layers of clouds dimmed the daylight, and chilly breezes danced along the hillsides. Snowfall from a few days past had softened the ground, and any creature that did not move and step carefully left tracks to follow.

Whirlwind rubbed his knee. It was getting better each day, though he kept it wrapped tightly. Frequent stops to rest helped greatly. At the moment, the warrior felt no particular urgency. His quarry was moving slowly, and for now it was only important not to lose his trail. In any case, Whirlwind sensed that the white man was heading for the mountains—the Black Hills.

The Black Hills. A place that a medicine woman some-time in the dim and faraway past had seen in a dream. It was her dream, some of the old ones would say, which drew the first Lakota to the prairies west of the Great Muddy River—in the time long, long before the coming of the horses.

Whirlwind had traveled to those great, shadowy mountains several times. From a distance, the giant pines on their slopes gave the great mountains a blackness. In the eye of the beholder, that blackness hovered between the prairie and the sky, signifying the place those mountains held in the heart of the Lakota. For Whirlwind, it was a place of peace and a place of song. The quiet strength of those great mountains brought him peace, and the bright voice of the wind in the pines made his heart sing. Each time he went there he had felt a welcome that only a mother could give. More than once he had climbed to a rocky precipice to do nothing more than sit and become a small part of everything around him. In one mountain meadow, he had seen elk, buffalo, deer, and antelope grazing together in herds so thick that it seemed a man could walk across their backs to the opposite end of the meadow. There was a quietness and a serenity here that reached deep into every being's soul and strengthened the bond shared by every living thing. Nowhere else had Whirl-wind felt such communion.

Now he was trailing a killer whose path might lead him to the Black Hills. It was not the way he wanted to return to that place.

Voices suddenly pushed into his thoughts. Voices from far away. Wolves. They were singing, many of them. Singing the song of a good hunt. Whirlwind touched the small bag hanging around his neck. He could feel the fang inside as the wolf songs drifted on the wind for long moments. Songs of joy. Songs of family. Songs of strength.

After a time the wolf songs faded. Whirlwind looked up into the gray sky, and his lips parted slightly in surprise. Just above the northern horizon was a long gray-black cloud in the shape of a running wolf. He watched until it was a wolf no more. Then he quickly removed his shirt. With the point of his flint knife, he gouged out ten pieces of flesh from each upper arm just below the shoulder. He laid the offering on a small, flat stone.

"Grandfather," he whispered, "you have given me a difficult path. But you have also given me hope and reminded me how to walk that path. For that I give you thanks and this pitiful offering of my flesh . . ."

A single, long howl rode the wind. Whirlwind smiled, gathered his things, and put on his shirt. He would travel a little further and then make camp for the night. There he would fashion a bow from the good strong ash sapling he had cut this morning.

Floundering on the sharp incline, the bay slipped to one knee on the treacherous mud and pitched its rider into the muck. Bruneaux landed with a heavy thud but came immediately to his feet, struggling wide-eyed to catch his breath. Moments later, after regaining his composure and his breath, he unleashed a string of curses. The horse eyed him warily.

Jerking the reins, the man led the horse up the incline to a narrow bench and tied him to a lone scrub oak. He had tried to cradle and protect the rifle when he had fallen. Landing on his own forearm, he had knocked the wind out of himself.

Bruneaux hurriedly checked the weapon. He found no damage and breathed a sigh of relief. Squinting up at the sky, he decided it was time to make camp for the night. Besides, he was hungry.

If there was anything Henri Bruneaux was skilled at, it was making a well-concealed night camp. He looked about until he spied a small, tight grove of oaks in a narrow draw between two low hills.

"You must conceal yourself well at night," a man named Letellier had told him. "Them brown-skinned, sneaking heathens will find you if you do not." Letellier ran a small trading post on the outskirts of the Saint Louis settlement. In his younger days he had been a voyageur and liked to brag of many close encounters with "sneaking heathens." One such encounter had cost him his entire right ear. A young Ojibway warrior had stolen into the night camp of Letellier's party and sliced off the ear of the sleeping voyageur.

Bruneaux grinned at the memory of the one-eared man's words of caution. But he took them to heart. Good advice. And hiding was easier than fighting.

By sundown he was inside the shelter made of dried brush, interwoven upright between four small oak trees standing close together. The bay was nearby, concealed by a similar structure. Even in the daylight, the most discerning eye would have had difficulty detecting the Frenchman's hideout. At night it was nearly impossible, unless someone took the trouble to follow the smell of smoke or cooking meat. Or the big man's body odor. Still, it did not enter Bruneaux's mind to obliterate the tracks he and the horse had left in the mud where he had fallen.

Bruneaux kept his small fire going as he chewed on his last two strips of deer meat. A hindquarter of deer did not last long for someone with a large, constant hunger. He glanced at the flintlock. He would get more fresh meat tomorrow. It was easy enough, with the gun. Deer were plentiful. Maybe there were not as many as along the Mississippi River breaks, but enough. And they were too dumb to stay out of range. Wiping his mouth with a sleeve, he yielded to a stray thought and opened his shot bag. There were thirty-six lead balls. His eyes narrowed as he remembered that several of the previous balls had been lost on that ridge, when those Indians had nearly killed him. A hand moved to the long wound on his cheek. At least he had gotten one of them then, and another one later. Perhaps.

The one who had fallen down the shale embankment had to be dead. If getting shot had not killed him, then the fall would have. Bruneaux could still see the immense splash as horse and rider had hit the water. No one could have lived after that.

Bruneaux picked up the very last piece of deer meat. Getting fresh meat would be the first thing to do tomorrow. But then what? Winter was nearly here. Perhaps he should find a place to hole up—like last winter along the Mississippi. That lean-to he had built was snug, and the deer were thick along the river bottoms. Food was plentiful here, too, but his ammunition was low. And he had only three more horns of powder.

He chewed and swallowed the last piece of meat while reaching a decision. West. He could keep riding west for a few days to get further away from that village and de la Verendrye's friends. De la Verendrye! That pup! He sent those heathens! A curse erupted from his face as images of Spanish gold coins and a pretty, black-eyed girl vividly appeared in his mind. He smashed a fist into the wall of his shelter, driving away the images. For several long moments, he glared into the fire. West. He would ride west for a while longer. Then he would decide where to hole up for the winter.

Whirlwind sat outside the opening to his night shelter, watching the last remnants of day's light yield to the darkness. Since before sundown, he had been working on his bow, and thinking of home. By now, he felt, the Wolf Tail band would be on their way to the winter campsite—if they were not there already. Seasonal moves were always exciting. It was during such a time that he had courted Her Good Trail, during the Winter of the Glowing Black Stone. The

Wolf Tail people had been summering north of the White Earth River, two days' ride west of the Great Muddy. Bear Looks Behind was the war leader at that time when three young men from the Speaks Red People, whose lodges were somewhere west of the Black Hills, came to show three fist-sized pieces of shiny black stone. They had traveled far to the west, to mountains filled with bighorn sheep, and found the stone, they had said. That stone made good knives and arrowheads, because it kept a sharp edge for a long time. That autumn, early in the Moon of Falling Leaves when the people traveled to a winter camp near the White Earth River, was when Whirlwind first took his place in line at the lodge of Hollow Horn.

His best friend Goes in Center told him that Noisy Hawk had already offered more horses than anyone ever had for a wife, but his heart told him he had to try to win Her Good Trail—the girl whose eyes glowed like the shiny black stones from the mountain country, and whose walking was like a graceful dance. And Whirlwind did win her, after his father had let him use the elk-hide courting robe painted by the Elk Dreamer, Sees at Night. "I used it to court your mother," Spotted Calf had said. "It worked because you are here." Later, those words had a stronger meaning, when Her Good Trail's stomach swelled with their child, for especially then she seemed to dance as she walked.

He wanted to stay in the warm valleys of those memories, but a sudden breath of cool air brought him back to the half-light between sundown and darkness. Still, he wondered how many young men were impatiently waiting outside the lodges of this or that eligible young woman back in the village of the Wolf Tail people. But the tragedy suffered by the High Hawk family, the same tragedy that had brought him here to this lonely night camp, had surely dampened the usual excitement of the Wolf Tail people's move to the winter encampment. For a moment, Whirlwind stopped his work and sat with the flint blade in his hand poised above the ash stave.

Images of the dead face of High Hawk's mother swirled through his mind. He shook them off, but he could not erase the effect that one death had had on an entire village. High Hawk's family was not alone with their grief. That was the way of the Lakota—to share grief. But beyond the grief, there were other things. Like Walks High's confusion over Sun Rise Woman's silence.

Whirlwind resumed his work, trying to ignore the sadness he felt for his old friend High Hawk. The sun was well down now, and a far-off screech owl raised his trembling voice to acknowledge the night. A glance inside his shelter at the fire revealed that the bed of coals was nearly ready. He turned and crawled into the shelter.

Narrow gullies and ravines were best for secure and well-hidden night camps. Whirlwind had learned this from his father. Such narrow ravines already had two sides and a closed end. With a well-made roof of shrubs, deadfall, and leaves and a snug door, such a shelter was good even during a hard winter. Whirlwind looked around as he crawled inside. All that was lacking here was the warmth of Her Good Trail lying next to him. But the way of the warrior was filled with many lonely nights.

He closed the door behind him, after one final look into the night. The screech owl was still crying, and a coyote yipped somewhere nearby.

The ash stave was a good one, with only a few knots on it and about half the size of his wrist. He had a bit more work to do before he could begin the drying process. With his flint knife, Whirlwind had shaved away layers of wood from one side of the stave. He left the bark on the opposite side. Over his good knee, he tested it. It was coming along.

Low flames danced lazily from the bed of coals. Whirlwind had dug a long, shallow firepit against the side of the ravine and slowly developed a bed of coals. He added a few small twigs to it and hung the skewered rabbit on the spit.

He planned to work far into the night. As soon as he was satisfied with the bend in the limbs of the bow, he would hang it over the bed of coals to dry, cure, and harden. While it was drying, he would make arrows.

Outside, darkness covered the land. Inside his cozy shelter, the warrior was warm and safe. Warmer images and thoughts of Her Good Trail surged in on him as he worked on the bow. And amidst those thoughts came another. The warrior wondered if the white man he was hunting could build his own holy iron.

Twelve

Walks High was nearing the end of his watch. It was dawn. Cool, gray daylight grew over the eastern horizon. Night was departing under a clear, blue-black sky. Stars in the western half of the sky were sharply bright. There was a promise of a clear, warm day.

The camp was along an old watercourse, a long stone's throw from the White Earth River. Three large piles of old, old driftwood provided ideal shelter and concealment. Walks High had spent his watch sitting near his war horse, depending on the tall black's keener senses to help him.

A slight rustling came from near the fire. Someone was moving. Bear Heart glanced toward Walks High and moved off into the thick willows. Red Lance cautiously pushed aside his elk-hide robe and sat up. Only the white man, now referred to as Beard, was still asleep, an arm protectively wrapped around his borrowed holy iron.

Walks High left his comfortable perch and walked to the smoldering ashes in the firepit. They had eaten late last night, long after sundown. But hot peppermint tea on a morning like this would chase away the lingering night chill. He stirred the coals and added kindling. Soon, flames flickered up out of the gray coals.

Bear Heart, at the end of his watch, had warned Walks High of heavy rustling noises to the south across the White Earth River. He suspected bear. And during his watch, Walks

High heard the snorting of buffalo bulls, somewhere off to the west. Though the horses peered off intently into the darkness a time or two, nothing seemed to have come close to the camp.

Returning to camp, Bear Heart loudly cleared his throat, causing the white man to stir. He was the only one of the group who did not have a night watch.

After they had made camp, de la Verendrye had worked on the holy iron. Bear Heart had watched with particular interest, though he kept silent. Red Lance, however, did not hide his curiosity. And to his credit, de la Verendrye answered all of the young warrior's questions.

An involuntary moan escaped the white man's lips as he sat up. Red Lance glanced knowingly at Walks High. They knew that his wound was much more painful than he let on, but he had not complained or asked that they slow down their pace.

De la Verendrye squinted at Walks High. "It is cold," he commented.

The young warrior nodded. "I will boil water for tea."

"Good," replied the white man, carefully pushing himself up to a sitting position, "that will warm me."

Bear Heart dropped a handful of small, round stones next to the fire—his contribution to the task of boiling water. When the fire was hot enough, Walks High would place the stones in it. Once the stones were hot, he would drop them into a water flask made from buffalo bladder. Dried wild peppermint leaves would be added after that. Hot tea was a welcome brew on such a morning.

"Will the holy iron work?" asked Bear Heart suddenly.

De la Verendrye nodded, without looking at the warrior. "Yes. I could see nothing wrong with it. It should work."

"Perhaps you should try it. Today."

De la Verendrye glanced in Bear Heart's direction. "Yes, I will. Perhaps after I drink some tea."

The two younger warriors glanced at one another with a mixture of expectation and apprehension. They had heard the sound of the holy iron when Lone Elk was wounded. Now they would hear it and see it up close.

"Who makes holy irons?" Bear Heart wanted to know.

"Men who have learned to do so," replied de la Verendrye.

"Can any white man make a holy iron?"

De la Verendrye shook his head. "No. Only a very few."

"Huh!" snorted the warrior. "Among us, every man has the knowledge and skill to make a bow. Some are more skilled than others, like this young man's grandfather," he noted, pointing toward Walks High. "How is it then that many white men have holy irons if only a few can make them?"

"We trade for them," the white man replied. "Or . . . pay for them. Furs, yellow stone."

"Furs, I know. What is yellow stone?"

"Yellow stone is found in the ground. It is melted and made into round . . . circles. My people consider it to be worth much."

Bear Heart appraised the man's words for a moment. "Yellow stone is considered to be worth more than holy irons? That is hard for me to understand. But it is good to learn that furs are worth something to those who have holy irons to trade."

De la Verendrye nodded. "Yes. Some people would rather have yellow stone than holy irons." He suddenly remembered the gold coins in his pouch and fumbled for one, finally pulling out a Spanish gold piece. "I was given this for working on a boat on the Grandfather River, four winters ago."

Bear Heart lifted an eyebrow. "And *that* is better to have than a holy iron? What can it do?"

The white man handed the coin to the warrior. "You can . . . ah . . ." he struggled to find the right words. "You can buy many different things with that." He pointed at the coin, which Bear Heart now handed to Red Lance.

"The only thing *we* buy is a wife," pointed out Bear Heart, looking doubtfully at the white man. "And then, only if the offer is acceptable to the girl's family. But even then a man does not *own* his wife. I think buying means something different to your people. In our way, if we want something like a horse or a bow from someone else, we trade for it—two young colts for a grown horse or a horse for a good bow. Trading benefits both traders. Since both people end up having what they each want or need. In your way, it seems that only he who has the most round yellow stones can end up having the most things."

De la Verendrye could only nod, yielding as much to the warrior's forcefulness as to his logic.

Red Lance, meanwhile, rubbed the coin, then bit it before he passed it on to Walks High. "My grandfather, who died two winters ago, had an old arrow with a point made of something like this. I forget what it is called, but he said it was a pale red. But now that arrow point is a strange color of green. Could it be the same kind of thing?"

"No. I do not think so," replied de la Verendrye. "Where did your grandfather get the arrow? Did he make it?"

Red Lance shook his head. "No. He traded for it when he was a young man. He was told that it came from east of the lake country."

"Yes," de la Verendrye said. "Among the Dakota, there are many objects made from that iron that turns green. Things that were traded. The Dakota do not have that iron in their country."

Walks High returned the gold coin to the white man. "Is this yellow stone better than the iron that turns green?"

De la Verendrye nodded. "In some ways."

Bear Heart pointed at the holy iron. "That is made from iron and wood. Is that iron different than yellow stone?"

"Yes. That iron is stronger. Harder."

The two young warriors exchanged glances. The council of old men had been right, after all. There was much to be learned from this white man about his kind.

The older warrior measured the white man with a long, even stare. "Do you know where a man could find holy irons to trade?"

De la Verendrye cast a nervous glance toward the river and nodded. "Yes, I do."

"Where is that place?" There was a strange light in the warrior's eyes as he waited for the answer.

The white man cleared his throat. "South," he said, "and east. At a white man's town along the Grandfather River."

"How far?"

De la Verendrye looked hard at the fire, as if the answer were there. "Twenty, thirty days' travel," he said quietly. "If you push hard. More, if you do not."

Bear Heart smiled. "Far into Pawnee country. It will be an exciting journey."

Walks High noticed that there was an edge in the older warrior's voice and a look of helplessness in the white man's eyes. He motioned toward the white man, pointing to a spot on the opposite side of the fire away from Bear Heart. "Sit there," he said, as he put stones in the fire. "Soon we will have tea."

Bear Heart saw the younger warrior's maneuver but said nothing. He looked into the fire. A hard set came to his mouth, but there was a glow of victory in his eyes.

From inside the willow thicket, Red Lance looked west and waited for the thunderous voice of the holy iron. The white man had cautioned that horses were always afraid of the noise and might run. Consequently, the warriors had tied all their horses securely to clumps of willow stalks. Twice the white man would shoot the holy iron. Walks

High and Red Lance would take turns remaining with the horses to calm them.

BOOM! The crashing noise reverberated up and down the valley of the White Earth River. Within the same heartbeat as the noise, a spout of water erupted from the river's surface near the opposite bank—exactly where the white man had said the iron ball would hit. A cloud of white smoke drifted away on the breeze, and a slight burning smell reached the two warriors' noses.

The horses had only flinched a little. Red Lance was relieved. "The Thunders make greater noises than that every summer," he shouted to them.

De la Verendrye started reloading, knowing that Bear Heart was watching his every movement.

"Beard," Walks High said quietly. "When you shoot the holy iron, I see how it pushes you back."

"Yes," de la Verendrye replied. "It kicks. Every holy iron does that."

De la Verendrye rested the end of the stock on his foot and poured a small amount of powder down the barrel. Then he pulled a ball from the shot bag and fit it into the end. Pulling the ramrod he shoved the ball down into the barrel, tapping the ball a few times with the rod to make sure it was well seated.

He nodded to Walks High, who trotted away toward the willow thicket. Soon after, Red Lance arrived.

De la Verendrye replaced the ramrod and held the weapon barrel up as he pulled back the striker with his right thumb. He nodded toward Bear Heart and Red Lance. "I will aim for the water near the bank on the other side," he said.

As he pulled the butt against his shoulder and placed his cheek firmly against the stock, de la Verendrye suddenly realized he had probably outlived his usefulness to the warrior Bear Heart. He decided to find a way to tell Walks High about his very first conversation with Whirlwind's rival.

BOOM! White smoke belched from the flashpan an instant before the weapon fired. Another spout erupted upward from the water.

Red Lance regarded the weapon with wide eyes. Bear Heart seemed unimpressed with the weapon's performance. But de la Verendrye knew that the older warrior was very shrewd, and that worried him.

When the last echoes of the shot had faded into the hazy distances of morning, a silence came to the valley as if the land itself were recoiling from the presence of an intruder. De la Verendrye looked down at the weapon. "The bad thing about this," he said, "is the noise it makes. Now if Bruneaux is in the area, he knows that someone else has a holy iron."

Bear Heart spun on his heel and walked toward the camp.

Red Lance turned a puzzled face toward the white man. Perhaps Walks High was right, he thought. Something might have happened between the white man and Bear Heart.

A bright midmorning sun warmed the land, chasing away the memories of the early season snowfall days earlier. The group had split up to cover more ground in the search for Whirlwind's trail. Walks High and the white man were south of the Smoking Earth River. Bear Heart and Red Lance were working to the north of it.

Walks High loped his horses to the river's edge. Red Lance was already on the opposite bank and motioned with a hand sign that something had been found.

Bear Heart was sitting cross-legged near a stand of willow and ash trees. He stood as the other three arrived and dismounted. "Our war leader has been here," he said to them. "Perhaps two days ago."

The older warrior led them to a stand of young ash trees and pointed to a freshly cut stump. "I think he will make a bow," he pointed out. "But there is a better sign over there." He pointed to a bare patch of earth. "Two footprints are here," he said, touching the slight indentations in the dirt. "Right. Left. This," he said, touching a small round hole next to the right footprint, "was made by a lance or a cane. Maybe a lance he is using as a cane. See how the right footprint is deeper than the left. He is walking with a limp. He was hurt in the fall down the embankment, after his horse was shot."

Walks High contained his excitement by studying the tracks in the dirt. "Thank you," he said to Bear Heart.

The older warrior nodded. "I think that the other white man is riding west. Our war leader knows that. I think he will stay on the man's trail for a while. Then he will ignore the trail and travel straight—to close the distance between them."

Walks High nodded. "Perhaps we should do the same. If we move faster and travel in a straighter line, we would reach my father before he catches up with the white man."

Bear Heart agreed. Then he glanced toward de la Verendrye. "As Beard has shown us, the holy iron is a powerful weapon. Your father may need help if he is to capture the killer of High Hawk's mother."

The warrior moved toward de la Verendrye and spoke with a fierce whisper, "I want you to see what a Lakota warrior would do to some . . . thing . . . that is not welcome in our land."

Thirteen

Three old men sat in the windbreak of an ancient pine and talked of the news brought to them from a Lakota band that lived to the north along the Great Muddy River. Two messengers had come just after the Wolf Tail people had arrived at their winter encampment, two young men from a Mniconju band—Those Who Plant by the Water. The messengers had come with an invitation for the Lakota from white traders of the south country somewhere along the Grandfather River. The traders wanted the Lakota to gather next summer where the White Earth River flows into the Great Muddy River to trade for furs. Two white men had traveled far up along the Great Muddy, accompanied by two men from a tribe to the south. A tribe unknown to the Lakota.

White Crane added wood to the fire and pulled his elk-hide robe tighter around his thin shoulders. Stone and Spotted Calf were also wrapped in robes. There was a thin layer of ice on the river this morning, and a low, gray sky hinted at snow or even a late autumn rain. Smoke from the lodges rose straight upward in the cool, calm morning air, while in the distance it appeared as though one gray cloud was dangling fringes toward the Earth.

White Crane shook his head slightly. "As for me, I do not think we should go to this trade gathering," he said.

Stone nodded. "I think the same. But we cannot tell the people what to do or what not to do. If the council decides it is not a wise thing to do, many of the people will not go. Still, I am afraid some will go."

Spotted Calf nodded beneath his frown. "Yes, some will," he agreed. "There is much curiosity about white men since my son brought the one to our village. The people have seen that the white men have different ways and different things. Goods. Objects made of iron. Holy irons. It will be difficult to hold back such curiosity."

"I am worried," Stone said, "because I know some of our people will go to this gathering. And I am afraid that what the white men may have could be harmful to us."

"Also, their ignorance of our country could be harmful to everyone, including them," pointed out White Crane. "Do they not know that the Great Muddy does not stop overrunning its banks until late summer? To camp near it during its flood time is not wise."

"Still, this is something we must talk about at the meeting of the old men," Stone added. "Myself, I am worried about how we are faced with so many things concerning the white men in such a short space of time. I have a feeling they can be like the first mosquitos of spring. Very hungry."

They fell silent as a woman approached. It was Her Good Trail, carrying a small paunch of buffalo meat and wild turnip soup. The enticing aroma of it reached them before she did. She stopped in front of the three old men and smiled, though she did not look directly at them. Skillfully, she pounded four willow stakes into the ground, evenly spaced in a square. On the stakes she tied the four corners of the paunch. Then she placed three large buffalo-horn spoons in the soup, handles protruding upward.

"Granddaughter," said Stone, "we thank you."

"I know that this is a favorite of my husband's father," she said, addressing them all but directing her words toward

Stone. It would not have been respectful of her to speak directly to Spotted Calf, her father-in-law. "I know that my husband's mother liked to prepare it for him on mornings like this. But, of course, my soup could never be as good as hers used to be."

Spotted Calf smiled and nodded, never really looking in his daughter-in-law's direction. But it was acknowledgment enough. As she walked away, he said to his friends, but loud enough for Her Good Trail to hear, "The day my son took her for his wife, *my* heart was singing."

Her Good Trail, walking away with eyes lowered, smiled shyly. Then she looked north and sent up a prayer for four Wolf Tail warriors pursuing the killer of High Hawk's mother.

The Wolf Tail people had quickly settled into winter camp. Tall, pine-covered hills on either side of the river acted as windbreaks, making this area known as Spring Creek ideal as a winter haven. Moreover, cottonwoods along the river and creek bottoms would feed the horses if deep snow covered the grass, and many white-tailed deer lived in the pine-covered draws. It was, like the summer encampment, a very fine home.

Even now, as Her Good Trail walked toward her lodge, there was much activity for a cold, late autumn morning. Many older boys, fourteen to sixteen winters, were already with the horse herd, helping the younger warriors as they stood guard. A few women and girls were out gathering firewood, being careful to stay within the ring of sentinels encircling the camp. Beyond the outer lodges to the west, a group of smaller boys were playing the arrow-in-the-hoop game, trying noisily to be the first to send an arrow through a small willow hoop rolled along the ground. Like most games played by Lakota children, it had an added purpose— to sharpen the eye and quicken the hand of those on whose skills the safety and well-being of their people would one day depend.

At the inner row of lodges to the north, Her Good Trail saw the Not Afraid family bringing out the Winter Count robe for display. She paused to watch for a moment.

Once again, it was time for the people to consider what was to be painted on the Winter Count to help remember the thirteen moons that were now nearly over. One full winter. She had an idea that the symbol painted for this winter would have something to do with the death of High Hawk's mother or the coming of Beard, the white man. Last winter was known as the Winter of Countless Buffalo. During the Moon of Geese Returning, the Wolf Tail people had delayed in moving from winter camp because a herd of buffalo had taken seven days to pass north of the encampment. The land was black from horizon to horizon, and the Earth shook when they ran. Four winters ago was the Winter of Whirlwind's Victory, because he had killed a white man and captured a strange new weapon.

She watched as Grandfather Not Afraid and his wife, Two High Geese, hung the elk-hide Winter Count on its frame. Makes the Fire was helping, a young man who had been taken in by Not Afraid after losing his mother and father some eleven winters ago. Now Makes the Fire was learning the stories of the Winter Count, just as Not Afraid had when he was a young man. It was generally accepted among the Wolf Tail people that Makes the Fire would be the next Keeper of the Winter Count. He had drawn and painted the pictures that showed the last two winters, working under the patient and watchful eye of Not Afraid. Most importantly, Makes the Fire told the stories truthfully.

Her Good Trail remembered her chores and headed for her lodge. There was a bundle of dried meat she wanted to send to the High Hawk family. She looked about for Red Legs. He was a good boy, always ready to help her. One day he would be a fine warrior. Now he was probably playing the arrow-in-the-hoop game. She could wait.

White Crane loudly sipped his soup and nodded in the direction of the Not Afraid lodge. "My cousin has put out the Winter Count robe, I see," he said. "I hope that we can find something good to remember this winter by. And I hope that my dream will not come to be."

Stone nodded, remembering his friend's dream of the Wolf Tail people taking two different roads. "It is something we should pray about," he said. "Tomorrow we will have a sweat, and pray."

Spotted Calf agreed.

Her Good Trail saw a shadow block her open door and looked up just as she heard polite scratching on the lodge cover. It was Yellow Earrings. In spite of the old woman's smile as she entered, Her Good Trail could see the pain that was still behind the eyes. The death of Walks Far had been difficult for many people, especially for Yellow Earrings.

"Aunt, it is good to see you," the younger woman said.

The old woman nodded in acknowledgment of Her Good Trail's greeting. In a moment she seated herself at a backrest close to the fire. Her white-gray hair was short, cut to her shoulders, as she had cut it once before after the death of her husband. In the years since, it had grown back down to her waist. She held out her palms to the fire and then removed the deer-hide robe from her shoulders. "Your fire is warm. Your home has a certain peace," she said softly. "It is good to see you, too, Niece."

"I have some buffalo meat and turnip soup." Her Good Trail took a bowl from a hide case and reached for the buffalo-horn soup ladle. She had been only a girl when Yellow Earrings had accompanied the war party that traveled in search of her husband, Blue Thunder. He had been missing for days, and she had ridden just as hard and fast as the warriors, and endured the same hardships, until her husband was found. Later, when a foolish young man teased

Blue Thunder about being rescued by a woman, his only reply was that every man would be fortunate if they could win such love from a good woman.

Her Good Trail filled the bowl and held it out toward the older woman, taking a quick glance into the old woman's eyes. The same fire was still there, but it was noticeably dimmed.

A momentary sparkle returned to the old woman's eyes. "Thank you," she said. "No one makes turnip soup like yours."

Her Good Trail smiled and turned to finish preparing the bundle of meat for the High Hawk family. In a while, after a few sips of soup, the old woman put down her bowl and leaned back.

"I was just visiting with my niece," Yellow Earrings said, pointing in the direction of the High Hawk lodge. "Walks Straight was there. Sun Rise Woman, too."

Her Good Trail waited through the long, heavy pause. The old ones did not do things for no reason. She knew that Yellow Earrings had come calling for a purpose. But it was difficult for her to talk about anything related to the death of her cousin, Walks Far.

"Sun Rise Woman told me something," the old woman went on, pulling herself back from some far-off place. "She told me that she had asked your son to put off their marriage ceremony for a while. Thirteen moons, she said."

Her Good Trail nodded. She had not wanted to ask her son about what was troubling him. There was a good reason for his silence and the pain in his eyes.

"But," Yellow Earrings said, "she has spoken with her mother and father. They agree that it would be wise for her to change her mind. She thinks that early summer would be a good time to have a marriage ceremony. Still, she feels bad that she cannot tell your son."

"It will be the best news he could come home to," replied Her Good Trail. "I hope that my future daughter-in-law's family is doing well. Things are so painful sometimes."

The old woman glanced at Her Good Trail, giving her a soft smile with many feelings behind it. "They are sad. But time will weaken the pain. Then remembering will be easier. And the happiness resulting from a marriage between your son and my granddaughter will help heal our hearts. Life goes on. And perhaps I will see you become a grandmother before I leave this world."

Her Good Trail smiled, finished tying the bundle of meat, and laid it aside. "Thank you . . . for telling me. My son was troubled, and now I know why. Still, I wish I could tell him, to ease his mind. But he and his father and the others will be home soon."

Whirlwind selected a target, a small, rotted stump some twenty paces away at the base of a slight rise. He was ready to test the new bow.

For an entire night he had stayed awake drying and curing the bow over a bed of coals. As the bow dried, he made arrows. After sunrise, he had let the coals die out and slept. The sun was well past the middle of the sky when he awoke, though he could barely see it through the low, dark clouds.

After cutting in the string notches, two at the bottom and one at the top, and attaching the spare sinew string, there was nothing left to do but test the bow.

As he shot, the bowstring twanged, and the arrow flashed toward the stump. A miss. High. It was a good miss. The bow was stronger than he expected. Whirlwind nocked a second arrow, lifted the bow, pulled, and released. This time it was a direct hit. So were three other shots.

He retrieved his arrows and returned to his shelter. There he carefully inspected the weapon. Whirlwind had made many bows before—good bows, thanks to the patient teaching of his father. But no bow was ever more important and necessary than this one.

It was a beautiful weapon, even when unstrung as it was now. Both limbs curved gracefully away, looking like two thin crescent moons end to end. Where they touched was the handle. Whirlwind had tied the green stave to a length of stout wood in that position. The high, steady heat of the coals had quickly dried the stave, causing it to keep its curvatures even after Whirlwind untied it.

As Spotted Calf pointed out often, there was something else just as important in the making of a bow—the spirit it was given by its maker. Since the wood used to make the bow had once been a living thing, its spirit and its life had to be honored by making the best bow that skill and knowledge could produce. In doing so, the bow-maker gave it a new spirit, which came from his heart and mind. If the heart and mind of the maker was not good, the spirit of the bow would be weak. If the maker cleared his heart and mind of anger, selfishness, and impurity, the spirit of the bow would be strong. As Spotted Calf liked to tell, the best bow he ever crafted was the one he made just after Carries the Medicine told him she was going to have a baby. That bow was not the strongest nor the most beautiful he had ever made, but it sent arrows faster than any of his other bows. It fit in his hand like no other one did. Now, though it was well over forty winters old, it still effortlessly sent arrows flying.

Whirlwind had been careful of his thoughts as he had worked on the bow. He had pushed anger and revenge from his heart and remembered that to everything there was a purpose. He had prayed that he would always think to use the bow to bring about something good.

Although the bow looked unfinished, because the back still had a layer of bark, there were no flaws that he could see. Whirlwind decided that the bow was done, except for one last step. Taking a short piece of antler tine, he began to rub the front, or belly, of the bow. This would give the wood a hard, shiny finish and prevent it from getting soaked too quickly if submerged in water, or if it became wet during a heavy rain- or snowstorm.

As he worked, his thoughts returned to the larger task at hand—the white man who had killed an old Lakota woman. This new bow greatly improved his chances of capturing that killer. Still, Whirlwind knew that the white man would fight because he had a holy iron. But that weapon was not as fearful to him as it once had been. Knowledge of how it worked and what it could not do was important. Now, though Whirlwind was still afraid of the holy iron, he was no longer afraid of an unknown thing. As many, many old warriors had said, knowledge was a warrior's best weapon. Knowledge was the way to move past the fear and do what must be done.

Whirlwind's thoughts drifted back to times past, and he could see himself as a thin, spindly boy of fifteen winters. Images of a tall, strong warrior named Brings Three Horses filled his mind. Brings Three Horses was an uncle, his mother's older brother, a stalwart warrior who had taken a liking to the boy called Badger before he had earned the warrior name of Whirlwind.

Badger had learned much from Brings Three Horses, more than he could ever remember. "Always look behind you, at your back trail," he said many times. "What you cannot see can often be more dangerous than what you can. Fewer things will surprise you that way. If death surprises you, it will only happen once." Whirlwind could hear that deep voice, even now: "Remember that the power of a true warrior comes from what is in his mind and heart, not from what is in his hand," that powerful warrior had emphasized. But Spotted Calf had also passed much on to his son. And one day, he stood with his brother-in-law to present a young warrior named Whirlwind to the Wolf Warrior Society.

Whirlwind could still clearly remember that day as he stood in the lodge of the Wolf Warrior Society. An old, old man named Kills Plenty spoke to the gathering:

"The wolf has always been our relative," he said. "But his people have walked this Earth far longer than we have. Because of that, he is wiser than we are. Someday, perhaps we will be as wise. But for now we must strive to be like our brother, the wolf.

"The wolf always looks out for his people, and his family. He defends them against hunger, and cold, and loneliness, and enemies that would destroy them. He hunts, he builds warm lodges, and no wolf child is ever without a mother or a father. And he does not count his enemies; he simply defends all that is precious to him.

"My grandson, to be a Wolf Warrior you must pledge that you will do the same. No one should go hungry as long as you have the ability to provide. No one should be cold as long as you can offer a warm lodge, even if you must give away your own. No one, young or old, should cry out of loneliness without your heart hearing it. When a child without one cries 'Father,' you must hear, and answer.

"You must understand that dignity is more important than any honor you might win. That wisdom and knowledge are the best weapons you can carry into the hunt and into battle, and throughout your journey on this Earth.

"Finally, you must always be the first to answer the call when your people are in danger. And you must always know, even though you are a pitiful being, that the greatest gift you offer to your people is your life. Though you will be afraid, do not hesitate to give it.

"You have chosen a most difficult path, Grandson. There is no harder way to travel than the trail of the Wolf Warrior. I pray that the Great Mystery will give you the strength and the courage to walk on that trail, with purpose and humility."

Whirlwind shuddered as the images of the past faded. Old Kills Plenty had been right. A Wolf Warrior's trail was very difficult. Brings Three Horses had died searching for a lost child, fourteen winters past. Whirlwind had always envisioned that this hero of his youth would die on the field of battle or during a buffalo hunt. Instead, that stalwart warrior had frozen to death after breaking his leg in a fall while leading a search for a small child lost in a blizzard. Whirlwind had found the warrior's body, and nearby, huddled inside a tangle of driftwood, was the lost child—still alive. That winter, Not Afraid had painted the likeness of Brings Three Horses on the elk-hide Winter Count. And that winter was known as The Winter Brings Three Horses Died and Found Little Deer Woman. As for Little Deer Woman, she was always the first into the dance circle whenever any honoring song was sung, calling out the name of the warrior who had saved her life even after he had died.

Whirlwind looked out across the wide, flat valley of the White Earth River. It was as Her Good Trail had said one day long ago. Brings Three Horses had not really died; he had simply found another place to live. She was right. Death was simply a doorway from one life to another. And one's place in that other life depended on how well, or how poorly, one lived when the spirit was with the body in this life. Brings Three Horses had lived well, as had Whirlwind's own mother, Carries the Medicine. He wondered if he could live as honorably.

A movement across the river caught his eye. Buffalo, slowly moving toward the river. One by one they emerged from the trees until they filled a wide draw—over one hundred of them. The first to the water was a wary cow, testing the wind for the scent of danger. A while later there were hundreds of them, and Whirlwind knew there were many, many more beyond the hills to the north. Now they filled the valley of the White Earth River as far as he could see to the west and to the east.

Fresh meat of the buffalo was a meal he did not often turn down willingly. He could more than likely move close enough to bring one down, if he had time to shoot three or four arrows at the same animal. But the meat of one buffalo far exceeded the needs of one man. To kill one now would be senseless, because a true hunter took only as much as he really needed. So he sat and watched the great animals moving about with their air of self-assurance. They reminded him of his first buffalo hunt with his father and Brings Three Horses.

It was in the Moon of Cherries Ripening, in the Winter of Living with Four White Wolves. The Wolf Tail people had chosen a summer camp in the same valley as a family of wolves with four snow-white cubs. That summer, Brings Three Horses had presented young Badger with his own buffalo-hunting horse, a swift brown and white mare, eight winters old. And Spotted Calf had given him a short, stout, sinew-backed chokecherry buffalo bow. It was so strong that Badger could barely pull it. He had spent that summer practicing with both the horse and the bow. When the old men picked the time for the hunt and the scouts returned with news of a large herd to the north, Badger tossed and turned for several sleepless nights.

"Remember," Spotted Calf said to his young son, "after you pick out your animal, let your horse do the rest." On that warm autumn day, they were on a hill looking east as the herd darkened the Earth all the way to the eastern horizon. Because Badger was a left-handed shooter, Brings Three Horses had trained the mare to approach from the left side of a buffalo.

Badger took deep, nervous breaths as they walked their horses into the fringes of the herd. For about the tenth time he checked to make certain that his quiver of sixteen arrows was tied securely to the front of his waist, and that he was holding his new bow properly. He gathered all the courage of his fifteen winters as the buffalo began to move. They only trotted at first, but in a few heartbeats they were at a high gallop.

"*Hokahe!*" yelled Spotted Calf from somewhere in the rising prairie dust. Looking right, the boy spotted a cow as it sprinted away from him. He leaned forward, low over the mare's neck, signaling her to follow the cow. The mare's sudden burst of speed caught him off guard, and he nearly fell. By the time he regained his balance, the mare was closing in at an angle on the cow. Badger drew an arrow from the quiver and let go of the single jaw rope. Now he was totally without a rein, and the mare was doing exactly what she had been trained for over half her life.

Dust and thunder filled the air. Though he was in the midst of thousands of animals and twenty or so other riders, all he could see clearly was the cow he was chasing. Beyond that was nothing but dark shapes fading in and out of the dust. He nocked an arrow to the string as the horse took him closer and closer. He could plainly see the black curly hair on his cow and the dark swatch of sweat beginning to form on her flank. She was a giant. The top of her hump was even with his chest, and he was on a horse!

His arms strained, and his string hand shook a little as he drew the bow and picked out a spot just behind the cow's front leg. Now he was less than ten paces from the cow. TWANG! The mare moved to the left, after hearing the bowstring. Fletching and a spot of red from his arrow's crest appeared in the cow's side, not far from where he had aimed. He pulled another arrow from the quiver and leaned right to signal the mare to go at the cow again. His second arrow embedded itself close to the first. So did the third and fourth. He only faintly heard the cow's bellow of rage and pain. Reaching down, he grabbed the neck rope to steady himself and found the jaw rope. Only when he began to guide the mare toward the edge of the herd did he realize that the rhythm and intensity of his heartbeats nearly matched the constant thunder of hooves. Only then did he taste the dust in his mouth and feel the sweat running down his face. He felt powerful and small at the same time.

By midafternoon he had finally found his cow. She had run far with four arrows in her, over a ridge and nearly halfway across a low valley.

Late that night, as his mother Carries the Medicine cooked the meat from his first kill, he felt no sense of victory. He felt, instead, a sense of purpose, as if he were part of something indescribably big and endless. His father had hung the cow's raw liver from the longest pole of a willow tripod to show that it was his son's first buffalo kill. Brings Three Horses and other hunters came and each took a bite of the liver, to acknowledge the gift of life from the buffalo as well as to show that Badger was now one of them. A buffalo hunter.

Whirlwind looked again at the valley full of buffalo and reluctantly let the sounds and images of his first buffalo hunt fade away.

He decided to remain one more night in his snug shelter built into the narrow draw. Although there was now much less stiffness and discomfort in his injured knee when he walked, another long night of rest would be good. Besides, he could take the opportunity to make more arrows. Whirlwind felt a renewed sense of confidence as he looked down at the bow in his hand. Because he did not know how many iron balls the white man had for the holy iron, he had to assume that he had many and, accordingly, make as many arrows as his quiver would hold. The most he had ever carried in his war quiver was forty-four. At the moment, he did not have half that many.

Yes, there was still much to do to prepare for the fight he knew would come. Yet he knew he could win. He did not know exactly how it would happen, only that he could win if he did not turn reckless. Seeing the wolf-shaped cloud had told him that. Once he had watched two wolves and followed them for an entire day as they trailed a wounded elk. They brought the old bull down in the end, not because they could tear and slash with their great fangs, but because they persevered. So, too, must he persevere. Then he would defeat the killer.

But even while he watched the valley of the White Earth River turn dark as the buffalo continued to fill it, he could not help but think of his dream. The dream of the wolf fighting the gray dogs. One white man could be easily defeated, or easily accepted into a Lakota village. But if an uncountable number of them were to come, what then? And what else did they possess, beyond the holy iron, that was powerful and dangerous? And would the Lakota have to fight like the wolf in his dream?

Whirlwind stood and grabbed his new bow. It was time to check the snares. He kept among the trees, carefully and instinctively picking his trail in order not to make noise. This country was familiar to him. On either side of the river were rough, broken hills covered with soapweed and cactus. Antelope hunting was good here. Away from the river valley there were few trees. From any high point it was possible to see great distances in any direction since unbroken, grassy prairies stretched as far as the eye could see. Breezes wandered over those vast spaces, singing of the freedom of the open lands.

As he came to a clearing in the trees, he could see a sudden commotion among the buffalo. Some along the western edge of the great herd were running away from the river. Whirlwind thought perhaps he had startled them. Soon the thunder of running hooves filled the river valley as the buffalo fled in panic. Eventually they all disappeared beyond the northern horizon, leaving only a wide, dark swath on the Earth and a thin cloud of dust to show that they had been in the valley.

Whirlwind studied the landscape, but he could not see what had driven the buffalo away. It worried him, though, because anything feared by those great animals would certainly be a danger to a lone two-legged hunter.

He started walking again. By the time he finished checking all of his snares it was nearly sundown. He returned to his shelter by another route, carrying the four rabbits he had trapped. He felt good. There were enough hides to make moccasin liners to keep his feet warm during the cold days that were hiding just behind the sharp gusts of wind. And four rabbits cooked this night would be food enough for three or four days.

Whirlwind took a last look around before crawling into the snug shelter. It was now quiet in the valley. Deathly quiet.

Fourteen

Whirlwind finished wiping out all signs of his fire and the camp. He had scattered the deadfall he had used for the shelter and buried the fire. There was nothing left to show that he had ever been here. But he would remember this place because there were many unknown tomorrows, and the path of a warrior sometimes doubled back on itself.

This was the coldest morning so far. A heavy frost covered the land and the trees, and Whirlwind knew there was a thin layer of ice on the river. He climbed a low rise and looked out over the land. A coyote warily approached the river. Antelope stood on the crest of some low hills to the north. And there was a stillness everywhere.

The warrior walked into a stand of oaks and picked up his things. There was a bow in the case now and sixteen arrows in the quiver. During the night he had also built a willow back frame, to which he tied his rawhide case, his extra food, and four rolled-up rabbit hides. Overall, his pack was not heavy, but he did not want it to be cumbersome or restrict free use of his arms and hands. He slipped the carry strap to the bow case and quiver over his head and onto his left shoulder. In that way, the bow and the quiver hung at his right hip, pointing forward. This would enable him to move through brush and trees without getting caught on branches and have the bow and arrows within easy reach.

Although his injured knee was still tender to the touch, it could bear more weight now. He needed to use the lance as a cane, but not as much as before.

An eagle feather tied at the back of his head hung downward, fluttering now and then in the early morning breeze. From inside the stand of oaks, he surveyed the land, squinting a little from the reflection of the sun off the frost. After several moments, Whirlwind turned his face to the west. His brown eyes were alert and calm, and below the slightly hawk-like nose, his lips were set in determination.

Whirlwind resumed his pursuit of the killer white man. Soon he was moving rapidly with only a slight limp. Ever vigilant, he kept a steady watch on the skyline around him and paused frequently to look at his back trail.

By midmorning he came to an area where the White Earth River flowed through a broad, grassy plain. Sunlight glistened off the frost-covered land, but though the sun was bright the air was still cold.

Near an old watercourse he paused beside the gray remains of an ancient cottonwood giant, a stump slightly taller than a man. As he glanced back to the east, a movement to the north caught his eye. Instinctively, he stayed motionless, moving only his eyes at first. Then he turned his head slowly. Death was watching him, from a short stone's throw to the north.

Only the massive head and shoulders of the bear were visible at first. The animal tested the wind and caught the scent of the two-legged. With agility that belied his bulk, he leaped to the top of the bank and walked cautiously toward Whirlwind.

The bear stopped but continued to cast about for scent. Whirlwind slowly pushed himself against the giant stump, knowing that the bear had not clearly seen him yet. When the animal turned his head to the east for a heartbeat or two, Whirlwind quickly ducked around the stump. Now, though he was completely out of sight, it was only a momentary reprieve.

Cautiously, the warrior edged his head around the stump until he could see the bear. The bear had returned his attention to the stump and was a few steps closer.

Whirlwind ducked back and looked to the south. There were no trees nearby, nothing he could climb. He looked back around the stump. The bear was closer, about fifteen paces away. He had caught Whirlwind's scent now, sniffing along the path the warrior had walked. With a loud snort and a half growl, the bear stood upright.

Whirlwind's stomach tightened. The bear was one and a half times the height of a man.

Even as his hand went to pull the bow out of its case, Whirlwind decided against it. Wounding the bear would only make the situation worse. His only hope was to stay out of sight. Whirlwind began to back away from the stump with his lance ready, keeping the stump between himself and the bear's line of sight. A sudden roar shattered the cold stillness and froze the warrior in his tracks.

Whirlwind was certain that the bear would come charging around the stump. He started to back away again, keeping a watch on the stump. His only immediate hope was to widen the distance between him and the bear. Slowly, he stepped backwards again until he was forty paces from the stump. A quick glance behind revealed a clump of soapweeds nearby. Whirlwind jumped behind it.

Any thought that he might have escaped from the bear vanished like a fleeing antelope. The bear was back down on all four feet as he came around the stump. Now he was purposefully following Whirlwind's scent, snorting as he walked with nose to the ground.

There was no time for indecision. Whirlwind pulled the bow from its case and strung it. He also pulled out four arrows and placed them in his bow hand. Then he looked around once more for an escape route, but there was none, unless he crawled. If he came to his feet, the bear would see him, and there was no hope of outrunning the animal, even without an injured knee. In his youth, he had seen a charging bear catch a galloping colt.

To the north was the old watercourse, a dry creek bed with a low bank. For the time being, it was his best hope. With the bow and arrows in his right hand and the lance in his left, he began belly-crawling toward the dry creek. He could feel and hear his own heart pounding.

A glance to the right revealed that the bear was still trailing him by scent. He kept crawling, being careful not to make any sudden noises. By the time he gained the creek bank and ducked behind it, the bear had reached the clump of soapweeds. The fresh, strong scent put the bear in a frenzy, and a roar erupted from his great chest as he stood upright and slashed at the air.

Whirlwind knew that any hesitation would lessen his chances of escape. On his hands and knees he crawled along the low bank of the creek bed until it was too low to hide him. He was now about eighty paces to the northwest of his pursuer.

To his dismay, the bear was still following his scent, moving slowly toward the dry creek.

Six winters ago, while hunting elk in the Black Hills, he and Walks High had hidden behind a boulder and watched a bear walk by close enough for them to touch. He knew that bears were always wary of people, often going far out of their way to avoid contact when they caught the scent of a man. Never had he heard of one tracking a man. Until now.

Hoping that he would live to tell the story of this strange-acting bear, Whirlwind looked to the southwest and saw a high, grassy knob a long arrow's cast away. If he could reach that knob, he could at least observe the bear approaching.

He began crawling through the grass and soapweeds, pausing frequently to look at his pursuer and to watch for cactus. Fortunately, it was past the season for snakes. Although his injured knee began to throb, he kept moving, knowing that the pain of his leg could never be as bad as being slashed by an angry bear the size of a horse.

The bear was now moving along the bank of the dry creek, still trailing Whirlwind by scent.

Whirlwind paused in a low spot to catch his breath. The grassy knob was very close now. Rising cautiously above the grass, he saw the bear's back as the bear continued to move along the creek bed, about sixty paces away.

The warrior looked around, suddenly realizing that an uneasy silence had descended, as if every living thing was holding its breath to await the outcome of this contest between bear and man.

He began to crawl again toward the grassy knob. TIK-TIK-TIK-TIK! A sudden explosion of wings startled him, making him jump to his feet in surprise. Grouse. Three of them. He watched them for less than a heartbeat before he remembered the bear. It was too long. The bear was now coming toward him at a gallop.

Whirlwind knelt down, never taking his eyes off the bear. He nocked an arrow on his bowstring and pulled his quiver to his left hip, being one of the very few who pulled and shot the bow with his left hand.

Closer and closer came the great bear. Whirlwind watched, gauging the distance and timing the animal's jumps. Disregarding, for the moment, that his chances of defeating the bear were next to nothing, he decided that his best hope for an effective shot would be to hit the throat.

At twenty paces, the gigantic bear stopped and raised up again on his hind legs. This close, Whirlwind could see flecks of foam at the corners of his mouth.

Snorting, and with an occasional roar that echoed over the broad grassy prairie, the bear began to circle the man. Whirlwind lifted his bow, aiming at a spot to the left of the animal's breastbone. He turned slowly, keeping the bear to his front. It would take at least three fast shots to do any damage, and every shot would need to be a direct hit in the area of the heart and lungs. The first shot was a sure hit at this distance, but the second and third would be difficult. Whirlwind knew that the bear could close the distance between them in only three or four jumps, three or four heartbeats. Three or four heartbeats were, more than likely, not enough time for two more shots.

Roaring, the bear continued to close in on Whirlwind. Then something caught the warrior's eye—a rock as high as a man's thigh. Very cautiously, he moved to it. Slowly, he stepped up onto the narrow top of the sandstone boulder and pulled himself up to his full height. Suddenly, he was as tall as the bear.

The bear ceased his roaring and stared at his prey, which had suddenly grown larger.

Whirlwind slowly raised his arms and locked his gaze on the bear's dark eyes. "I AM WHIRLWIND!" he suddenly shouted. "I AM WHIRLWIND! WHO ARE YOU?"

The great animal hesitated for only a moment longer. He answered with a long roar and walked away, glancing back only once.

Whirlwind's legs were weak, nearly shaking. He stayed on the rock with his arms up until the bear went out of sight behind a rise.

Climbing down, he retrieved his lance. Glancing in the direction that the bear had gone, he trotted away slowly toward the west, realizing now what had stampeded the buffalo the evening before.

Trotting only as far as his throbbing knee and pounding heart would permit, he found a narrow, eroded bank on the crest of a low rise and stopped to rest. Looking up into the bright blue sky, he smiled and nodded. "Yes, Grandfather," he said, "life is precious. Life is good."

The image of the great bear's open mouth and glistening fangs stayed in his mind, like the lingering flash of a sunset. To calm himself and drive away the memory of the bear, Whirlwind looked to see that he had all his weapons and other things with him. He took a long, deep breath and leaned back against the eroded bank. A flash of movement drew his eyes upward, just in time to see a red-tailed hawk set his wings, pulling them in close until his body looked like a stone arrowhead. He streaked toward the prairie floor, almost too fast for Whirlwind's eyes to follow, and disappeared behind a rise. A short time later, he reappeared, wings beating mightily as he struggled to regain the sky. With gratitude for his own escape, Whirlwind observed how the young prairie dog skewered in the hawk's talons hung lifeless as the bird rose higher and higher.

From the top of the grassy knob, slightly to the south and east of Whirlwind, two pairs of dark eyes watched where the lone warrior had sat down to rest. Two men lying flat amidst the sparse grass had been watching the lone warrior and the bear.

Black Lodge turned to his companion. "Lakota. But why is he alone and on foot?"

Looks Twice, the older of the two, shook his head. "That is not important. And it is better for us. It was a Lakota raiding party which killed my son, when he was out hunting alone. The Great One has decided to give me revenge."

"Revenge?"

"Yes," replied Looks Twice. "The life of a Lakota for the life of my son."

"But I think he must be a very brave man to face a bear the way he did."

Looks Twice smiled. "Better to take revenge on a brave man than on a coward."

After a while the two Arikara left their lookout. They hurried away to a hidden draw, from which they soon emerged mounted on their horses.

Fifteen

As the echoes of the flintlock's boom reverberated across the rolling prairies, anger flashed through the shooter's eyes. One of the ducks had taken wing and was already far from the narrow little stream, while pieces of the other were still falling back down to the water.

Bruneaux cursed. He had aimed below the bird, hoping that a near miss would stun the duck. Instead, the ball had gone high, hitting the bird squarely.

Two ducks on the narrow creek had been the only game close enough for a decent shot in the last three days. There were plenty of antelope. Thousands of them. But they were so wary they dashed away at the sight of a man on a horse. Infuriatingly, they would stop just out of range to look back.

Bruneaux was hungry. He had last eaten yesterday, and that meal had not been substantial since the musket ball had blown apart most of the rabbit. He had not seen a deer since he had veered westward away from the river he had been following. This morning he had seen a few buffalo, but the bay horse had become skittish when he got close to the animals. Bruneaux had angrily abandoned his buffalo hunt after his horse had nearly thrown him. He now regretted not having taken at least the other hindquarter of the deer he had killed days ago. But it would have been too cumbersome to carry on the horse, and too troublesome to skin the hide and prepare the meat. It seemed senseless to take a whole carcass with so much game around. It was easier to take only a piece or two. As long as a man could get close enough to shoot something, that is.

Bruneaux looked around at the rolling, open prairie and the distant horizons. The land was so open, and the sky seemed somehow larger than anywhere else. Buffalo, antelope, and deer were around, but the openness was their ally. It was hard to get close enough to kill them, even for a man with a gun. He preferred the forests near the Mississippi. There it was easy to hunt. All a man had to do was wait in the thick, dark underbrush until a deer walked by. Then . . . boom! Food!

De la Verendrye had talked of the open prairies as if they were God's gift to man. He could have them. Man was not meant to live here. Only animals and heathens. Like the . . . Dakota, was it? Yes. The tribe whose language the little pup had learned. He could still hear the little runt droning on about his time with those heathens.

Bruneaux grunted in disgust. He preferred Letellier's approach to the problem of heathens. "Shoot them all!" the one-eared trader had said. "They are evil, like wolves! They live in the wilds and eat their meat half raw. Vermin! All of them. Soon'r we get rid of them all, the better this place will be. They got no place among civilized people!"

Bruneaux glanced toward a far horizon. There were no civilized people here. There was no tobacco for his pipe, and he missed the sound of a human voice. There was nothing but the occasional screech of some bird in the sky and the grunting of buffalo. Even de la Verendrye's voice would be a welcome change, for a little while at least. No, the man's gold would be better.

At the bottom of the rock outcropping above the stream, he stopped to reload the flintlock and check his supply of powder and shot. There was plenty of powder. With some difficulty, he counted the musket balls—thirty-four. Some had been lost back on that ridge, where the sneaking heathens had almost killed him. Bruneaux touched the fresh scar on his left cheek, where an arrow had sliced his face open. Well, at least he had gotten one of them then. And another one was probably lying dead in the river. The one riding the gray horse.

He touched the fresh scar again and scanned the eastern skyline. Antelope dotted the slopes, and something that looked like a coyote was moving below the crest of a low hill far off to the southeast, stalking the antelope. Bruneaux suddenly realized that it was a wolf. He moved slowly and deliberately, and then suddenly disappeared in a clump of grass. Bruneaux lost interest and looked northeast, but there was nothing to see. At least not a man on a gray horse. Then a thin, distant bleating reached his ears. He looked back south in time to see the wolf trotting away with a young antelope in his jaws—killed in just a few blinks of an eye. The surviving antelope were running and were soon out of sight over the northern horizon. Bruneaux watched until the wolf had also disappeared and then finished reloading his weapon.

His stomach growled.

Yesterday he had followed a creek into a strange area where there was only bare earth and tall, stark hills with no trees or grasses. There was something eerie about the bizarre-colored place he did not like. The bay had been edgy, too. The trouble was, he had seen lots of deer in there.

Perhaps tomorrow he would go in there again after the deer. Tomorrow—in the daylight.

Bruneaux walked to the creek and took a long drink to fill his growling stomach. Near the bank was a piece of the duck he had shot—about as large as his thumb. It was, he decided, better than nothing.

Whirlwind looked down at the tracks in the hardened mud. A horse had slipped, and someone had fallen. The warrior guessed it was the man he was following. It had all happened no more than three days past, since the snowfall was four days ago. Whirlwind could see that a horse and his rider had come here after the snow had melted and softened the ground. After the rider fell he had led the horse up a narrow gully. Following the tracks with his eyes, Whirlwind saw the brush shelter among the oaks.

The sun was still high. Whirlwind knew he could cover a good distance before he had to make camp for the night. He was anxious for a warm fire and a good meal. Yesterday's encounter with the bear had reminded him that the simple things were often the best part of life—like a warm fire, a good buffalo-hide robe when the blizzards howled, a quiet morning, a bright autumn sunset, and the first cool drink after a long, hot journey. And best of all, a long walk among the river willows with Her Good Trail.

Whirlwind climbed to a brush-covered rise and sat down among short, leafless stalks. For a long while he surveyed the land, studying the way he had come. Far off to the north and east a large herd of deer lay in a grove of trees, patiently waiting for dark to begin their nocturnal browsing. Out of the blue sky came the whistle of a hawk, riding the high winds on outstretched wings. To the west was a small dust cloud—buffalo he guessed. The moon was a thin sliver of gray-blue just above the eastern horizon. At tomorrow's first light it would be hanging above the western horizon, keeping its place in the vast circle of everything that lived and moved. Whirlwind suddenly felt so very small.

Did white men feel these things? he wondered. How did they look at the world? Did they know of the Great Mystery? Did they know that the Great Mystery was the Father of all life, and that the Earth was Mother? Did they feel a kinship with everything around them, like the Lakota did? If they did not, then they must be a poor people, without a path to walk in this life. Perhaps he would ask the wounded one about these things.

Whirlwind had not seen the strange white man who was thought to be a sort of holy man. That was seven winters ago, when the Wolf Tail people camped for the summer north of the Bad River. He traveled alone and wore a long black robe, like a woman's dress. Spotted Calf reported that he had a long beard and seemed very angry. Some of the old men thought his mind was gone. The black robe did not speak Lakota, but that did not stop him from standing in the middle of the encampment for most of a day haranguing. And his most prized possession was a strange little four-cornered object wrapped in a black hide, with flat, white wings inside that fluttered in the wind. The people said he talked to that object continuously.

Then one day the man had left, after putting his hands on some of the people's heads and saying strange words.

Whirlwind shook his head as he remembered the story. Three moons later, a Wolf Tail hunter had found the remains of a man near the Great Muddy River. The bones were scattered about, and there was a strange little object among them, an object that fit in the palm, about the size of a small medicine hoop. It was made of iron and resembled the crossed paths of the medicine hoop, though one arm of it was longer.

Why would a man travel alone in a land unknown to him? Whirlwind wondered. Perhaps it was a test of manhood. Perhaps the black robe was lost and crazy. The wounded one he had found in the cottonwood grove was also far from home and his own kind. The trapper he had killed was alone, too, and gathering furs—perhaps to trade somewhere. Maybe it was the nature of white men to go to places where they were not invited and to take things from the land without permission. What purpose did white men see in all this? It was another thing to ask the wounded one about.

What was clear to Whirlwind was the fact that each white man he had seen or heard of had brought hardship to the Lakota in some way. One had nearly killed him, and another had killed an old woman. Although the one who spoke Lakota had not done any harm himself, it was his onetime friend who had killed the old woman. And the Lakota who had been touched by the strange holy man had come down with a severe coughing sickness. Only the skill and knowledge of Stone had saved their lives. Perhaps it was the fate of white men to have trouble follow them like a black cloud. There was at least one of them who would have trouble returned to him, of that Whirlwind was certain.

He reached into his rawhide case and grabbed some cooked rabbit. After a few bites he put away the uneaten portion and drank from his water flask. A noise behind him, to the south, caught his ear. A large flock of grouse were taking wing. After a moment they flew over him and finally landed far to the north on a grassy slope.

Quickly, he pulled his bow from its case and strung it. Perhaps it was the bear again, or another one. But anything could have chased those birds into the air—a coyote, mountain lion, short-tailed cat, badger. Or a two-legged hunter. For a long, long while Whirlwind did not move. He listened and tested the wind, but no more sudden noises could be heard, and no unusual smells reached his nose. Whirlwind carefully looked all around. Although he could see no immediate danger, he had learned long ago that the most dangerous thing was that which could not be seen, or heard, or smelled. The hunter or the warrior who did not think so or act accordingly did not live to see his grandchildren. Sometimes he did not live to have children.

Staying low, he moved out of the brush and down to the bottom of the slope. Settling into an easy trot, even with a slight limp, he quickly moved far away from where the grouse had been frightened. He didn't stop until he came to a grassy flat, and when he saw a clump of soapweeds, he dropped down next to it. A duck whined overhead, and somewhere a prairie dog whistled. Whirlwind smiled, as he saw the discarded skin of a snake near his knee. He was glad it was not summer or autumn since he did not like snakes.

Further off to the west was a long slope up from the floor of the wide valley he was in. Halfway up the slope was a grove of cedars. The cedar trees were old and tall, and their spreading branches would be good shelter for the night.

Suddenly, hoofbeats reached his ears as he was rising, and two riders appeared before he could duck out of sight. They were galloping straight toward him. In this open grassy area, there was no place to hide.

Throwing off his pack, he pulled his quiver to the front. His bow was already strung. Kneeling, he nocked an arrow on the string and put three more in his hand against the back of the bow.

One rider was slightly ahead of the other and low over the neck of his horse, with a lance in his hand. The other had a shield over his left arm and a long war club in his right hand.

Whirlwind pulled his lance closer without taking his eyes from the approaching warriors. They were now at a hundred paces and would be on him in a few heartbeats. He decided he would shoot first at the one on his left, and then swing right to shoot at the other.

He lifted his bow, drew, and released. Even before he knew the first arrow was a miss, he flicked another onto the string and shot again. The second arrow did not miss. The warrior with the shield took the arrow through the right lung and fell from his horse.

Whirlwind flicked a third arrow onto the string, but there was only time to dive out of the way. Horse and rider were a dark blur above him as he felt a hot pain. The warrior's lance sliced across Whirlwind's right shoulder.

His arm was not broken, but the wound in his shoulder was deep, already darkening his shirt. As he scrambled for his lance, he saw the warrior slide his horse to a stop and turn around.

Whirlwind realized he could not use his bow again. But he knew that he had evened the odds. The fallen warrior was either dead or too badly wounded to fight. However, his companion, still mounted, had now strung his bow and was reaching for his arrows. He was less than fifty paces from Whirlwind.

Unable to use his own bow, out in the open, and without a good buffalo-hide shield, the Lakota warrior was an easy target for the mounted enemy with a bow. Instinct told Whirlwind not to wait for his enemy to shoot. He did not ponder, even for the most fleeting moment, what his next move would be. In the heat of battle, the slightest hesitation and doubt were enough to cause defeat and death. Whirlwind sprang to his feet and sprinted toward the enemy.

As he ran, he watched the horse. A nervous horse in battle had more control than its rider. Though this one danced and jumped about, he kept his ground.

The mounted warrior drew his bow and sent an arrow hissing toward Whirlwind.

Whirlwind dived to his left and rolled over his left shoulder. Panic, excitement, and uncertainty usually caused warriors shooting a bow to miss to their left because they did not release the arrow smoothly. Whirlwind rolled and came up running.

Realizing there was no time to nock and shoot another arrow, the mounted warrior threw aside his bow and pulled a war club from his belt. But even those two swift motions were not fast enough. The mounted warrior's war cry turned into a grunt of surprise and then pain as a swift, blurred form suddenly filled his vision. Whirlwind jumped without hesitating and thrust the lance under the enemy warrior's breastbone. His momentum carried him and the dying warrior over the horse.

As they slammed to the earth, Whirlwind grabbed the horse's long jaw rope and hung on desperately as the frightened horse dragged him a short distance. He waited for the horse to calm down before he painfully pulled himself to a sitting position. His own breath came in short, shaky gasps as he struggled to calm himself. Finally, he stood up and instinctively pressed his hand to his shoulder wound to stem the flow of blood. But in spite of trembling legs and a slight dizziness, his warrior instincts prompted him to immediately search the open areas and the horizon for signs of more enemies.

All was quiet. Only a prairie dog scurried through the grass nearby, and the first warrior's horse was still standing where he had stopped some hundred paces away.

His attackers, Whirlwind realized, were Arikara. He walked, leading the captured horse, toward the body of the warrior he had killed with his lance. With some difficulty, Whirlwind recovered his weapon, which was protruding from the man's chest. The point had been buried in a back rib.

Whirlwind studied the dead warrior's face for a moment. He was neither young nor old. His light brown eyes stared blankly toward a far horizon.

A war club and bow lay off to one side. There were still thirty or more arrows in the dead warrior's quiver. Whirlwind grabbed the shafts at the fletching and pulled them out of the quiver. Only then did he realize that he had lost his bow case and quiver somewhere.

He disdained anything else that the dead warrior had, keeping the arrows and the horse. His shoulder throbbed with each heartbeat, but it was not bleeding heavily. Leading the horse, he walked to the other body. He was a young man, and still alive. Whirlwind knelt to steady himself, as Walks High's face came into his mind.

The first clear image which formed in the young warrior's vision was of the stars over a distant, dark horizon. Is this death? he wondered. A hot pain in his right chest told him that it was not. Confusion swirled in his mind, until he remembered riding at the lone Lakota.

Little by little, the young warrior realized his predicament and remembered the circumstances which had brought him to this moment of pain and confusion. He and Looks Twice had followed the lone Lakota for more than a day, waiting for the right moment to attack. Where was Looks Twice? Black Lodge moved to sit upright, but the pain stopped him. Although he could not see clearly in the darkness, even with the moon's light, he reached for the spot of pain and touched the binding over his wound. He also realized that someone had covered him with his own robe.

He had been wounded, and Looks Twice must be caring for him, he thought. But where was Looks Twice? It was not like Looks Twice to leave him here alone. Black Lodge slowly pulled his right arm out from under his robe and saw that a rope was tied around his wrist. He pulled on the rope and heard a movement nearby. Turning his head slowly, he saw his horse. Its jaw rope had been tied around his wrist.

Now he was very confused and began to be afraid. Looks Twice was not here. It must have been Looks Twice who had cared for him. But why was there not a fire? In spite of the questions whirling in his head, Black Lodge's pain and exhaustion compelled him to drift off to sleep.

At daybreak sunlight warmed the young warrior's face. As he opened his eyes, the first thing he saw clearly was the arrow at his feet, an arrow impaled in the ground. From its appearance and its markings, he knew it was the arrow of a Lakota warrior.

Sixteen

The sun's rays pushed through the branches of the giant cedars and splashed sudden light on Whirlwind's face. He awoke with a jerk and a moan as waves of pain emanated from his shoulder. Lingering images from his dream began to fade. He tried to pull the images back: Eyes, large, luminous yellow eyes. And a voice which had spoken without speaking. Then warm, soothing moistness on his wounded shoulder.

Consciousness chased away the dream images. Whirlwind looked about. The deer-hide robe had slid to his waist. He was half-reclining on a makeshift backrest set against the trunk of a tree. When he glanced down at his right shoulder, he immediately noticed that the poultice had fallen away. Strangely, the wound was cleaner than he remembered it, and the congealed blood was very dark—an encouraging sign that the wound had stopped bleeding.

Whirlwind pulled the robe up over his injured shoulder to protect it from the morning cold. A snort startled him, until he remembered the Arikara horse, which he had tied to a nearby tree.

Off to the east, under the brightening sky, a buffalo bull bellowed a challenge. An angry bellow soon answered, matching the tone of Whirlwind's mood. It was possible that his pursuit of the killer white man was over. He had fought the Arikara in spite of a bothersome, injured knee, but the wound in his right shoulder was much more debilitating. The Arikara's lance had sliced deeply into his shoulder just below the collarbone. Because of the wound he could not shoot a bow, and any movement of his arm caused pain and bleeding. Pain he could bear, but too much bleeding was dangerous.

The bright sky held promise of another warm day, but it was nearly the Winter Moon. There would not be many more warm days such as this. When the days became steadily colder and the snow arrived, it would be difficult to be in the open country—difficult even for someone without the burden of a bad wound.

That he was alive was incredible good fortune. How was it that the two Arikara got close without him knowing it? Was his anger with the killer white man dulling his senses? If he had not ducked when the Arikara warrior had charged at him, he would be lying out on the prairie cold and lifeless. By now the coyotes would have picked his flesh and left him an unrecognizable pile of bones. No one from the Wolf Tail camp would have known how or where he died. His life would have ended in mystery for Her Good Trail, and Walks High, and Spotted Calf.

Whirlwind was happy to have defeated his enemies, but he was not glad that he had had to kill. Life was to be defended to the utmost against any enemy. However, that did not mean that a warrior should find joy in killing, any more than a hunter should find joy in killing. One did not take any life, animal or human, simply because one could. One took a life only when there was no other way to survive. Perhaps that was why he had aided the young, wounded Arikara. Whirlwind smiled wryly. Bear Heart would label him weak and perhaps even call him a coward for not killing the wounded Arikara, but there were always choices. Yesterday, Whirlwind had decided to cool the fevered blood of the warrior and let his heart speak.

Killing was not the only way to defeat an enemy. Two days ago the great bear had retreated. No one had been hurt, and Whirlwind had won the encounter. It might turn out differently with the next bear, but his encounter with the great bear had reminded Whirlwind that victory could sometimes be gained without a weapon, and without taking a life. What was in the heart was stronger than what was in the hand. If he could have eluded the Arikara yesterday, he would have considered that a victory. To outwit an enemy and live to tell about it was, to Whirlwind, the best victory of all. To kill an enemy was sometimes necessary, but this was a dark, hollow victory—one that invaded sleep with shadowy dreams. The words of Grandfather Walks High, his son's namesake, echoed through his memory: "The hunter lives for the hunt but not to kill. Only to provide. And the warrior is not bred for war, the warrior is bred to defeat it."

To continue his pursuit of the killer white man now would be foolish, unless he did not travel for several days to allow his wound to start healing. It was the kind of a wound that would take time to heal, even under the best of circumstances. In a few days, however, the trail would be very cold, which would reduce his chances of capturing the man. That meant that the killer would escape and not have to answer for the killing of a good woman.

Whirlwind made his decision. He was a warrior. More than that, he was a Wolf Warrior and sworn to defend his people. He would continue to pursue the killer because he now had a horse to ride, but he would need to travel slowly in order to avoid jostling his wound.

Through the swooping branches of the cedar, he could see no clouds. It would be a warm day. He would rest often and let the sun help heal his wound.

Whirlwind sat up slowly. First, he would build a fire and eat. Then he would cut up the bloodstained shirt for bindings to help keep his arm in one position as he rode. Fortunately, he had a spare shirt.

Building a fire was a painful process. The bow drill fire starter required that one hand hold down the spinning drill stick while the other worked the bow. It was helpful that Whirlwind was one of those few who were left-handed, since he could work the bow with his left hand while holding down the spinning drill with his right. Even so, with his injury it was still hard to apply enough pressure with his right hand to produce the necessary friction.

Then he remembered something an old man had done whose hand had been badly mangled by a bear. He had built a special device, with two long, springy sticks, to brace the bow drill while holding the base.

Whirlwind looked around. There was plenty of wood. He found two pieces a little longer than finger tip to elbow. On the underside of one thick end, he carved a hole where he would fit the top of the drill. To the thickest end of the second stick, he attached the grooved base for the drill. Then he tied the two narrow ends together, very tightly, with strips of leather cut from his blood-soaked shirt. After that, he pried apart the untied, thicker ends and forced the drill into the hole at the top and the grooved base at the bottom. In this manner, it was not necessary to apply downward pressure with his right hand.

The new device was slightly awkward to handle at first, but it worked. Without further injury to his wound, Whirlwind eventually had a fire—a small victory but a victory nonetheless. This triumph gave him the resolve to continue his pursuit of the killer, for without fire in the winter, death was only a matter of time.

The soft crackle and occasional hiss from the flames brought a certain sense of calm. It was a connection with where he wanted to be—home in his own lodge with Her Good Trail. At home, the fire in the lodge reminded him of the many lonely camps he had endured. Here, at this lonely camp, the fire reminded him of home. It was his prayer that when he came to the end of his journey through this life, it would happen at home beside a warm fire, with Her Good Trail beside him.

He could not bear the thought of living without Her Good Trail. Although she kept the lodge clean and orderly, was a good cook, and her quillwork was the envy of many, her place in his heart was not because of such things. It was because she filled an emptiness and made him feel whole. Because she brought a stirring inside of him each time she looked at him or touched him. Because her spirit calmed him whenever he was in turmoil. For those reasons, he was prepared to die for her, with the hope his deeds would measure up to all that she meant to him.

Whirlwind lost himself in the undulating flames. Covering his injured shoulder with the robe, he sank back against the makeshift backrest. Out of the corner of his eye, he could see that the horse was dozing. That was a good sign. He closed his eyes.

When he awoke, the sun was at its halfway point. Whirlwind began preparing to travel. He tied the poultice over the wound for when it bled again, although he planned to travel slowly and avoid using his right arm. He disliked the limitation, but he well understood that the injury could have been much worse—like a broken leg.

Whirlwind used his own jaw and neck ropes on the Arikara horse. A tall and steady brown and white paint gelding, he had stood his ground to allow his rider a chance to defeat an enemy, and defeat had been the fault of the rider not the horse.

The paint was a fast walker, and he had a smooth gait. Whirlwind urged him into a lope and then a gallop, but only briefly to learn how the horse moved. By late afternoon they reached a plateau northeast of the desert-like badlands that

Stone had called the Stronghold of the Spirits. Spotted Calf had described the badlands as the loneliest place he had ever seen, with one bare hillside after another where grass could not take root and where the winds moaned with a hollow, heartbroken voice.

Whirlwind found a sandstone outcropping and stopped to rest. After hobbling the horse, he crawled to the top of the outcropping and scouted the land around. Although he had never had a bad experience in the Stronghold, the place did seem to reach out to a man and push him away at the same time. It was a place both pleasing to the eye and sometimes unsettling for the spirit. He guessed that the white man he was following would be wary about going into the Stronghold.

The sun was very bright and warm. A long, low dust cloud hung just above the ground, far off to the south. Whirlwind guessed that it was a large herd of antelope on the run. Buzzards were circling to the west. To the north, just below the horizon, was a layer of dark color—buffalo. This area had many grassy bottoms and plateaus that were good grazing areas in the winter, especially for buffalo.

Whirlwind leaned against a low, vertical wall and exposed his injured shoulder to the sun's rays. While he rested, he kept an eye on the horse since a horse's senses were far better than any man's.

Whirlwind thought he imagined the sound of a holy iron a great distance away. The paint brought his ears forward and looked off to the west. Perhaps it was not his imagination. Whirlwind turned, keeping his left ear to the west since a slight breeze was coming from that direction. Long, long moments crawled by as he sat without moving, and then the sound came again. For the second time, the paint brought up his ears and looked west.

It could only be the killer white man.

Whirlwind tied the deer-hide robe over his shoulders and climbed slowly down the outcropping. Before he mounted the horse, he carefully checked the neck rope. Everything was still tied on securely—his pack, lance, and war club. The bow, in its case, and the quiver now bristling with arrows was hanging at the small of his back.

"Well, my friend," he said softly to the horse as he untied the hobbles and mounted, "I know you probably have never seen a white man. But soon you will."

Seventeen

Walks High and de la Verendrye arrived at the Antler Tree before sundown and set about preparing the camp. They had been south of the White Earth River, riding west and looking for Whirlwind's trail. Bear Heart and Red Lance were north of the river, doing the same. They had agreed to meet at the Antler Tree.

The Antler Tree, a stout cottonwood with twin trunks, was on a bench about a stone's throw south of the river. Caught in each trunk was the antler and skull of a white-tailed buck, a testimony to an ancient battle when the tree was only a few winters old.

De la Verendrye finished gathering firewood. He glanced a few times at the tree with the antlers imbedded in each of its trunks as he dug a firepit. Like anyone basically knowledgeable about the wilderness and animals, he knew that buck deer sometimes interlocked their horns while fighting. But he had never seen a sight like the Antler Tree.

Walks High came with an armload of wood to build a heat reflector and immediately noticed the white man's fascination with the tree.

"My grandfather showed me this tree when I was eight winters old," he informed de la Verendrye.

De la Verendrye nodded. "How do you think it happened?"

Walks High talked as he worked on the heat reflector. "They came together like this," he said, imitating two sparring bucks by extending his fingers and then interlocking them. "The tree was in between them. It was just a young tree then but stout enough so they could not bend it to free themselves from it."

"How did they die? Starvation?"

Walks High shook his head. "No. A bear came. Or the great cat or wolves. But the deer did not die of starvation. Later, the coyotes came. And ravens, buzzards, and hawks. Then the insects. The deer bones were carried away until only the skulls and antlers remained. As winters passed, the tree became larger and grew around the antlers, as you can see. In the end, it was the tree that won."

"How long ago do you think it happened? The deer fighting."

Walks High shrugged. "Hard to say. But my grandfather, who is almost seventy winters old, says the tree is older than he is."

De la Verendrye settled into finishing his task. When the firepit was ready, he worked on a fire. Soon smoke swirled from the base of the bow drill fire starter.

Walks High finished the reflector and took a long, careful look around. Bear Heart and Red Lance should be showing up soon. Before they did, he wanted to ask the white man to explain something.

"Beard," he said quietly.

"Yes," De la Verendrye did not look up. He was blowing gently on the tiny embers among the kindling.

"Beard, you said something this morning about Bear Heart. You thought he was angry because my mother let you use the holy iron."

De la Verendrye looked up briefly and nodded.

"Why would he be angry?"

The kindling caught. De la Verendrye blew on the flames and added bigger kindling. When the fire was well started, he sat back and looked at Walks High.

A look of relief flickered in the white man's eyes as he began to speak. "Some days ago, before High Hawk's mother was killed, he told me he would trade for your father's holy iron. Ten horses, he said. He was sure he could trade for it, and when he did, he wanted me to teach him how to use it."

Walks High nodded. "Now I understand why he does not like you."

De la Verendrye decided not to tell the young warrior about Bear Heart's threat. It was enough, for now, that Walks High understood the reason for the bad feelings between him and Bear Heart. "I have seen many like him," he said. "Many who want the holy iron. Bruneaux wanted it. Men like Bruneaux are nothing with it. That is why I cannot understand Bear Heart. He is a fierce warrior. He does not need the holy iron to be a warrior, and a man."

Walks High looked down into the growing fire. "My father does not want it."

"I think that soon many of your people will have it by trading for it. Hunting will be easier. You won't have to try so hard to get within arrow shot of a deer or an elk. And your enemies will not bother you if they know that you have warriors with holy irons."

"True. But there is something about the holy iron, more than what it can do. There is a different power that it has, a power that comes from the fear of it."

"It is only a weapon. A thing to be used."

"Yes. Yes. And by watching you use it and handle it, I can see that it does not have its own life. It is just . . . a thing. But I also saw a change in you. You were different without it. Helpless. Powerless. As for me, I am a true hunter, and I have always hunted with the bow. As a true hunter, I know that I need to be worthy of the life that I take. Our way of hunting helps me to be worthy. If hunting becomes easy, then maybe I will begin to feel a power that I truthfully do not have. That is why my father does not like the holy iron, and I understand his thinking."

De la Verendrye nodded. "You are right," he admitted, a little ashamed. "When you had Bruneaux trapped on that ridge, all I could do was watch. I did not feel part of it, because I did not have a holy iron. Now it is different. If I see deer, I look at them differently." He shrugged. "Maybe it's because I know I can kill them, if I wanted to."

Walks High nodded emphatically. "I think my father sees something about the holy iron that others do not. And will not."

"I think your father is right," de la Verendrye replied. "I have seen men who are meek and fearful without a holy iron become loud and boisterous when they have one in their hands." He paused to gather his thoughts. "There are many people on this land. To the east, far beyond the Grandfather River, there are many different people speaking many different languages. And your people are here, and there are others to the south. I know that all of you have been here for a very long time, long before my kind of people came here. And you lived without any of the things that white men have."

Walks High stared long at de la Verendrye, suddenly realizing that this white man had traveled far, very far. And he had seen much that Walks High did not know about, or could not imagine. "Tell me," he said. "Are there many of your kind of people?"

"Yes. Many."

"More than my kind of people?"

De la Verendrye thought for a moment. "I do not know. There are many white men living on the lands along the great water. But the further west I came, the fewer white men I saw."

"Your kind of people, are there . . . different types or only one?" Walks High quietly persisted.

"We are many different types."

"Different languages?"

"Many."

"Where do you come from?"

De la Verendrye grabbed a stick and drew a rough map in the dirt, approximating one he had seen of the eastern coastline. "This is the land, far to the east, along the great water. East of where the land ends, there is nothing but water. Much, much water. I rode on a large boat. I got on the boat where my homeland touches the great water. The boat traveled on the great water for eighty-seven days before it reached this land here." He pointed to a spot on the Acadian coastline on his crude map.

"Eighty-seven days! Perhaps you were going around in circles," observed Walks High.

"Perhaps," allowed de la Verendrye. "The man who was in charge of the boat was not a good thinker. But I do know that this great water is larger than any lands I have ever heard of."

"Larger than this land?" Walks High scoffed with his eyes. "I do not know if that could be true. I have traveled as far north as the Knife River, and the land goes beyond that. My father has been south of the Running Water. The land goes beyond that. My grandfather has said that the land goes so far east, beyond the Grandfather River, that it might take several moons to travel that far and back. To the west there are other mountains further than the Black Hills. And you say there is a great water larger than all of that?"

De la Verendrye shrugged. "It does not matter to me. I will never be on that water again." He waved his hand around. "This land is more beautiful than that dark, angry water."

Walks High agreed. He tilted his head toward the west. "That way, to the west, are the great hills. Some call them the Black Mountains. Others say Black Hills. It is a good place to be. Stone says it is where the spirit of the Earth itself lives. My mother says those mountains are like a womb."

The smile faded from de la Verendrye's face at the sound of splashing as Bear Heart and Red Lance crossed the White Earth River. He looked down at the fire, uncertain as to what Bear Heart's mood would be.

"My friend," Walks High said softly, "there will be no trouble over the holy iron. You asked my mother's permission, which is a proper thing to do. She let you use it."

"Good," replied de la Verendrye. "But . . . but there was a day when I . . . I thought of just taking the holy iron . . . from your father's lodge."

Walks High looked long into the white man's face. "What do you mean?"

De la Verendrye cleared his throat. "I saw the holy iron in your father's lodge, hanging behind the dew liner, the first day I was in the camp, the day High Hawk and his family returned from the north. I began . . . to think of ways to steal it."

"Why?"

"To . . . take revenge on Bruneaux."

"But you changed your thinking?"

"Yes. But not about taking revenge on Bruneaux."

Red Lance shouted a greeting as he and Bear Heart dismounted nearby. Walks High waved and looked back at de la Verendrye. "As I said, there will be no trouble over the holy iron."

Bear Heart had taken an antelope. It was quickly skinned, butchered, and cooked. The three warriors ate until they couldn't eat anymore, a common practice when on a long trail, since there was often no time or opportunity to preserve meat. They would take with them what was left.

De la Verendrye ate well, too, but could not eat half as much as the other three. For the rest of the evening he busied himself with the fire, and silently envied the easy comrade-ship of Walks High and Red Lance. He had been alone all of his life—as the youngest child in his family and as a lone traveler. He had borne his burdens and celebrated his victo-ries alone. Subsequently, he had found a home among the Dakota, but, in spite of their warm hospitality, a barrier to communication and communion remained. He was uncer-tain who should cross it first, so he held back. Perhaps such a barrier existed because the differences between them were thought to be greater than they actually were. For the most part, it seemed to be the same here with these Lakota, although the conversation he had had with Walks High was easy and friendly.

White Hare, the Isanti Dakota warrior, had liked to visit late into the night sometimes, de la Verendrye recalled fondly. He knew that White Hare was curious as well as friendly and that he had disappointed White Hare by not revealing more about himself. But he had never considered his life before coming to America worth talking about.

He looked at Walks High. Beneath the imposing image of the warrior was a shy and gentle young man, with even a touch of boyishness that showed in the mischievous twinkle that flashed occasionally through the young warrior's eyes.

De la Verendrye's face suddenly warmed with embarrass-ment, remembering his thoughts about Sun Rise Woman. He could never tell Walks High about that. Admitting those thoughts to him would surely be a barrier to many things, especially since he was beginning to think that, perhaps, he had found a friend—something he had never had.

De la Verendrye looked up and saw Bear Heart's dark, steady stare. Another barrier. And what of Whirlwind? What did the war leader of the Wolf Tail people really think of the white man he had saved? Perhaps he regarded all white men to be like Bruneaux. For certain, Bear Heart did.

"Beard."

De la Verendrye smiled inwardly at the sound of the name he would apparently be known by among the Wolf Tail people. He looked up into the intense eyes of Red Lance.

"Beard, you will have second watch."

"Good."

Red Lance pointed at the moon. "When it is there," he indicated a spot in the western night sky, "I will wake you."

De la Verendrye nodded.

The sun was barely above the horizon when they broke camp the next morning. Preparations had been made with hardly a word being spoken, and then only to the horses. De la Verendrye was the last to be mounted but only because his wound still prevented sudden movements.

They rode with Red Lance in the lead and Bear Heart as the rear guard. Half a morning passed as they alternated between a fast walk and a slow lope. Only Bear Heart interrupted the pace as he paused a few times to study the eastern skyline. Walks High kept watch to the north and south, with de la Verendrye helping.

As they crossed a creek that eventually flowed into the White Earth River, Red Lance signaled a halt and pointed to the west. De la Verendrye held the horses as the three warriors dismounted and crawled up a low hill.

"A horse," Walks High told de la Verendrye when they returned, "standing by itself. We have to see about it."

They spent the rest of the morning sneaking up on the lone horse. He was standing near a rise, and all that could be seen from the east was his head and back. Red Lance and Bear Heart went north while Walks High and de la Verendrye went south. They had a simple plan: Each pair would ride a wide half circle, and they would converge at a point to the west of the lone horse. Moving in wide half circles would enable them to see what else might be hiding somewhere.

A thin layer of clouds began to slide in from the southwest when Walks High caught sight of Red Lance. They had completed the circle. They had seen nothing, save a few prairie dogs and a large herd of antelope. The lone gray horse was still standing where Red Lance had first spotted him.

They encircled the horse and moved in. De la Verendrye had the holy iron ready, and the three warriors had bows strung and arrows nocked. At the sight of other horses, the gray neighed a greeting. Though he seemed a little nervous, he was reluctant to move.

They all saw the body at once, a man lying face up.

"Arikara," said Bear Heart.

"He is not breathing," pointed out Red Lance.

"That is why." Bear Heart pointed to the large, dark stain of dried blood on the dead man's chest.

Dismounting, Bear Heart bent to untie the horse's jaw rope from the man's wrist. He had not moved because he was tied to the dead man. Bear Heart paused as he coiled up the jaw rope, staring intently at an arrow impaled in the ground near the dead body. He dislodged the arrow, held it up, and glanced at Walks High.

Walks High's mouth tightened. "My father's arrow."

"Yes," whispered Bear Heart, touching the red and black beneath the fletching. "This is your father's mark."

Walks High's eyes flashed as he took the jaw rope of the gray from Bear Heart. "There is only one thing to do," he said. "Backtrack this horse."

Eighteen

It began just after midday, and by the middle of the afternoon the snow squall had completely covered the tracks Whirlwind had been following. Still, he had been able to gain ground on the killer.

At first the tracks led west into the Stronghold, but then they turned sharply north. Whirlwind seemed to have guessed right—the white man was afraid to go into the Stronghold and was heading back toward the prairie. Along the northern edge of the desert-like formations, he found a deer carcass. Three coyotes and several ravens fled as he approached. Without dismounting, he could see the work of a rough hand. Only one hindquarter had been taken. The most telling sign was the hole in the animal's rib cage. It had been killed by a holy iron, probably the one he had heard yesterday.

Whirlwind had a thought and carefully dismounted. The deer meat was still good. He quickly sliced off the remaining hindquarter, tied it to the neck rope, and remounted with a grimace of pain. "I have left some for you," he said to the coyotes and ravens. "I know that you will not dishonor our relative here," he said, pointing to the dead deer, "by letting his flesh go to waste. The white man is a strange being. He does not understand how things are." The coyotes and ravens reclaimed the day-old kill after he rode away.

Mounting and dismounting were the most difficult activities for Whirlwind as far as his injured shoulder was concerned. To help keep his shoulder from moving, he held his right hand inside the makeshift belt tied around his deer-hide robe. Nevertheless, his shoulder was still very tender and throbbed with each heartbeat.

Steadily falling snow soon obscured the horizons, and the flakes grew smaller, a sign that the snowfall would probably last most of the night. Finding shelter now became the most important task. There was no sense of panic, however, since Whirlwind knew this country well.

He kept moving west until he came to a deep, narrow gully as deep as a man's waist. Coaxing the horse down into it, he rode northward. The gully grew deeper and steeper the further north he went. He had been here before, many times.

The horse moved willingly, undaunted by the uncertain footing of the gully floor. As the trail became steeper, Whirlwind kept his eyes more and more straight ahead. Though the snowflakes remained small, the snowfall was getting heavier. Soon, it was very difficult to see much beyond the end of the horse's nose.

As the horse carefully picked his trail, Whirlwind began to recall details of the secluded grove of pines at the end of this gully hidden in a hollow at the top of a sharp butte. The butte's sides were bare, except for an occasional cactus. From a distance, it did not attract the eye, because it looked like many other bare buttes. But at the top of this butte was a bowl-shaped hollow thick with pines, which for some reason grew only as tall as the rim of the hollow. It was good shelter, for both two-leggeds and four-leggeds. Two or three winters ago, Whirlwind had seen many signs of deer inside the grove.

A low branch, hanging out over the gully, suddenly appeared out of the whiteness. Whirlwind ducked just in time and smiled. That branch over the gully meant he was nearly there.

With an effort, the paint climbed a sudden incline. Whirlwind had to lean far over its neck to keep from sliding off backwards. Suddenly, they were in the thick grove of pines where there was shelter and relative safety and plenty of firewood.

Whirlwind pulled the horse to a stop and listened. The hollow was utterly quiet. Dismounting, the warrior pulled his war club and led the paint through the trees, weaving his way in and out. Finally, he was satisfied that he and the paint were alone in the grove. Tying the horse to a large, bare branch, he began to gather firewood.

Red Lance looked to the area where Walks High was pointing. He saw hoofprints of a lone horse.

"My father was here," decided Walks High. "Spent the night. Had a fire." Relief brightened the young warrior's face.

Earlier, they had backtracked the gray to a grassy bottom where Bear Heart had shown them signs of a fight. Below a low bank nearby, they had found a second Arikara body covered with a thin layer of dirt. "Your father killed this one and only wounded the one we found this morning," Bear Heart had observed. "He let the wounded one go, perhaps because he himself was wounded." Then he had pointed to the southwest and said, "I found drops of blood there." From there, they had followed hoofprints to the grove of cedars on the east slope of a long, low hill.

Walks High followed the hoofprints only far enough to satisfy himself that his father was still heading west. Snow began to fall heavily as he rejoined Red Lance and Beard. Bear Heart had ridden south to scout.

De la Verendrye pointed to a track close to the fire. "Do you think this wolf was here before or after your father came here?"

The two young warriors looked. "Is it the only one?" Red Lance wondered, looking around.

Walks High nodded. "Yes. A big one, too. Wolf, for sure. Perhaps my father made the track. The wolf is his spirit helper."

The other two men yielded to that logic and set about preparing camp, as the snow came down heavier and heavier. Walks High picketed all the horses nearby while Red Lance gathered firewood. Using the shallow firepit they had found, de la Verendrye built a fire.

Outside of the grove, the land turned white and then disappeared, as if, for the three men, the world suddenly diminished to the size of the cedar grove. A few snowflakes came down through the branches, vanishing with a sizzle as the flames ended their long, earthward journey just before they could reach their destination. The three men settled in, intending to make the most of their sojourn amidst the tall, silent cedars.

"If your father is hurt, it must not be too bad," Red Lance pointed out. "It did not stop him from following that white man."

Walks High nodded. "You are right, I think. And now he has a horse, it looks like."

"Do you suppose he has weapons?" de la Verendrye asked.

"Yes," Walks High replied. "He would have at least made a lance. A war club, too. The first Arikara we found this morning was shot with an arrow not stabbed with a lance. Perhaps my father has made a bow."

"I think he did," Red Lance said. "There was a bow left behind with the second body. The one we found this morning had his bow, too. Your father did make his own bow."

"How?" de la Verendrye wondered. "Does he have any tools?"

"A knife," Walks High said.

"A knife? What can he do with a knife?"

Walks High smiled. "Make a bow. Arrows, too."

One of the horses nickered softly. Bear Heart came into view, leading his horse. "This will fall all night," he said. He returned after tying his horse to the picket line.

"Beard," the older warrior said, after sitting down by the fire. "I have decided that I will borrow the holy iron from you."

The younger warriors fell silent as de la Verendrye took a deep breath and rubbed his forehead.

"Yes," Bear Heart continued. "Someone among the Wolf Tail people must deal with this straight on. That will be me. I am not afraid of the holy iron."

Images of his first meeting with Bear Heart swirled in de la Verendrye's memory. "It does not belong to me," he pointed out, softly.

Bear Heart glanced quickly aside at Walks High and then returned a hard gaze to the white man's face. "Not yours? How so?"

"I borrowed it from Walks High's mother. When we return, I will give it back."

Bear Heart looked to Walks High. "Is this true?"

Walks High nodded.

"Still, I will borrow it."

De la Verendrye nervously cleared his throat and shook his head. "No. I cannot lend you something that I borrowed."

A hard stare from the older warrior nearly pushed the white man away from the fire. Finally, Bear Heart looked sideways to Walks High. "Then I am asking you," he said, his voice low and angry. "I will borrow the holy iron from you."

Walks High looked out into the snowfall briefly and then toward the older warrior. "This white man, Beard," he said, "came to my mother's lodge and asked to use the holy iron. My father was not there to speak for our lodge so my mother did. She decided to lend it to Beard. So it is for him to say 'yes' or 'no' to you. . . . I heard him say 'no.' "

"You think like the white man."

"No," Walks High replied evenly. "No, I think for myself. I think that the white man's reply was proper for him."

Bear Heart smiled. But it was a thin, hard smile. "You are a young man," he said. "You will have a long life, if you are not killed on the warpath, or under the hooves of the mighty buffalo. In your life, you will see many things, many changes. You are seeing one now." He paused a moment to point at the encased weapon next to the white man. "That. And it will not be the last one you will see. Many more will come into our lands and into our lives. We cannot be afraid of them—like your father is." He stabbed the air with an angry gesture toward the weapon. "It is only a thing! But it is a way for our people to be strong! The Pawnee and Arikara would stay out of our country if they knew that many warriors in every Lakota encampment had holy irons! What would they think now, if they knew that a Lakota war leader was hiding such a weapon, afraid to use it?"

Red Lance grabbed the head of the war club at his belt and glanced nervously toward his best friend. Walks High, meanwhile, who rarely touched another person, put a reassuring hand briefly on Red Lance's shoulder.

Bear Heart slowly rose to his feet, with Walks High following his move. Both warriors were tall, although Walks High was slightly taller and larger than the older warrior.

"Is it because my father is afraid that he is pursuing a white man who has a holy iron?"

"I know your father is a brave man. Once I saw him stake himself to fight the Pawnee. But it is easier to fight something that is seen, that can be understood. It is not so easy to fight something you do not understand. Your father is afraid of the holy iron because he fears the changes it will bring."

"Perhaps. And perhaps he is right. It seems the holy iron has changed you because you want it so badly."

Bear Heart's gaze was hard and unrelenting. "I could have taken the weapon from this . . . this . . . white man many times."

Walks High returned the older warrior's stare. "True. But that would have been a wrong thing to do."

Though he now spoke to de la Verendrye, Bear Heart kept his eyes on Walks High. "What do you say, white man? Will you give me the holy iron?"

Red Lance glanced at de la Verendrye and shook his head, just as Walks High spoke again. "No. No, because I will not let him. And I will not let you take it."

Bear Heart measured the young warrior across the fire. The snow was falling more heavily. There was no sound, except for the crackling flames, until he spoke for the last time. "This thing with the holy iron among us, among our people, is not over. There will be a time when it must be settled. It will not be now, but there will be a day."

He backed slowly away from the fire, keeping the two younger warriors in view. After several steps he spun on his heel and hurried to the picketed horses.

Walks High and Red Lance glanced at one another as Bear Heart led his horses away and disappeared into the whiteness. Soon it was quiet again.

"Beard," Walks High called softly.

"Yes. What?"

Walks High waved a hand at the fire. "I think we need some more wood. Unless you want to freeze."

De la Verendrye performed his small chore. Walks High had retaken his seat by the fire. The white man glanced at the thick, white snowfall. "Where is he going?" he asked.

"Home," replied Walks High.

"Home? You mean he will not follow us?"

"I do not think so," said Walks High. "He could not get from you what he really wanted. There is no longer a reason for him to travel with us. He will go home."

De la Verendrye glanced at the snow again. "Why does he dislike your father so much?"

Walks High smiled, and Red Lance replied, "Because my uncle Whirlwind was selected as our war leader. Bear Heart thought he should have been picked instead of my uncle."

De la Verendrye nodded and was quiet for a time. "There is something else I would like to ask," he said.

The two young warriors nodded and waited.

"How did your father get his name?" he asked Walks High.

The warrior smiled again. "When he was a young man," Walks High said, "before he and my mother were married, he went with a war party into Pawnee country. The war party was led by my father's uncle, a very fine warrior who later died in a blizzard. It was a revenge raid because the Pawnee had attacked and killed some of our people. Our warriors sneaked into a Pawnee village and turned horses loose, to lure their warriors out into the open. But it was a large village with many warriors, and they surrounded my father's war party. So the Lakota leader, the one who died in a blizzard, staked himself to fight."

"Staked? What does that mean?"

"All of us who are Wolf Warriors carry a long rope," explained Red Lance. "Sometimes, in a battle, some of us will decide not to retreat, even if we must die. We pound a stake into the ground and tie ourselves to it with that rope. When that happens, either a warrior dies fighting where he stands or the fight is won. The third way is for another warrior to pull up the stake."

De la Verendrye nodded, trying to make images in his mind to fit Red Lance's words.

Walks High continued the story. "My father was going to pull up the war party leader's stake, but the man refused to let him. So my father, who was called Badger then, stayed and fought beside him. His uncle told later how my father fought so fiercely that he moved like a whirlwind. The Pawnee so outnumbered the Lakota that they could have killed them all, but they were impressed by the bravery of our war party leader and my father and let the Lakota go."

A slight hiss came from the fire. De la Verendrye let the powerful images of Walks High's story slowly fade away. He looked across into the young warrior's face but said nothing. He could see that Walks High was still reliving his father's battle with the Pawnee.

Whirlwind leaned against the backrest beneath the shelter he had built in the hollow. His fire was blazing high, and deer meat was roasting on a spit. It had been awkward, painful, and slow to build his camp. The snow was much heavier now, nearly ankle deep by the time daylight began to fade.

Perhaps, he thought, I will be here for a few days. That possibility was not a bad thing since he needed to rest and care for his wound. Making camp with one arm had not been easy. But making camp was one thing, fighting was another.

If he had to fight the killer now, he would be limited to a lance or a war club. With a wounded shoulder his accuracy with a bow would not be good, if he could even use one at all. So the snowfall was like a truce. He could not travel in it because the whiteness would soon turn him in circles. There was no choice but to stop and wait for the snow to stop falling—and to rest.

He dozed for a short while. When he awoke with a start, he saw a dark shape out of the corner of his eye—a wolf, visible for a heartbeat or two before it faded into the whiteness.

Whirlwind smiled and closed his eyes once more.

Again he had the dream of the wolf fighting the gray dogs. But this time the gray dogs retreated into a mist, and from the mist emerged a white man whose face could not be plainly seen, except for the insidious, evil smile which was more like a snarl. In the white man's hands was a holy iron, pointing at the wolf. Suddenly, the man turned toward Whirlwind and aimed the weapon straight at the warrior's heart.

Whirlwind awoke with a jerk and a slight moan. The movement brought a hot pain to his wounded shoulder. He sat up and poked at the fire. Even as the flames grew, so did an anger deep in his heart. The mother of High Hawk should still be alive, and the horse standing nearby should be a tall, swift gray roan.

Nineteen

Spring Creek Valley was hushed as slowly falling snow-flakes floated to the Earth. Its pine-covered hillsides lost their hard darkness as the land began to turn white. Three figures among the leafless willow stalks near a bend in the Smoking Earth River looked up at the sky, two old men and a boy. The old men drank in the quiet beauty of the moment. Though they had seen many, many like it, every new snowfall to them was a new memory and a new awakening. The boy, as yet unaware that he was gathering his own memories, simply stuck out his tongue to catch snowflakes.

Stone glanced around and then pointed to a thick clump of willows. "We can make a fire there," he said.

Spotted Calf nodded. They were still a long walk from the winter encampment. A spirited morning hunt for cottontail rabbits had brought them to the edge of hunger and fatigue. Food and a little rest would ease the walk home.

"Grandson," called out Stone. The boy had discovered a promising sign on the soft ground. He held up crooked fingers on either side of his head to show that a buck whitetail had passed by here. "Grandson, we need wood. Before everything gets too wet to start a fire." The boy nodded and took a last look at the tracks before he attacked his task.

Spotted Calf picked two rabbits from their morning's take of eight and headed for the river. There, at the cold water's edge, he skinned and washed the gutted carcasses. He returned with bundled hides and meat ready for cooking. Stone, by then, had a fire going and was putting together a makeshift shelter. Beneath it they could rest and cook their food. Red Legs brought a third armload of wood and found a spot to sit under the shelter.

Spotted Calf built up the fire and skewered the rabbits on sticks to hang above the flames. For cooking only, he would have waited until there was a thick bed of hot coals to cook the meat. But since they needed to warm themselves as well, he simply hung the meat high above the dancing flames.

Red Legs unstrung his bow. "Are you cooking the two I shot?" he wondered.

"I do not know," replied Spotted Calf.

"You shot six," he told the old man. "Someday I will be as good as you are with the bow."

Spotted Calf nodded and smiled. "Yes, you will. And after that, you will be better."

"I once saw my cousin here shoot so fast that he put two arrows in the same deer," Stone said. "One on each side."

Red Legs's mouth fell open. "How did you do that?" he asked Spotted Calf.

Spotted Calf only smiled as Stone continued the story. "We were near the Great Muddy. It was autumn. The deer was coming up the draw where we had been waiting all morning. When he got close enough, this grandfather," he said, pointing at Spotted Calf, "shot and put the first arrow through his left side. The deer was so surprised he jumped and turned in the other direction. By then, my cousin's second arrow was on the way, and it hit him in the same spot on the right side."

The boy looked at Spotted Calf with unconcealed awe. He knew that the father of Whirlwind was the best shot among all of the men in the Wolf Tail band. Once Walks High had told how his grandfather had taken a duck on the wing.

Spotted Calf turned the meat. "Like I said, Grandson," he remarked, "someday you will be so good with the bow that you will make me look like a child."

Red Legs shook his head. "I do not know," he muttered. "I do not think anyone can be as good as you."

"Not true," returned Spotted Calf. "There was a time I thought like that. I saw my grandfather hit a coyote at over eighty paces."

"Eighty paces!" Red Legs looked around, measuring eighty paces with his eyes. "A coyote is a small thing to hit at that distance."

"Yes, but my grandfather did. I was with him, and I thought that no one could ever be that good. When I said so, do you know what he told me?"

The boy shook his head.

"My grandfather said that we will never be as good as we will be with a bow until we die."

Stone leaned over. "What that means is that we should always try to improve. Much depends on it. Being a poor shot with a bow means your family will go hungry. Or an enemy might kill you in battle."

"My grandfather won a horse with that shot at the coyote," Spotted Calf went on. "It was a time when there were only a few horses. It would be like winning ten or twenty horses now."

"A wager?" Red Legs wondered.

"Yes. My grandfather and his brother-in-law had just buried part of the carcass of a buffalo they had killed. The other part was loaded on his brother-in-law's horse. I was with them, and I was seven winters old then. We were going to take some of the meat back to the village and then return for the rest. But from the top of a small hill we saw a coyote digging at the buried meat.

"My grandfather only wanted to scare the coyote away, not kill him. So he took out an arrow with a blunt head. As he was getting ready to shoot, his brother-in-law said that no one could hit a coyote at that distance. My grandfather asked if his brother-in-law was willing to wager his horse against one shot. The man said 'yes,' if my grandfather was willing to wager two bows and fifty arrows. It was agreed."

Spotted Calf paused as he traveled back into the days of his boyhood, savoring the memory as he told the story. "My grandfather laid the arrow on the string, took aim, and let it go." The old man motioned with his hands as he talked, imitating drawing a bow and an arrow flying off from the string. "I watched that arrow," he went on. "It went up . . . and came down. It hit the coyote on the side. The coyote yelped and ran away. And my grandfather was the owner of a horse, one of only eight horses in our encampment then."

The boy's eyebrows tightened as an intensity came into his eyes. He was imagining an arrow flying over eighty paces on its way to a coyote. "That was a very good shot," he murmured. "Because it hit a coyote and won a horse."

"Yes," affirmed Stone. "If my cousin's grandfather had not always tried to get better and better, he would not have made that shot. He would not have earned that horse."

A few quiet moments passed. The two old men listened intently for any sounds that did not belong. From the north came the faint cry of the great cat. Only the distance weakened the strong voice of that great hunter. But there was no need for worry. He was a long way off, and he respected the two-leggeds as much as the two-leggeds respected him. Of all of the beings who shared the Earth with the Lakota, the great tawny cat was the best at moving silently and striking swiftly. His way was a strong lesson for two-legged hunters and warriors. As his proud, heart-stopping cry pierced the quiet winter morning, a white-tailed buck stamped a hoof and woofed somewhere inside the shadowy pine-covered hills. He had heard the cry of the great cat, too.

Red Legs watched as Spotted Calf turned the meat, which was nearly cooked. "Why were there only a few horses in your grandfather's time?" he asked.

The two old men looked at one another, and it was Stone who replied. "There was a time when the people did not have horses at all," he said.

"No horses? How can that be?"

"It was," replied Stone. "No horses."

"What did the people do without horses?" the boy wondered.

"They walked."

"Was it difficult?"

"No," answered Spotted Calf. "Is our life difficult now because we do not have the holy iron? No. Long ago our people lived well without the horse. They did not know of the horse. They did not know what they did not have. They hunted. They moved their lodges. Dogs helped them carry their belongings. They were happy, as we are now."

"How did the horse come? Was it hiding from the people?"

"From the south country," said Stone. "There are stories of strange people who traveled across the deserts far to the south, in places not known to us. They wore iron clothes and rode horses."

"What kind of people wear iron clothes?"

"A kind of white people, I think," said Spotted Calf.

"They carried fearful weapons. Holy irons. They killed."

"And they gave horses to our people?"

"No, I do not think so. I think some horses were taken away from them, by our kind of people. After many winters, herds grew as colts were born. Our kind of people raised the horses and traded them. Different tribes traded with one another until the horse came up into our country."

"When did they come?"

"My grandfather said he first saw a horse when he was a young man. That was over eighty winters ago."

Stone agreed. "Yes, but at first there were only a few. My father said that his village had a herd of twelve horses when he was a boy."

"Now we have four hundred in our herd," the boy pointed out.

"Yes. And at a summer gathering two winters back, when six bands of our people came together, there were two thousand horses," Stone recalled.

"It's a good thing the horses came," observed the boy. "We would still be walking everywhere."

Spotted Calf chuckled. "We still walk. Like now. We did not bring horses with us. Remember this, Grandson. Horses are a good thing—very powerful and fast. But they did not change us. We are still the same people. We still hunt. We still move our camps. The things we believed in did not change just because horses came. But they did give us a way to do things better and faster. Our lodges are bigger, because horses can carry bigger loads. With the help of horses, our warriors can protect the people better. In a way, horses came and joined us on the path we were following, to help us along."

Silence returned. The boy nestled his chin on drawn-up knees as he stared into the crackling fire. Spotted Calf continued to turn the meat, careful to keep it above the flames. In a while, the boy spoke again.

"I do not know how it is without horses," he said.

"Yes. They will always be a part of your life," Stone said. "Horses are important to us. With them we can travel fast and far. They make our warriors better able to fight for the people. They take us into the running herds of buffalo. They can pull an entire lodge rolled up on drag poles. But horses can only help hunters and warriors. Remember that a man without a horse is not less than someone who has one. A warrior without weapons is still a warrior, if he understands what it truly means to be a warrior. Grandfather Spotted Calf is the best shot with the bow. He does not need a horse for that. As a young man he was one of the first among us to ride his horse into a herd of buffalo and one of the first to train a horse to chase the buffalo. His horse helped him to hunt the buffalo in a different and better way. But his horse did not give him his skill with the bow. His horse did not give him the heart to be a hunter or a warrior. A horse can never do that."

"I heard Bear Heart say that the holy iron is much more powerful than the horse," the boy said, after a moment.

"True," replied Stone. "The holy iron has its own kind of power, like the horse. We must be careful of it. The holy iron cannot replace the heart of a warrior. Those who think that it can are wrong."

"Is Bear Heart wrong?"

"Bear Heart can think how he chooses. We all can." Stone glanced knowingly at Spotted Calf as he spoke. "We can think what we choose. We can do what we choose. But we must be ready for what happens to us because of what we think and do. That is the price. Wise thinking will help to bring good things our way. Foolish thinking will bring more bad things than good things. That is how life is."

"Bear Heart does not like my uncle, Whirlwind."

Stone nodded. "That is true also. Since they were boys Bear Heart has carried those feelings. And when High Hawk passed the eagle feather lance of the war leader on to Whirlwind, Bear Heart was angry. High Hawk made his choice because of what he saw in each of them. He saw that Whirlwind did not need anything but what was in his heart to make him a warrior. He saw that Bear Heart needed other things to make him a warrior. Other things that gave him a power he could not find within himself."

"I want to be like Whirlwind."

"You will," assured Spotted Calf. "Your grandfather and I will make certain of that. So will Walks High and others. But you already have some of what a true warrior needs."

"What is that?"

"A good heart," replied Spotted Calf.

"Was my father a good warrior?" the boy wanted to know.

Stone stared off into the falling snow. His grandson's question brought the image of a face to him suddenly, like the sun sliding out from behind a dark cloud. He vividly recalled Otter, a warrior who did not return from a raid into the south country, at a time when he was already dying of a broken heart. The loss of his wife and new daughter during childbirth was a wound for which Otter could find no medicine. Even the strength and understanding of his best friend and teacher Whirlwind could not pull the son of Stone from the black depths of grief. He knew well Otter's reason for joining the war party into the south country, against the Pawnee. And when Whirlwind returned alone from his long search, Stone could do nothing but remind himself of the words he often spoke to others: "We cannot fight against death, we can only fight for life."

Stone reached out and squeezed his grandson's shoulder, touching part of a beloved son that was still left in this world. "Yes," the old man replied, softly. "Your father was a good warrior."

"My son and your father were good friends, like you and Windy Boy," Spotted Calf said. "Whirlwind rode into the south country after your father was gone for two moons. He could not find him. That is why, after he returned, he gave you an eagle feather—though you were only three winters old."

Red Legs returned his gaze to the fire, letting the dancing flames kick up many thoughts and images in his mind. After a long while, he heard Grandfather Spotted Calf say that the meat was done and they could eat.

The three figures under the makeshift shelter ate rabbit meat and looked out at the snow. Spring Creek Valley lay hushed beneath a thickening robe of white. Somewhere off to the north, the great cat screamed again.

In a while they finished their meal and felt rested. They put out the fire and buried it. Gathering up their bundles and weapons, they set out for home amidst the falling snow. The boy walked between his grandfathers, remembering their words as images of horses, hissing arrows, and powerful warriors danced in his mind.

Twenty

There was grass beneath the snow in the hollow. Sounds of the paint pawing away the snow to find the grass woke the warrior. The fire was low, and the sun was still in the morning half of the sky. After two days the snow had finally stopped.

Mindful of his wound, Whirlwind ducked out of the low brush shelter and wrapped the deer-hide robe around his shoulders. The paint greeted him with a low, throaty nicker and returned to the task of finding food under the snow. Whirlwind smiled, and looked for a path through the trees and up to the rim.

A shimmering white robe covered the land under a bright blue sky. Beneath the endless bowl of blue, hawks and eagles rode the high breezes as they hunted in slow-moving circles. To the north, a gray form suddenly appeared on the crest of the butte and stood motionless in the deep snow—a coyote intently and curiously watching the two-legged.

In every direction, the land was glistening, an image that immediately burned itself into Whirlwind's memory. He returned to his camp and added wood to the fire.

Two days ago he had improved the heat reflector. Yesterday he had worked a little on his shelter. So, though the air was cold, he had been comfortable beside the fire and under his deer-hide robe. He had enough food for several more days, then he would have to find more.

Whirlwind sensed that the killer white man was close, perhaps less than a day's ride to the west. He smiled at the irony of sharing meat with the killer, as he was certain that the deer kill had been made by the man.

Whirlwind guessed that the white man probably had not traveled during the storm. But if he had, he could be anywhere, or dead. Suddenly, a feeling of uncertainty touched him like a cold hand, and he softly voiced a question to the wind.

"Why have I come to this place?"

Then again he remembered the dream of the wolf fighting the gray dogs. It was that dream which gave him courage and determination, and kept him in pursuit of the white man. Still, was trailing the white man the same as fighting the gray dogs?

"Why have I come to this place?" he asked again.

Finally, he realized that only he could give an answer. Only he could give purpose to the task he had chosen for himself.

He would face the killer of High Hawk's mother when he found him. Deep snow could have covered the killer's tracks. But if he were nearby, then the snow would make tracking easier. His intention was to capture him and take him back to the Wolf Tail village to face the judgment of the old men. But the man would most certainly not allow himself to be captured. There were ways to deal with that, however. Whirlwind knew how to make many different traps. Still, there was the holy iron.

Yes. The holy iron. It was all about the holy iron, beginning with the one in his lodge—the one which had nearly killed him four winters ago.

The white man he had rescued had told how the holy iron worked. There was no mystery about it. It was a man-made thing and had no power that a man did not provide in some way. Iron had been heated and shaped to build some of its parts. A large part of it was wood. The round balls were sent by the black powder which caught fire easily.

If the mind of a man could conceive the holy iron and the hands of man could build it, there was no mystery. Sooner or later, even without help, the mind of another man would learn how it was built and how it worked.

There was also no mystery about how the weapon seemed to change people. Many warriors had offered numerous possessions for the one he had captured. Many warriors wanted to possess it and to possess its powers. Perhaps their desire was more to possess the power of mystery.

Yes. This was all about the holy iron. Not so much about its power to kill but about its power to change. Because they had many holy irons the Ojibway had changed the lives of the Nakota and Dakota by driving them from the lake country to the northeast. That was one kind of change. But what had happened, Whirlwind wondered, to the Ojibway warriors on the inside? Did they lose their respect for life, because it became so easy to kill with the holy iron? If so, then perhaps what a man believed was not as strong as the unseen power of the holy iron.

Whirlwind had only seen one holy iron. He knew of only two to ever come into the territory of the Sicangu Lakota, including the one which had been used to kill the mother of High Hawk. But he had also watched the first small waves of a spring flood lead the way over the dike of a beaver's pond. He had watched the beaver work hard to turn back the flood, only to be swept away in it.

Perhaps if the beaver had built a stronger dike it would have held back the flood. But then, who knew how powerful a flood would be? Whirlwind knew that the same beaver would work just as hard the next time a flood threatened his home and his pond. And if a flood swept him away again, he would once more fight to stay afloat.

Part of the answer, then, was not to fight the flood. And to learn to swim in rough water.

If I am here to stem the flood, Whirlwind told himself, then I am wrong. If I am here because someone must answer for killing an old woman, then I am right.

Whirlwind climbed to the rim again. There were no clouds in the sky, although that could change quickly. But more snow was not the danger. It was the wind. The wind could create a world of no directions, just by blowing the snow already on the ground. A world of moving whiteness just above the ground and just below the sky. A world where even the great buffalo sometimes lost his way.

Whirlwind returned to the camp to make preparations. First, he sliced up the remaining meat and began cooking it. While he waited, he gathered and tied several bundles of kindling and firewood. Out of a stout piece of dry wood, he carved a hoof scraper, to scrape off the snow and ice that would build up on the bottoms of the horse's hooves. He carved a covering for his eyes from pine bark, to prevent snow blindness. As he worked, he also fashioned a plan.

He would ride straight west only as fast as the horse could travel easily since it was not wise to tire a horse in the cold when there was little forage for him. He guessed that the white man was heading for the mountains, the Black Hills. It was to his advantage that Whirlwind knew where the mountains were, and the white man did not. It was at least a two-day ride before the mountains would appear on the western horizon. In that time, the white man would be searching, casting about—giving Whirlwind time to gain even more ground.

Just past midday Whirlwind led the paint down the gentler western slope of the butte. He had not been able to entirely avoid using his right arm while making his preparations. The wounded shoulder throbbed heavily, even bleeding a little, but, once mounted, he would not have to use it.

The snow was deep, nearly knee high to the horse, but it was powdery. Although movement was slow, it was not difficult. Whirlwind had to rely on his knowledge of the area, mainly to avoid places where the snow had filled in a deep gully or dry creek bed. Even so, now and then the horse went belly deep into a low spot.

Walks High rejoined the white man and Red Lance where they waited in the cedar grove. "I think he went south," he said, referring to Bear Heart. "I think he will go back to the winter encampment." He took the jaw rope of his war horse from Red Lance, and the three rode out of the grove.

Red Lance and Walks High took turns breaking trail in the deep snow. By midday they had left a long, meandering trail along the crests of low hills and through old flood plains and creek bottoms. All three wore coverings for their eyes, made by the white man—a skill he had learned from the Dakota.

At the base of a hill, Walks High signaled for a stop. "Deer," he whispered. "We need fresh meat." He pointed to the encased weapon tied to de la Verendrye's dun mare. "I know it makes noise, but we do not have time for a long stalk."

The white man nodded. "Show me where they are."

They found a spot downwind from the six deer. Walks High estimated the distance at eighty paces. The cracking boom of the weapon sent the group of deer in several directions, except for one large doe. By midafternoon the gutted out doe had been loaded and tied onto de la Verendrye's bay gelding. Walks High imitated the flash of the powder with his hands, and how the deer twisted in the air before she fell. "Fast," he said. "In the corner of my eye I saw the white smoke at the same time I saw the deer fall. Very fast."

Red Lance smiled at the white man. "You made a long shot."

"Not so long, for this," he said, patting the flintlock. "For a bow, it would have been a long shot."

"I would like to shoot it sometime," Red Lance admitted.

De la Verendrye nodded. "We will trade. You teach me how to shoot a bow, and I will teach you how to shoot this."

Red Lance nodded. "Yes. We will trade."

Whirlwind had found tracks just before sundown and pushed the paint hard until the light began to fade. There were no footprints. Only hoofprints. But he knew the horse was being ridden by the white man, or at least some man, because the hoofprints where in places a horse would not go on his own. Also the hoofprints went on endlessly, for as long as he followed them. Whirlwind knew that no Lakota, or anyone who understood the worth of a horse, would ride one endlessly in deep snow without walking himself now and then to lighten the horse's load. He was certain he had found the killer's trail.

He made camp in a valley sliced by a wide, meandering creek. A thick grove of young cottonwoods offered a good windbreak and cover. Whirlwind dug a deep hole for the fire and kept the flames low. Hastily built heat reflectors on either side of the fire would keep him from getting too cold. They would also cut down on the glow from the fire.

Coyotes were all around, barking and howling. A nearly full moon meant a very bright night. The paint interrupted his browsing now and then to listen to the thin, strident cries of the coyotes. Whirlwind had tied him to a long lead so he could paw at snow to get at the grass beneath it.

It would be a cold night. Whirlwind took advantage of the remaining daylight to set a few snares nearby. He returned to the camp with another load of firewood. There was nothing to do now but eat, stay warm, stay alert, and make snowshoes. He would pick up the killer's trail again at dawn.

"I hope your father is warm," Red Lance said, as he held out a chunk of roasted rib meat to Walks High. "I hope he is not hungry."

"I have never known my father to do anything foolish," observed Walks High. "At least not since I was old enough to think for myself. He will find a way to survive . . . to be warm and to have food."

Red Lance handed deer ribs to de la Verendrye. "Were the winters in your homeland like this?"

The white man took the meat and shook his head. "I do not think so. They were hard, yes. But the hardest winter I have ever known was along the Grandfather River."

"Lots of snow and very cold?"

De la Verendrye glanced at Red Lance and then stared into the fire as he gathered the memories of that time. "Yes," he said, "deep snow. And the coldest I have ever been."

"Were you alone?" Walks High wanted to know.

"No. I was with four others. It was after the time I worked on a flatboat on the Grandfather River. Five of us were in one small place." He paused. "We ran out of food, and the snow was so deep we could not hunt."

"What did you do?" asked Red Lance.

After a long moment, de la Verendrye replied. "We ate a horse. It was fortunate that it was a big horse. It was skinny, and the meat was stringy. We were down to the ribs and fighting one another for every bite it seemed. One of the other men wanted to trade the iron balls for his holy iron for my share of food. When I refused, he said he would kill me. After that, I was afraid to sleep, and for several days I did not. Then the weather broke. I went out hunting, alone, and I did not go back to them."

The two warriors glanced at one another, seeing that the telling of the story was difficult for the white man. "My grandfather says that anything which does not kill you makes you stronger," said Walks High.

The white man smiled. "Yes. Then I can understand why your father is so strong. He has seen much, lived through many difficult times. But then, facing Bear Heart the way you did was no small thing."

Walks High nodded. "I see now that his only reason for riding with us was to take the holy iron."

"I thought he would fight you for it."

"I thought so, too, but he is a shrewd man. He only fights when he can win, and he was not sure he could win."

"But he said it was not over."

"True. But I think he meant everything that has happened because of the holy iron. I am afraid he is right. It is not a simple thing. We do not all think alike when it comes to the holy iron." The warrior paused to listen to the night and then returned his gaze to the white man. "For Bear Heart, there is more to this whole thing. His thinking is shaped by the fact that he does not like my father."

De la Verendrye looked away to hide a twinge of sadness mingled with envy that came upon him like a sudden, cold wind, prompted by the sound of Walks High saying "my father." He looked down at the fire, watching the flames dancing together, before he spoke again. "Your father . . . he . . . if it were not for him, I would not be here."

Walks High glanced at the white man as he held his palms out to catch some warmth from the fire. He smiled. "Then there is something we share, you and me. I can say the same thing, in a way. He gave you back your life, and he gave me mine."

De la Verendrye reached out toward the dancing flames. The warmth of his palms was strangely reassuring, as he quietly contemplated the young warrior's words. Suddenly, he could see his own father and mother standing by their gray stone cottage, shrinking in size as the distance between he and them increased. Although he knew he would never see them again, he no longer had any regret about that separation. Looking at Walks High, he spoke again, trying to keep the hoarseness out of his voice. "Your father gave me more than my father or mother gave me," he said. "Because he had a choice . . . he . . ."

The firelight glowed in the eyes of Walks High. "It seems he made a good choice, Beard."

De la Verendrye kept his eyes down, trying to find words worthy of the feeling inside. He couldn't. The best he could do was nod.

Red Lance added wood to the fire and looked off into the bright, moonlit night. "Winter is my favorite season," he said, "even on a cold night like this." He tipped back his head and blew, turning his breath into a stream of mist. "These are the times when I give thanks for being Lakota! And I feel so good I will take the first watch!"

Whirlwind moved behind a leafless cottonwood and put a hand lightly over the horse's nose. He looked through thick branches at the man he had been watching since the middle of the morning.

The bearded man on the bay horse was big. Whirlwind had seen him from about sixty paces, on the ridge near the valley of the two rivers. He was at about that distance now, and he could hear the man as the bay horse floundered in belly-deep snow. The words were strange, but the rage was plain enough. Loud, angry words came from the man in dark buckskins as he pounded his horse's rump with a stick. The horse was out of the deep snow in three jarring jumps, nearly throwing his rider on the second jump.

It had been three days since Whirlwind had picked up the killer's trail in the deep snow, a day's ride into the Black Hills. He had spent two days closing the distance between them. This morning, he had found him.

So, thought Whirlwind, this is the man who killed the mother of High Hawk, and stole the girl who will be my daughter-in-law. How, he wondered, has he lived this long in this country?

The white man continued through a narrow valley between two mountain ridges. Tall, thick pines darkened the slopes of the ridges. Long afternoon shadows brought an early darkness to the mountain valleys. Only occasionally did the man on the struggling bay look to the right or left.

Whirlwind kept his hand over the paint's nose as he looked back carefully over each shoulder. The entire landscape was black and white—shadow and snow. Even an eagle hovering above a ridge appeared as a black crescent against a fading blue sky. Whirlwind watched the bird give up its hold on the sky, gliding down until it blended with the blackness of the ridge. Perhaps your hunt is over, Whirlwind thought. "Mine is not," he whispered.

The warrior shifted his gaze back to the white man, just as horse and rider went into a deep shadow. Unless he backtracked, the man could only follow the narrow valley. Sooner or later he would have to stop to find shelter and make camp—unless he was stupid. For the time being it was only necessary to keep him in sight. After the man made camp would be a good time to move in.

Whirlwind took another long, careful look around, searching the shadowy slopes for other interlopers. Satisfied that his only enemy was the loud white man on the bay, he turned to the paint and rubbed its neck. "Come," the warrior said, "we must find a place where there is grass for you."

Twenty-One

Far into the night, dogs began to bark among the lodges. The cold, crisp air carried the sharp sounds quickly throughout the encampment. Here and there, a picketed war horse snorted. Warriors inside the lodges awoke and glanced toward their weapons hanging next to the door. They waited for a cry or alarm as they silently slid from their warm sleeping robes, trying not to wake their sleeping families. Then a firm but muffled voice silenced the dogs. Quiet returned, and the warriors went back to their sleeping robes.

Light Haired Woman heard the slow, creaking footfalls on the cold snow move toward her lodge. A low, sharp word and the dogs stopped their barking. She heard a horse's halter rope being wrapped and tied around the picket pin just outside the door. He was home.

She untied the inner door covering and moved it aside as her husband opened the outer one. Before he entered, he pushed off his deer-hide robe and shook off the snow. Inside, he put down his weapons, folded his hide loosely, and laid it to one side, along with his coyote-hide gloves.

"Husband," she whispered. "It is good to see you."

Bear Heart nodded. The hardships of his journey were drawn on his face, though his features softened at the sound of his young wife's voice. "It is good to be home."

He removed his winter moccasins and watched her build up the fire. His anger over his failure to take the holy iron from the white man still simmered, but the warmth of the lodge and his wife's warmer welcome diminished it for the moment.

"I will cook . . ."

Bear Heart shook his head and held up a hand. "No. No need," he said. "I am not hungry. And it would be good to share the warmth of the robe with you. It has been a hard trail."

Sleep came quickly for the tired, angry warrior. Inside its shadowy valleys he dreamed of the long, dark weapon with the thunderous voice. It was in the hands of the white man, Beard. Bear Heart tried to take the weapon, but he could not, no matter how hard he tried. He awoke with a jerk and then remembered he was home. The faint light through the lodge covering above the dew liner told him it was past dawn.

Morning's gray light was still new when Stone heard the scratch on his door. "Come in," he said. Red Legs looked up from his morning meal as Bear Heart entered. The medicine man nodded a greeting and motioned toward the willow backrest at the rear of the lodge.

Bear Heart's face was a polite mask, but there was a turmoil behind the blackness of his eyes. He arranged the robe over his left shoulder and cleared his throat. "Grandfather," he said, "I have done some thinking."

Stone nodded as he slowly poured newly steeped tea from a large bowl into a smaller one. He set the small bowl with its hot, steaming liquid before his guest. "I am anxious to hear your thoughts," he said.

Bear Heart cleared his throat and glanced nervously at Red Legs.

"Grandson. I am worried about our new colt. The one born in early autumn."

Red Legs set down his bowl and reached for his deer-hide robe. "I will go see about him," he said, grabbing his bow and arrows. "And I am hungry for rabbit." He pushed out the door, and soon his crunching footsteps in the snow faded away.

The warrior sipped his tea and gathered his thoughts. "Grandfather. I have decided to leave. Some of my relatives live along the Bad River to the north. I am going there."

The old medicine man's eyes narrowed as he deliberately added wood to the fire. "The older I become, the harder it is to stay warm. This is not a simple thing—leaving."

"It has been much on my mind."

"It will not be easy for us to lose a man like you. You are a Wolf Warrior. The reason for your leaving must be very strong."

The momentary flash in the warrior's eyes could be easily seen. Bear Heart pushed back his anger until his face was a mask without thoughts. "Things have happened. Things have been done. Some of those things I would have done differently. But I cannot change anything of yesterday." His voice was flat. As flat as his face was false.

A moment passed. Stone let the silence settle heavily before he took a deep breath and spoke. "What do you know of Whirlwind and the others? Can you tell me of them?"

The mask did not leave the warrior's face. "I did not see . . . our . . . war leader," he replied. "But his son, Red Lance, and the white man have surely caught up with him by now. The killer of High Hawk's mother is moving fast, toward the Black Hills. Whirlwind was injured and his horse killed. But he still pursues the white man. He will catch him. That is all I know."

Stone stroked his chin, allying himself with the silence once again. There was more significance in Bear Heart's silence than meaning in his words. "That is good to hear, Grandson. It is good that you have returned unharmed. It is good that the others are well. And it is right that he who killed such a fine woman is brought back here to answer for his deed. Do you find wrong in these things?"

"No, Grandfather. I do not see wrong in those things."

Stone nodded. "Some say that we are free to choose the road we must travel. Others say it has already been chosen for us. I think the truth lies somewhere in between. I cannot understand your reason for leaving because you have not spoken of it. You are free to remain silent about your reason or to reveal it. And you have chosen a road you want to travel. Grandson, I will pray that it is the right one for you. One thing I must tell you is this: remember that something which is hidden today always finds a way to reveal itself in some tomorrow."

Annoyance flashed through Bear Heart's black eyes, like distant lightning inside an approaching storm. "Grandfather," he said, "I am not going away like a beaten dog with my tail under my belly. I will come before the old men leaders and tell them, if it is necessary. But, as I said, things were done that I cannot accept. A white man has come among us, and he has brought only difficulty. But that does not bother me. What disturbs me is that which has been done, or not done, about the holy iron. I would have acted differently. But so long as my lodge is here, my voice and my thoughts are ignored by the old men. Perhaps when I am no longer here, the empty space I have left behind will speak louder than my voice. Perhaps then someone will consider that there are other ways to handle this thing with the holy iron. And, Grandfather, you know that some of the people agree with my thinking. There is change in the wind, Grandfather. We cannot turn it away from us."

The fire hissed and popped, throwing a thumb-sized hot ember onto the buffalo hide near the medicine man's foot. He reached down and took the ember in his hand and returned it to the fire. Bear Heart looked at the old man's hand. There were no burn marks.

Stone ignored the younger man's look of surprise. "Grandson, I will pray that the road you have chosen is the right one for you," he repeated. "But before you take one step on that road, be certain that you can tell yourself whether you are traveling to something, or running away from something. No one has that answer but you."

Two days later, Light Haired Woman struck her lodge. The morning was gray with dark clouds hanging low. Eleven other lodges were struck, too—mostly lodges belonging to relatives of Bear Heart but some belonging to those who agreed that the lance of the war leader should have been passed to him instead of Whirlwind.

Although those who prepared to leave smiled and laughed a little as they loaded their lodges and belongings on drag poles, the laughter was thin and the smiles faded quickly.

Red Legs helped his best friend, Windy Boy, cut out his family's horses from the large herd. Since Windy Boy's father, Cuts, was a good friend of Bear Heart, their family would travel with him. Together the two boys drove the horses to the traveling herd of nearly eighty horses being held east of the encampment. The boys sat on their horses silently, not knowing what to say. Red Legs finally spoke.

"Do you know where you are going?"

Windy Boy nodded. "North of the Bad River, I think. I know it is a long way—four or five days of traveling, I think."

"Did your father say why your family and the others are leaving?"

Windy Boy shrugged. "He did not tell me. My mother told me we were moving, but she did not tell me why either. I wish I could stay."

"You could stay with me and my grandfather," Red Legs said hopefully. "I know he would let you."

"My father would say no. I know he would."

Red Legs looked away, but a shout made him look back at the small column ready to travel. It was Bear Heart. He and several other warriors were giving instructions and motioning to the women and children. From the edge of the crowd, the warrior Cuts called to his son.

"I am going now," Windy Boy said. "Someday . . ." Although he had many more words to speak, he could not say them as he looked at his best friend.

"Someday I will come to visit you," replied Red Legs. "I have been to the Bad River country before and know the way."

They both brought smiles to their faces, smiles which covered the heaviness in their hearts. Windy Boy nodded and rode away.

Many of the people stood outside their lodges and watched the small column depart. Too soon it became a smaller and smaller line of darkness against the snow until it slid around a far hill to the north. Only the tracks in the snow could be seen, and the vacant spaces where twelve lodges once stood matched the emptiness in many hearts. A quietness descended on the village. Even the dogs were silent.

Half a day's travel from the winter camp Bear Heart and his people stopped to rest and eat in a meadow near the Smoking Earth River. Half of the sixteen warriors in the column took up positions surrounding the group. Four of the warriors immediately climbed to the top of the two highest hills nearby, while many of the older boys sat on their horses in a loose circle around the herd.

Bear Heart and Caught the Eagle walked among the people as the cooking fires were being lit. Satisfied that all was well, they returned to the fire at which Light Haired Woman was boiling tea and roasting meat. She had swept snow away from around the fire and rolled out three back-rests. The warriors sat down. "I hope you have a good journey back . . ." said Bear Heart, after a quiet moment.

Caught the Eagle nodded. "I will be home by sundown,"

he replied. "I hope you reach Badger Hill by then. It is a good safe place to camp for the night."

Bear Heart stared into the fire for a long moment. "We will be safe," he said. "No enemy comes this far into our country during the winter."

Bear Heart's words had an edge, and Caught the Eagle knew it was the front of the warrior's anger—anger over Caught the Eagle's decision to stay with the Wolf Tail village. Bear Heart had counted on Caught the Eagle's alliance.

"My friend," Caught the Eagle said. "I know you will protect the people. But protecting the people is more than knowing where the enemy is, or taking up the lance and the war club and the bow when he attacks. Protecting the people also means thinking wisely. A warrior takes up the lance when there is nothing else left to do. But if a man thinks clearly and makes wise choices, then it is sometimes not necessary to take up the lance."

Bear Heart pulled his robe up around his neck and stared harder into the flames. "Look around," he said, "we are not many. Only twelve lodges, eighty horses, sixteen warriors. You speak of choices. We few have made a choice. We do not agree with the thinking of the old men leaders and Whirlwind when it comes to the white man. The things that have happened because of the white man are not simple things. He should not have been brought into our encampment. Because of that a good woman was killed by another white man. I would not have brought the white man among us in the first place."

Caught the Eagle nodded his thanks for the bowl of tea and roasted meat on a stick which Light Haired Woman placed before him. He took a bite before he replied. "My friend, it is easy enough to say 'I would have done this' when something has already come to pass. I know you would have left the white man with an arrow in his heart. But that is only dealing with one white man. What about the others we know will come? Can we fight them all? Can we kill them all? Do you not see any wisdom in learning something about all white men from one white man?"

Bear Heart shrugged off his robe and reached for the bowl of tea. "The mother of High Hawk is still dead."

"Yes. But High Hawk agrees with the thinking of the old men leaders."

"He is getting old!" snapped Bear Heart. "His warrior heart cools with age!"

"Yes! And we will all reach that place in our lives. That is when wisdom must guide the mind and the heart." Caught the Eagle finished his meat and looked around. "These people are guided by you. But what is guiding you? Anger or wisdom? Be careful, my friend. The answer to that question could turn out to be their bones scattered on the prairie."

He turned to the young woman and spoke his thanks for the meal. A quick sideways glance revealed that Bear Heart was clinging to his anger, his mouth set in a thin, hard line. Caught the Eagle rose to his feet and spoke again, "You will always be my friend," he said. "I will see you again, sometime."

"And when I see you again," Bear Heart replied, "I will be carrying a holy iron. Maybe you will feast on the buffalo meat I will kill with it. And maybe you will dance to celebrate a great victory I will win with it."

Caught the Eagle pulled his robe tighter and looked around at the small group of people who were no longer part of the Wolf Tail band. "I would feast and dance with you," he told his friend, "for any good reason. But I do not want to carry you to your burial scaffold, after someone has killed you with a holy iron."

Bear Heart ignored Caught the Eagle's departure until he heard him untie his picketed horse. Only then did he stand

and watch Caught the Eagle mount and ride away up and over a distant hill. It was only when Bear Heart returned to his seat by the fire that he noticed the bowl next to the empty backrest. Caught the Eagle had not finished his tea.

Red Legs entered the lodge with a bundle of wood under one arm and his sleeping robes under the other. Her Good Trail smiled. The old men leaders were meeting in the council lodge tonight, and she had expected that Stone would send the boy over to her. "Thank you for bringing in the wood," she said. "Are you hungry?"

The boy nodded, put down his bundles, and darted back out the door, returning with his bow and arrows. He took a seat by the fire and sat quietly with arms folded around his knees as Her Good Trail arranged his sleeping robes and checked the meat roasting over the coals. "I saw Caught the Eagle when he rode in," he said suddenly. "He rode out a ways with . . . the others."

Her Good Trail studied the boy's face for a time. He seemed to be carrying everyone's confusion in his eyes. She remembered that in a few years he had parted with much that was important to him. His mother had died giving birth to a stillborn sister some six winters ago. And his father, the son of Stone, had never returned from a raid into the south country some time after that.

Red Legs blinked back the tears in his eyes. "Four or five days of travel is not long. I can do it," he said. "I am strong. I am ready to be a warrior. I can find my way to the Bad River country."

Her Good Trail could hear the sadness in his voice. "Yes, I know you can," she said, "but traveling to the Bad River means more than starting out and getting there."

The boy looked up. "What do you mean?"

"There is the journey in between." She looked around at the several bows in their cases and the quivers of arrows hanging from lodgepoles. "It takes more than bows and arrows, lances, and war clubs to be a warrior," she went on. "You are strong, but there is a kind of strength that has nothing to do with how far you can shoot an arrow, or how well you can fight with a lance or a war club."

Red Legs glanced up at the bows and arrows. Some belonged to Walks High, some to Whirlwind. "You mean courage?"

"Yes."

"I could fight an enemy!"

The sudden flash in the boy's eyes reminded her of her own son, now no longer a boy. "What about being lonely? Or being away from your family for many, many days? A warrior has to fight those things, too. If you go to see Windy Boy in the Bad River country, by yourself, being alone will be part of the journey."

Red Legs rubbed his eyes and looked at the empty backrests in the lodge.

"Sometimes, being alone can be harder than facing a Pawnee or Arikara warrior. That is the journey in between." She smiled gently and turned the meat. "I have lived with a warrior for twenty-one winters," she said. "I have seen my son turn from a boy like you into a warrior. My father and grandfathers were warriors. The way of the warrior has always been. It is a path that was already marked out for you before you were born. You are on that path, even now. And when I am an old woman and you are a mighty warrior, I will tell my grandchildren that you ate at my fire and slept in my lodge." She looked at the boy tenderly. "We will eat soon," she said.

The night was cold for early winter. Light from the half-moon glistened on the snow. Sentinels on the ridges around the village of the Wolf Tail Lakota built up their fires and kept their dogs close. Coyotes sang all around them. Here and there a sentinel pulled his buffalo-hide robe tighter and glanced to the north. Somewhere in that direction were the people who had left to follow Bear Heart.

Inside the council lodge the old men talked as the cold, bright moon moved across the star-filled sky. They talked of all that had come to pass since the white man had been brought to them.

Twenty-Two

"**C**ome in." Her Good Trail answered the scratching on the door of her lodge.

Leading with a smile, Stone entered. "I am up and about early," he said, by way of greeting. "I think it is a condition of old age."

"Sit down, Grandfather," she said, pointing to a backrest at the rear of the lodge.

The old medicine man went to the backrest, smiling down at the boy still asleep beneath the robes. "I hope my grandson has been a help to you," he said.

"Yes," she replied. "He has. And he keeps me from talking to myself."

"Granddaughter," the old man said, "I have come to make sure that the word I sent two days ago, about your son and husband, reached you."

Her Good Trail nodded as she prepared to heat a bowl of tea for her visitor. "Yes. It did. Thank you."

"Your husband is a strong warrior. His power comes from what he knows and how he uses that knowledge. Your son is much the same. Bear Heart said that, by now, your husband and your son are traveling together."

In spite of his words concerning Whirlwind and Walks High, Her Good Trail sensed that there was something else he wanted to say.

"Why did Bear Heart return alone, I wonder?"

"That, Granddaughter, troubles me," the old man said, glancing sideways at his grandson. "He came to my lodge to tell me that he was leaving, but he said nothing about his reason for leaving your son and the others behind."

Her Good Trail glanced at the spot where the holy iron had been hanging, before she let Beard use it. "Could it have something to do with the holy iron?"

"Yes, but that is only part of it. He was angry when High Hawk passed the lance of the war leader on to your husband. Bear Heart and your husband were never friends. What High Hawk did took them to the edge of being enemies . . . in Bear Heart's thinking. Then your husband captured the holy iron from the white man who nearly killed him, and when he chose to keep that weapon away from others, it only made Bear Heart angrier. To him, it was a sign of weakness, a sign that High Hawk made the wrong choice."

Her Good Trail handed a bowl of hot peppermint tea to her guest. "I was worried when he rode out after my son and the others. I knew he had a reason for doing that."

The old man savored the aroma of the tea for a moment before taking a sip. "Yes," he said, "and I have a feeling it had something to do with your husband's holy iron."

Her Good Trail paused, her eyes looking even more worried. "I hope I did not do the wrong thing when I let the white man use that weapon."

Stone was quick to shake his head. "No. You did not. The wrong is not yours."

In spite of the medicine man's assurance, a slight frown still clouded the woman's face.

"Granddaughter, without that weapon the white man would not be much help to your son, only a burden. You gave him a purpose by letting him use it."

Her Good Trail sighed and sat back. "Still, I wonder if the weapon had something to do with Bear Heart leaving."

"I am certain of that," the old man said. "But it does not matter how. Sooner or later, Bear Heart's injured pride and his jealousy would have caused discord. The holy iron and the white man were only small things. That which is in the mind and heart of Bear Heart drove him to leave."

Her Good Trail sat quietly for several moments. There was still worry on her face, but she saw the wisdom in the medicine man's words. "What will happen to us?" she wondered out loud. "Twelve lodges are gone. Forty-two remain." She glanced at the sleeping boy. "It was hardest on the children. Your grandson is making plans to travel north someday, to visit his friend Windy Boy."

A knowing smile came to the old man's face. "Yes," he said, "some things are hard to do, or live with. But we must not turn the young ones from the difficult things. Your father-in-law will tell you that the more he heats the limbs of a bow and the harder he rubs it with a deer tine, the farther and faster it will cast its arrow. It is the difficult things from which our strength comes. If my grandson does take the trail north, I will not stop him. There is much strength he can gain from that, to add to that which he already has . . . from his mother. And when all is said and done, can we ask any less of ourselves than of our children? We will adapt to this sudden change in our lives. We will go on."

At midafternoon the crier called for the people to gather in the center of the encampment. Under a warm sun and a cloudless sky, the people came together.

The crier, an old man named Red Hill, rode through the camp leading a prancing blue roan. Then he joined the High Hawk family in the center while the people stood in a large circle. He handed the lead rope of the blue roan to High Hawk and held high an eagle-wing fan as a sign he was about to speak.

"My relatives," Red Hill called in a loud voice, as he remained mounted on his own horse, "my cousin High Hawk has asked me to speak these words:

"Our family is grateful for all the help you have given us since we lost our grandmother. We thank you for sharing our grief. But today, for a short while, we will put aside our grief to honor one who stands among us. A young warrior.

"It is the way of the warrior to put himself first and last—first to defend his people and last to seek reward for his deeds.

"We would like to reward a warrior today, not to pay him for his deeds but, with the Wolf Tail people as witnesses, to let him know that we thank him for being a warrior. We thank him for helping to bring our daughter back to us. And we want him to know that the memory of his courage will always live in our family.

"This horse is a poor gift. It does not measure up to the greatness of a courageous deed. But this horse will be a symbol of our gratefulness. We hope that the warrior Lone Elk will come forward and accept it."

From somewhere within the circle of people, a drum pounded twice in acknowledgment of the crier's words, and the women trilled.

Before he could resist, two old women gently took the young warrior by each arm and led him toward the center of the circle.

High Hawk handed the lead rope of the prancing blue roan to Lone Elk.

"Thank you, Uncle. He is the best I have ever seen."

High Hawk, his hair cut short in mourning, smiled. Unspoken words danced in his eyes, but only for a moment. "I am glad to see that your wound is healing. I do not want it to hinder your dancing at the wedding of my daughter and your friend."

Lone Elk glanced briefly toward Sun Rise Woman, who shyly returned his smile. "Yes, Uncle," he said. "But I would dance at that wedding even if I had no legs."

The fire burned high inside the council lodge. White Crane, Stone, and Spotted Calf looked up and nodded their greetings as Not Afraid, Keeper of the Winter Count, entered with his helper, Makes the Fire. After he took a seat, Not Afraid spoke.

"I had thought to name this winter after one of two things—the death of the mother of High Hawk or the coming of the white man among us. Some of the people are in favor of one, some are in favor of the other. However, since some of our people have left with Bear Heart, I do not know."

Low sounds of affirmation rose in response to Not Afraid's words. Stone nodded in the direction of White Crane. "My cousin did dream about this," he said. "About our people coming to a fork in a road—some going one way, some going the other."

"Yes," agreed Spotted Calf. "But when the Mniconju messengers came with news of the trade gathering in the spring, up along the Great Muddy River, I thought then that his dream had come to pass. We were concerned that some of the people would travel to that gathering. But this thing with Bear Heart, it is a split. A fork in the road."

White Crane looked in the direction of Not Afraid. "Perhaps, my friend, we do have something to name this winter by. It is a thing I do not like, but it is something not likely to be forgotten. Perhaps we should call this winter the Winter of Two Roads."

Stone held his hands to the fire and shook his head. "Our people have taken two roads, that is true," he said. "Sometimes people take two different roads to get to the same place. Sometimes people take different roads and end up in different places. But there is a reason for taking those roads, for making those journeys." The medicine man paused, slowly rubbing his hands together as he carefully searched for the right words. "I know that the reason our people have taken two different roads is the same—the holy iron." He looked up and made a large circle in the air with his hand. "We are still here," he went on, "because our thinking is one way about the holy iron. Our thinking is that we must be careful about letting it into our lives. To us it is not a simple matter of trade. I think we want to be certain about what it will do to our minds and our hearts.

"Those who follow Bear Heart, I think, want to find the nearest white man trader and trade for holy irons. But as you can see, it is the holy iron which has divided our path, our thinking. As I see it, that shows that it has a power far beyond the noise it makes, and far beyond the way it can kill at great distances.

"Yes, my relatives, this is truly the winter of two roads. But the cause of that is the holy iron. I think when my cousin, Not Afraid, sits down to paint that which will describe this time the best, he should paint the holy iron. We should call these past thirteen moons the Winter of the Holy Iron."

"Yes!" said White Crane. "I agree. Look around us, my relatives. There are some who are missing. He who carries the wisdom of many, many winters, Circling Bear, is not here with us in this lodge. He is with Bear Heart. The holy iron has done that. But there is something else. To me, it is not only a question of two roads. We are coming to a turn in the road that rises up before us. We will travel in a certain direction, guided by our ways, but we will make a turn. The reason for that turn is the holy iron. I see a time when it will come into our lives—perhaps next spring, after the trade gathering up near the Great Muddy. So I agree with our medicine man. We should call these past thirteen moons the Winter of the Holy Iron."

Sounds of affirmation rose again in the council lodge. Not Afraid, Keeper of the Winter Count, cleared his throat. "I have a thought," he said. "I agree with the words I have just heard. I, too, think this time should be called the Winter of the Holy Iron. This thing, the holy iron, and this time should never be forgotten. Yes, I know that we are fearful of things we do not understand. For that reason, perhaps some of the people will not want me to paint the holy iron on the elk-hide Winter Count. Still, we owe something to those who will follow after us, those who will be the children and grandchildren of our grandchildren. We must let them know of our struggles with this thing. We owe them the truth, so we have to tell them about the bad times as well as the good times. The holy iron must be painted on the Winter Count of the Wolf Tail Lakota. If not, then we are turning our faces from what is happening to us. Even if I do not put the holy iron on the elk hide, this will still be the time of the holy iron. Better that we put it in front of everyone today—for all the tomorrows to come."

Old, gray heads in the council lodge bowed to the wisdom of Not Afraid's words. No one spoke. Some nodded, and some stared into the fire.

Twenty-Three

S ounds traveled easily in the mountains, especially with the deep snow. In the distance, Whirlwind could see an occasional flicker of flame from inside the white man's night shelter—a shelter well hidden in the tangles of an uprooted tree. Although he could not see the man, he could hear him. The man was scraping snow and grunting as he worked.

Whirlwind leaned back into the shadows between two boulders. He had watched the white man picket his horse out of sight behind a rock wall and the end of the uprooted tree. But it was still early. There was plenty of time to check on his own camp and even to rest a little.

He trudged through the snow almost leisurely back to his own secluded shelter. It was halfway up a steep slope, behind an upthrust of rock and several large pine trees. The paint nickered low and inquisitively at his approach. Whirlwind spoke softly. "Don't worry, my friend. I am not a bear."

Removing the snowshoes, Whirlwind eased himself under an overhang of large roots into which he had woven several dead branches. He added kindling to the glowing coals inside a ring of stones and blew gently. The fire came back to life.

His plan to capture the white man was simple enough. Tonight, after the man was asleep, Whirlwind would take his horse. Later, he would return in the dark and lay a false trail leading to a trap. Tomorrow, in the daylight, he would wait for the man to walk into the trap. Since he had much to do tonight, Whirlwind was glad for the moonlight. He noted the position of the moon as he added wood to the fire and laid down to rest.

Later, he awoke to dimly glowing embers. The moon was still high enough to cast good light. With thoughts of Her Good Trail flickering like persistent flames, Whirlwind left his camp. Perhaps she was awake at this moment, too, adding wood to keep the embers of the low night fire going. Or perhaps she was pausing to think about him. That possibility eased the pain in his shoulder for a moment and brought a smile to his face. At the bottom of the slope he stopped to tie on the snowshoes. Tonight he would need to use his injured shoulder as much as he could.

Whirlwind became a shadow in the night, blending with everything around him. Coyotes howled and barked all around. Now and then, the more resonant voice of a wolf joined the night voices. Only the hunters were singing. The hunted were silent.

When he came to a point about an arrow's cast from the white man's shelter, he removed his snowshoes and tied them to his willow pack frame. Also attached to the pack frame were several lengths of cordage and the jaw rope he had taken off the paint. The stone-headed war club was thrust into his belt next to the flint knife, while his bow in its case with a quiver full of arrows hung at his right hip. He felt that he could pull and shoot the bow at least three or four times before causing the shoulder to bleed badly, though at the moment, the pain in his injured shoulder pounded like a drum inside his head.

He moved up the slope, staying low and sometimes crawling in the snow. After a few stops to rest and to listen, he knew he was directly upslope from the white man's shelter and the fallen tree where the bay horse was tied.

Whirlwind chose his downward path carefully. He would follow it back up the slope leading the horse, so he had to choose a way that the horse could go without making noise or suddenly losing his footing.

Soon, the shadowy outline of the horse appeared, and Whirlwind could feel the animal's intent, uncertain gaze. He was about twenty short paces above the horse, and the white man's shelter was about the same distance below the horse. Whirlwind knew that the horse was more familiar with the sight of a man than a bear, a wolf, or a mountain lion and thus not so likely to be frightened of a man. Slowly, the warrior rose to his feet to let the horse see the outline of a man. The bay's ears were still pointed forward, and he had not yet snorted in fear.

Whirlwind stood silently, breathing evenly, allowing the horse to accept the sight of him. After a time, the bay lowered his head and looked away toward a slight rustling sound on the opposite slope. When he turned his gaze back, Whirlwind took a few tentative steps down the slope.

Proceeding a few cautious steps at a time, the warrior was soon close enough to touch the horse's neck. The horse stood fast, now more curious than afraid. With slow, deliberate motions, he untied the lead rope and gently tugged on it. Since Whirlwind was not certain how a different voice would affect the bay, he did not speak yet.

The horse responded, so Whirlwind began to lead him up the slope and then down. As he stopped to tie on snowshoes, he finally spoke to the bay. "I am glad that you were not afraid," he said. "I remember your owner saying once that you are a good horse. I believe him. Now, I will take you to meet a friend of mine."

As the bay and the paint began to get acquainted, the warrior retraced his steps. First, he wiped out his and the horse's tracks on the slope above the white man's camp. Then he circled the camp and approached it from the opposite side, across a narrow valley. He came so close to the white man's shelter that he saw him move a little in his sleep. At that moment, the shadowy warrior touched his bow. It would be an easy shot at ten or so paces. Someone who killed an old woman certainly deserved no better. But instead, Whirlwind turned and began to lay the false trail he hoped the man would follow. If this man were to die at the hands of a Wolf Warrior, Whirlwind wanted him to know the reason.

Dawn was approaching the mountains. In Whirlwind's valley it was cold and foggy as he peered from his shelter. The Earth wore only the colors of black and white on this dawn, and the shadowy places far outnumbered the patches of light.

He had slept fitfully for a short time, as fatigue and pain battled for his awareness and images of charging Arikara warriors pulled him from the edge of deep sleep. Whirlwind moved carefully, yielding to the tenderness and stiffness in his wounded shoulder. From his rawhide case he pulled a strip of cooked deer meat, wishing he had hot tea to go with it. But there would be time later, after the white man was captured, to hunt for fresh meat and enjoy a good meal.

Emerging from his shelter, he prepared himself for the warpath. Facing east, toward where the sun would rise, he lifted his voice into the mist. "Grandfather," he prayed, "among all who move on the Earth, I am not the most powerful or the wisest. Yet, I am thankful for what I am. On this day, I ask for the wisdom and strength to be a true warrior. And if it should be that I do not live to see the sun set this day, thank you for the trail you have given me to walk. Be with my family." After a quiet moment, he wrapped the deer-hide robe around himself, tying it at the waist. Then he thrust the war club and the knife into his belt and draped the carry strap of the bow and arrows over his left shoulder. In his right hand he carried his lance, in his left, his snowshoes.

The fog was perfect cover as Whirlwind walked along a winding trail to a slope across from the white man's camp. There was no smoke or the smell of fire. Either the white man was still asleep or he had frozen to death. Or he had already awakened and perhaps was following the false trail. A short moment of uncertainty ended with the sound of a sharp cough and a string of angry words.

Like a lumbering bear, a dark shape rose from the tangle of roots, then sank down again. For a time Whirlwind thought the man had crawled back into his robes, but after a long wait, a flicker of flame appeared through the fog. The man had been building a fire.

Suddenly, the man rose again and appeared to move away from his shelter.

Bruneaux stared in disbelief and rubbed his eyes. The horse was gone. He turned around. There were tracks, his and the horse's tracks leading to the end of the dead tree— but no further. He touched the thick stump of a dead branch to which he had tied the rope, but there was no horse.

The white man spun in his tracks and looked around. There was nothing but eerie, white fog and distant shadows. He hurried back to his shelter, grabbed the flintlock, and ran back to the spot where he knew the horse had been standing. There were tracks in the snow to show that the horse had been tied to the end of the deadfall, but no tracks to show which way the horse might have gone.

There was anger in the man's cold, gray eyes. But something else, too. Indecision. He went back to the fire and hunched down close to it.

Henri Bruneaux glanced about wildly, clutching the flintlock. The fog was thick all around. He nearly jumped into the fire at a sudden bellowing of a buffalo bull from somewhere in the confusing fog. Bruneaux pointed the weapon, uncertain of the source of the bellow.

As the bellowing faded, he buried his face in his hands and gathered his wits. Grabbing his deer-hide robe and throwing it over his shoulders, he jumped purposefully to his feet. Then he began to cast about for a sign. Almost immediately, he found the tracks of a man leading away from his shelter.

Eyes darting about, Bruneaux stared into the fog. His breath came heavily.

Whirlwind saw the big white man hesitate and then take a few indecisive steps. He stared at the man, knowing that sometimes the eyes had the power to draw the eyes of the enemy. But the man acted as if he were uncertain or afraid. Finally, he began to follow the false trail. The warrior watched for a little while longer, to make sure the man would keep to the trail. Then he faded away into the shadowy, pine-covered slopes.

A fast pace on snowshoes brought him to a snug hiding place he had picked last night, a good place to watch as the white man came to the rope. It was a simple trap, a rope stretched between two young pines and hidden beneath the snow. The footsteps in the snow were further and further apart as they led up to this spot, which would force the white man to lengthen his stride and walk faster. And when the man tripped on the hidden rope, he would fall down an embankment into a narrow creek covered with snow and thin ice—a deep creek. Whirlwind had poked a thin pole through the ice and was satisfied that the creek was at least as deep as a man's chest. And while the white man was floundering in the bitterly cold water, Whirlwind would disable him with his war club.

Bruneaux could not remember the last time he had walked so far. He had followed the footprints in the snow across a narrow valley, part way up a slope, and back across another valley. The flintlock was heavy. He stopped to rest and wondered if the fog would ever lift. Shadows, at the end of his limit of visibility, seemed to move now and then. Maybe it was the horse. Or maybe it was something else.

He caught his breath and moved on. Who took the horse? he wondered. Was it an Indian? But what kind? Or was it a bear or a puma? Either one could kill a horse, but that would have been noisy. And the horse had not been killed, at least not where he had been tied. No, the horse had been taken—stolen. Maybe . . . maybe it was the man on the gray horse! No! He was dead! He had to be!

The tracks were further apart, and Bruneaux was breathing hard. He could feel the sweat running down his back. At the top of a downslope barely visible in the fog, he stopped.

The fog thinned a little, and Whirlwind could see the area where the trap was hidden. He had been waiting for a long while, but the white man had not appeared. Up through the fog he could see the sun glowing brighter. Eventually, its warmth would burn off the fog.

Whirlwind came down from his hiding place. If the white man had turned back or turned aside from the false trail, he did not want to lose him. There was a chance he would return to his camp.

The fog was burning off quickly as the sun cleared the eastern ridges. Whirlwind untied the trip rope and followed his own false trail.

He veered away from the false trail and stayed near trees at the bottom of a steep slope. Suddenly, the dark, hunched form of the white man disappeared behind a rocky outcropping just ahead. Whirlwind ducked behind a tree, pulled his bow, and strung it. And waited.

He risked a look around the tree. The white man was slowly walking across a clearing between two ridges, with his weapon ready. With the fog thinning rapidly, the white man would have a clear view if Whirlwind stepped out of the trees.

Whirlwind wanted to make the man shoot and miss. But he remembered that he had managed to hit Lone Elk at a distance of about sixty paces. He waited until the man was nearly across the clearing.

The white man suddenly turned left and struggled up a steep slope to the base of a giant pine and sat down. Whirlwind could see that the man was panting. A thought flashed through his mind. It was difficult to aim a bow steadily if the shooter was panting. Perhaps it was the same when shooting a holy iron. There was also another way to spoil the man's aim by confusing him.

Whirlwind emerged from the shadow of the tree line, guessing the distance to the white man was about eighty paces. The warrior nocked an arrow and pulled the bow to test his shoulder. Hot, heavy pain coursed from the wound to the side of his head, but he had been able to draw the bow. The pine tree next to the white man was at least two times the width of a man. He had made shots at this distance before, and he needed to do it now. Whirlwind lifted his bow, pulled, and released the arrow.

Bruneaux heard a slight hiss, followed by a sharp thud. A shadow appeared in the corner of his eye. It was an arrow! An unpleasant memory of another arrow protruding from a bank just below his crotch popped into his mind and propelled him to unguided motion. His eyes fixed on the arrow which had hit the tree less than an arm's length from his head. As he struggled to coax unresponsive legs to move for cover, he saw the figure just below the tree line across the clearing.

Suddenly remembering the weapon in his hands, Bruneaux pulled back the striker and brought the stock to his shoulder. Just as his feet slid down the slope the cracking boom of the weapon filled the narrow valley.

Eyes wide and mouth gaping, Bruneaux realized that the figure was running toward him, running through the snow with a weapon in his hands. Managing to regain his feet at the bottom of the slope, he saw a narrow opening through the trees and ran for it. The second arrow went by his left ear with an angry hiss and buried itself in the snow up to the feathers.

The sound of the holy iron stopped them in their tracks. Walks High pointed to the west. They all dropped to the snow and looked around. "That was close by," de la Verendrye said. "West, I think."

Walks High nodded. "Come on! My father may need our help."

They stood and resumed following the tracks in the snow, this time at a trot.

Just after dawn they had ridden into a clearing as they followed Whirlwind's tracks. And it was Red Lance who noticed that the horses were particularly interested in something back in some trees. A cautious investigation revealed Whirlwind's camp and two horses, one of which de la Verendrye immediately recognized as his second bay horse. Leaving their horses in the camp with the other two, they continued to follow the tracks in the deep snow.

The tracks led them to a narrow valley and then up a slope near an uprooted tree. There they found tracks leading back down and onto the trail they had just followed. As they stood, momentarily confused, Walks High pointed to the tangle of roots and other deadfall.

"Smoke," he said.

They found a dying fire and more tracks. This time they led south.

"These are not my father's tracks," he said, pointing to a long, wide footprint.

"Bruneaux," whispered de la Verendrye.

"Are you certain?"

De la Verendrye nodded. "Yes. These are his tracks."

Red Lance had been studying the dark slope above them. "Nothing up there," he told the other two. "Where do we go now?"

"We follow the white man's tracks," Walks High replied. "And we need to hurry."

Twenty-Four

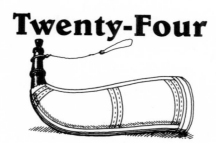

Whirlwind watched the white man climbing up between two rock walls. Once the man reached the ledge, about the size of a lodge floor, he would have time to reload the holy iron. Whirlwind could not allow him to do that.

The warrior peeked under his deer-hide robe. He knew the wound was bleeding, and now the dark red stain in his shirt was about the size of a hand. He knew he could still abandon the chase. But images of High Hawk's mother laying dead in the grass suddenly filled his mind, and he could hear the mournful keening of High Hawk's wife and daughter.

Whirlwind sprinted for the base of the rock walls, which were as high as the top of a lodgepole.

The white man was now very close to the top of the ledge but was having difficulty climbing with the holy iron in one hand. Whirlwind unstrung his bow and slid it into its case. His only chance was to climb fast and gain the ledge before the white man did. With an arrow held in his mouth, Whirlwind knew he could take the bow from its case and string it within a few heartbeats, before the white man could prepare the holy iron to shoot again.

Looking up, he saw the killer's face for the first time. It was a dark, meaty face with a beard and gray eyes. There was a bright scar across his left cheek. The gray eyes went wild with fright as the man lost a handhold and slid down a ways. A big hand flew up and caught an edge no wider than a finger. The man's face turned red with the strain of pulling himself up on top of the ledge by one arm.

Red Lance was the first to spot the two men climbing up the narrow space between two huge rocks. The one in dark buckskins was close to the top. Whirlwind was nearly halfway. De la Verendrye immediately realized the warrior's predicament.

"Listen," he said, pulling on Walks High's arm, "when Bruneaux reaches the top of the rocks, he must not have the time to prepare the weapon to shoot again. If he does . . ."

Walks High's eyes darted around. "How close are we? Close enough for you to have a good shot?"

De la Verendrye looked hard toward the two giant rocks. "Eighty, ninety paces maybe. Yes . . . I think."

"Good. You stay here and watch. When he gets to the top and starts to prepare the holy iron to shoot, then shoot him."

Walks High saw hesitation flicker in the white man's eyes. "You told me you wanted to take revenge," he said. "This is the way to do it. Do not let him kill my father."

"It is only that I have never killed a man," the white man admitted. "What will you do?"

"Climb after him, like my father is doing."

The two young warriors ran for the base of the rocks as fast as the deep snow would permit. The man in dark buckskins was now getting a handhold at the top of the ledge. Red Lance stopped about fifty paces from the rock base and took careful aim with his bow. At that moment, the man pulled himself over the edge and rolled out of sight.

De la Verendrye watched as Bruneaux crawled to the back of the ledge and began to reload the flintlock. He started counting.

Whirlwind caught sight of the movement from the edge of the trees—two figures running through the deep snow toward the base of the rocks. Something in the way one of them moved seemed familiar.

Walks High! It was Walks High and Red Lance.

De la Verendrye reached the count of thirty-five and aimed as steadily as he could at Bruneaux's chest. Bruneaux was finished reloading, and he could see him taking aim at the spot where Whirlwind would come over the top of the ledge.

Something hit the rock face just in front of Bruneaux. Flying rock shards stung his face. Then he heard it. BOOM! As he instinctively ducked for cover, he jerked the trigger of his own weapon. BOOM! The second thunderous voice echoed off the rock walls. Surprise crowded out any awareness, then he saw the warrior pull himself up over the ledge. He watched helplessly as the warrior pulled out a bow, strung it, and took the arrow from between his teeth.

Bruneaux pushed himself against the rock wall, looking for a way to escape. There was none. And the warrior was drawing his bow. Moving to the other edge of the ledge, Bruneaux glanced down. It was a very long drop.

Another warrior climbed up over the ledge. Then another. Now there were three drawn bows aimed straight at the white man's chest.

"Father, it is good to see you. Are you badly hurt?"

Whirlwind lowered his bow. "Keep yours on him and ready. No, it is only a little bleeding."

"What shall we do now with him?"

"There is nothing more to do, except take him back and let the old men decide what to do with him. Who shot the holy iron from the trees?"

Red Lance smiled. "Beard."

"Who?"

"Beard," the young warrior said again. "The white man you found. We have named him Beard."

"There is much for us to talk about, I can see."

Red Lance lowered a rope to de la Verendrye. After some moments of difficulty, the white man reached the top edge and pulled himself over. He looked at Whirlwind. "It is good to see you again."

Whirlwind nodded. "It is good to see you." He pointed to the other white man. "Did you miss because you wanted to?"

De la Verendrye was still down on one knee, still breathing hard from his climb. He shook his head. "No," he replied, "my aim was off." He turned his eyes toward Bruneaux. "Next time, I will not miss."

Bruneaux's eyes widened as he watched de la Verendrye reload his weapon.

De la Verendrye's hands trembled as he poured powder and rammed a ball down the long barrel. The image of his own flintlock being aimed at him exploded from his memory, filling his mind so much that it blocked out the three Lakota warriors standing nearby. He replaced the ramrod and cocked back the hammer. "I trusted you, Bruneaux," he said, as he snugged the stock against his right cheek and took careful aim for the big man's chest. Anger constricted his throat, and his next words came out in a loud, hoarse whisper. "At least I won't shoot you in the back!"

"No!" Whirlwind stepped toward de la Verendrye and grabbed the barrel of the weapon. "No!" The warrior looked down into the angry blue eyes. "I did not save you from death so you could be like him!"

De la Verendrye's lips trembled. He took a deep breath and nodded, but clung to the flintlock a moment longer before he pushed it toward Whirlwind. "This is yours," he said. "I borrowed it from Her Good Trail."

Whirlwind nodded. He pointed to the holy iron Bruneaux had dropped. "And that one is yours, I believe." He studied the white man's face for some moments. "I am glad you have ridden this trail with my son and my nephew. It seems like so long ago that you told me you wanted to help catch this killer and so you have. I thank you. In my heart and in my mind, you are a good man."

De la Verendrye rose stiffly to his feet. "My friend," he said, "I am glad to help. And you are right. In my heart I know I am a good man, and a good man does not kill simply because he can."

Whirlwind glanced toward the two young warriors still warily guarding their captive, and then back to de la Verendrye. "I am told your name is now Beard," he said, with a slight smile. "I can see why, and it is a good name . . . for now. Perhaps, in time, you will come to have another."

De la Verendrye nodded and pointed at the flintlock on the ground next to Bruneaux. "I want to look at it," he said. "To make certain he has not ruined it."

"Back at my camp where the horses are I have some sage," Whirlwind replied. "We will smudge your weapon, to cleanse it. The sage smoke will chase away anything bad he has given it."

Bruneaux sat with his wrists bound behind him, staring into the face of his countryman and former traveling companion.

"You are in more trouble than I can describe," de la Verendrye pointed out, almost gleefully.

"I see you have thrown in with these savages," retorted Bruneaux, having recovered some of his nerve.

"Yes, I have." De la Verendrye pointed at Whirlwind, who was reluctantly having his shoulder examined by Walks High. "He found me after you shot me. Took me back to his village, and they took care of me. And see that young man?" de la Verendrye next pointed at Walks High. "The girl you stole is going to be his wife."

"I did not steal any . . ."

"Oh yes, you did. And you murdered an old woman. That is why Whirlwind, the war leader over there, followed you. He . . . all of us will take you back to their village, and there a council of old men will decide what is to be done with you."

Bruneaux started to rise. Red Lance quickly drew back his bow and motioned for him to sit.

"I would not move, my onetime friend. That young warrior you shot back there when you let the girl go, well, he is this young man's very best friend. I think Red Lance here would love to sink that arrow in your gullet. In fact, I wish you would try something stupid."

Fear suddenly contorted the big man's face, but he fought to control himself. "You can't let them," he said. "Be sensible. We are civilized men. We must help one another. Why are you with these savages?"

De la Verendrye's eyes hardened. "You are the savage, Bruneaux. And I guess I am, too, because I am still sorely tempted to shoot you, right now."

"For God's sake, ask them to give me a fighting chance!"

"The same chance you gave me, Bruneaux? The same chance you gave that old woman?"

Henri Bruneaux turned away from Gaston de la Verendrye's withering stare.

De la Verendrye's voice was low. "I trusted you, Henri. You sat at my fire. You ate my food. We traveled together. Why, Henri? Why did you try to kill me?"

The big white man slowly lifted his eyes, and, for the briefest moment, there was remorse. Then his wild, gray eyes took on a dull flatness. There was no feeling behind them. "Your gold," he said. "Nothing more." His voice was as flat as his eyes. "I watched you for days, back there, near the Running Water River. After some heathen stole my gun. At first, all I wanted from you was your gun and your horses. But one day I saw the gold you dropped on the ground . . ."

De la Verendrye jumped to his feet. Whirlwind waited, ready to pounce like the great cat if the one now called Beard reached for his holy iron. Red Lance lifted his bow, aiming at the captive white man's chest. Walks High swiftly flicked an arrow onto his bowstring.

De la Verendrye felt the silence suddenly grow heavier. "I am only going to show this man something," he said to the warriors. Turning to Bruneaux, he pulled the pouch from his belt. "This gold?"

Bruneaux's mouth tightened.

De la Verendrye opened the pouch and shook six Spanish gold pieces onto his open palm. "This gold wouldn't buy you an old saddle—or a gun. And you tried to kill me for this?"

Bruneaux blinked. "You may be able to fool these savages, my friend. But you can't fool me. You've got more gold than that!"

De la Verendrye slowly shook his head. "No, Henri. This is all the gold I have." Dropping the six coins back into the pouch, he pulled the drawstring and tossed it at Bruneaux's feet. "It's yours," he said. "It's your 'thirty pieces of silver.' But then, someone like you wouldn't know anything about that."

Bruneaux looked down at the pouch. His lower lip trembled as indecision swirled in his eyes. He looked up at de la Verendrye. "Then, if you're giving me the gold . . . I want to buy my freedom!" he hissed. "I want to buy my freedom!" Ask them to let me go, without food . . . without anything. I'm willing to take my chances. Ask them!"

De la Verendrye shook his head, a slight smile growing on his lips. "Gold doesn't mean anything to them. Even if it did, they still wouldn't let you go. There is much you must answer for."

Bruneaux's jaw trembled. His gray eyes were wild from fear. "Ask them! Please!"

De la Verendrye looked down at the pouch and then into the face of the man who nearly killed him. "Once more, you will take something from me that I do not want to give you. Pity. Perhaps that is what 'thirty pieces of silver' can buy."

He turned to Whirlwind. "My friend," he said in Lakota. "This . . . man wishes to speak with you."

Whirlwind pulled the robe around his shoulders and stood. "Let him speak."

De la Verendrye looked with contempt at Bruneaux. "You're not fit to lick this man's feet, but he says to let you speak. So speak!"

A strange look came into the big man's eyes. "Ask them to let me go, without food . . . without anything."

De la Verendrye translated the man's words. The three warriors stared hard at the man. Whirlwind finally spoke. "Those are the words of a coward. However, I will give him an opportunity to win his freedom."

"How?" asked de la Verendrye.

"He must face me, man to man, with war clubs. If he defeats me, he can go. If I defeat him, he goes back with us to face the judgment of the old men."

Bruneaux's eyes darted about in fear as de la Verendrye translated Whirlwind's words. Whirlwind waved aside a look of concern from his son.

"Yes," Bruneaux finally whispered, "I'll do it!"

Whirlwind tossed off his robe and pulled the war club from his belt. "Give this . . . this man your war club," he said to Red Lance. "And do not worry, this will not last long."

Red Lance slid his war club toward Bruneaux as de la Verendrye untied him and stepped out of the way.

Bruneaux picked up the war club and noticed the warrior's bloody shoulder. His throat tightened. This was the man on the gray horse!

"You will lose, Bruneaux!" de la Verendrye chortled.

Bruneaux grasped the weapon at the end of its handle and waved it slowly back and forth to get the feel of its balance and weight. Nostrils flaring, eyes blinking, he took a shaky step toward the warrior.

Bruneaux was a big man, taller and broader than Whirlwind, but he had never learned the nuiances of single combat. Up to now he had always relied on the threat of his brute strength to back down opponents. He licked his lips and took another step.

Whirlwind noted the larger man's awkward stance. Though the white man carried the war club like it was nothing more than a twig, it was clear that he did not know how to use it. Still, the man was larger and probably much stronger. But Whirlwind guessed that his opponent did not know how best to use that size and strength, so it was all he had because there was nothing inside to give it meaning and to guide it. The man was not a warrior and would never understand what it meant to be a warrior.

The white man's initial bravery faded. He cast quick side glances at the edges of the rocky outcropping and at the faces of the four men who had him trapped. De la Verendrye was clearly sneering. The two younger warriors were ridiculing him with their eyes, confident of the outcome. Bruneaux turned an uncertain gaze toward Whirlwind and immediately felt the warrior's cold, measuring stare.

From amidst the craggy peaks came the bold song of a wolf.

"Hear that?" called de la Verendrye. "That is a good sign for him! Bad for you!"

Bruneaux waved the club faster and took a side step. Whirlwind stood calmly.

Again de la Verendrye called out, "Hey! If I were you, I would put down that weapon!"

Bruneaux's eyes widened as he hissed at de la Verendrye. "Shut up! Shut up!"

"You've got no chance! No chance!" de la Verendrye's derisive chuckle echoed off the granite wall behind Bruneaux and mingled with the call of the wolf as it drifted down again from the cold, shadowy peaks.

Bruneaux rushed at Whirlwind, wildly swinging the war club. But Whirlwind, almost effortlessly, sidestepped and delivered a cracking blow to Bruneaux's left elbow. With a bellow of fear and rage, Bruneaux retreated, his left hand trembling uncontrollably.

Whirlwind looked into the darting gray eyes of the killer white man. There was fear in them, but also a recklessness. And that made the man more dangerous. He dropped his gaze to the big man's chest and waited.

Bruneaux rubbed his elbow for a moment and repositioned his grip on the weapon's handle. He sliced the air with two vicious swings and then moved forward.

Whirlwind noted that the man was right-handed. There was much more strength in his right to left swing of the club. His backswing was slower and weaker.

Bruneaux moved slowly forward, drawing the club back toward his right shoulder. He was within three paces from the waiting warrior. Aiming for the head, Bruneaux swung with all of his strength.

Whirlwind bobbed backward, feeling the rush of air as the clubhead went by. Although the sudden movement brought a slicing pain to his injured shoulder, in less than a heartbeat he moved into the big man's backswing and delivered two swift, cracking blows. The first blow shattered the white man's left wrist while the second broke his upper right arm.

De la Verendrye was astounded. Whirlwind had delivered two blows in one blink of an eye.

Bruneaux cried out and backed away toward the rock wall, both arms dangling uselessly and his face contorted by fear and pain.

Whirlwind motioned for de la Verendrye. "Tell him these words," he said. De la Verendrye nodded.

Whirlwind moved toward Bruneaux, like a wolf certain of the kill. "You are a worthless thing. Any Lakota boy could defeat you. You kill. You take. You waste. In the next life, you will be a worm. If you keep fighting, I will break your other arm. Then your legs. Then I will leave you here, so the coyotes and the ravens can come and eat your flesh . . . while you are still alive. The choice is yours."

Pain and terror filled Bruneaux. He looked into the eyes of the warrior, and saw death. Before anyone could stop him, he ran toward the end of the ledge and did not stop.

His body turned once as he fell, and his upper right leg struck a rock face, breaking with a dull snap. Momentum pushed Bruneaux down between two walls of rock until he came to a stop on his back. The walls held him tight, and his feeble struggles were in vain, only heightening the pain in his leg and arms. His bellow of terror and agony echoed from one rock wall to another.

As his screams faded away, Bruneaux saw a slight movement out of the corner of his eye. Turning his head as far as he could, he finally saw the dark shape standing in the deep snow.

It was a coyote.

Twenty-Five

I t was morning. The land wore a glistening robe of white, for it was well into the Winter Moon. Forty-two lodges of the Wolf Tail Lakota stood east of some tall, pine-covered hills near Spring Creek, which flowed into the Smoking Earth River. On this new day the sun was bright and warm, although a few gray clouds were peeking over the southwest horizon.

There was already much activity. Boys were at the river's edge in groups, poking at the thickening ice with sharpened driftwood poles to keep watering holes open. A few younger boys helped older sisters or mothers gather and haul firewood to their lodges. Older boys and some younger warriors were moving the horse herd about a long arrow's cast to the north of the encampment. Even as they moved leisurely along, some of the horses paused to scrape the snow with their hooves to find the grass beneath. To the west, a small group of hunters walking on snowshoes disappeared into the pine-covered draws in pursuit of white-tailed deer. Closer to the lodges, among the leafless shrubs and thickets, boys with bows and arrows in hand stalked quick and elusive cottontail rabbits.

Outside the lodge of Her Good Trail, two war horses stood at their picket pins, resting from their eleven-day journey from the Black Hills.

Inside the lodge, the fire burned high. The war leader of

the Wolf Tail Lakota reached into a rawhide case and pulled out a red-painted eagle feather. He held it up, admiring its beauty. "Today," he said to his wife, "I have a promise to keep. Lone Elk's bravery against the white man with the holy iron, when we fought him at the ridge near the two rivers, is the kind that always stirs the heart—and will long be remembered. It is the kind of bravery that should be told in a song."

Her Good Trail looked at the eagle feather bonnet hanging from a pole at the back of the lodge, a bonnet made from forty-four feathers, representing forty-four brave deeds. Such as the time Whirlwind had stood with Brings Three Horses against the Pawnee. Or when he had ridden into a hail of Kiowa arrows to rescue the son of Stone. And there would be many more eagle feathers if he told about all of his deeds. She smiled. "He was brave because someone showed him how," she said.

Whirlwind looked into the fire for a moment, recalling the lonely camp beneath the cedars the day after he had fought with the Arikara warriors. He remembered the yearning in his heart to be where he was at this moment. With Her Good Trail. "Because he who showed him had the best reason to be brave," he said gently. "And he cannot ever do enough to show his gratefulness for that. All he can do is thank the Great Mystery for being such a fortunate man."

Her Good Trail felt her face grow warm as Whirlwind's eyes turned to her. She turned to him and held his gaze, a soft smile bending the corners of her mouth. He had returned again, as he had promised—as he promised each time he rode away for a hunt or on the warpath. Though from his fitful sleep, the wound to his shoulder, and the distant look that came into his eyes when he thought she was not watching, she knew this journey had been very difficult. But he was home, and she would do her best to help heal his wounds. She continued to hold his gaze, wanting this moment to go on because in his eyes she could see their life together.

"There is something that I must do," he said, now tilting his head toward the war lance tied to a lodgepole. "I know that the old men will not expect it, but I will give up the war lance that was passed to me from High Hawk."

Her hands went to her mouth, and tears welled up in her dark eyes.

"I have a reason to do so," he continued. "And like so many other times, I know that you will stand by me. Without that, without you, there are many things that I could not have done, or endured."

"I know that you must have a good reason for giving up the war lance," she said in a whisper. With her hands she wiped the tears sliding down her face. "Whatever the reason is, I will stand with you."

"I fought the white man," he told her, "the killer of High Hawk's mother. He was no warrior. I defeated him easily. After that, he killed himself. He was nothing without the holy iron. Like the trapper on the White Earth River, his power was the holy iron. If he had not had that weapon, he might have run when he saw me—or maybe tried to be friendly. But his holy iron guided his thinking, and he tried to kill me." The warrior paused and looked for a moment at the war lance of the Wolf Tail Lakota, then spoke again. "Those two white men, by doing what they did, proved to me something I already knew. The holy iron can have a power over a man's mind."

Whirlwind looked around behind him at the encased flintlock standing against a lodgepole. He turned back to Her Good Trail, with a sadness in his eyes she had never seen before. "I was wrong to hide the holy iron, to keep it away from the other warriors."

"Why? If it had been up to me, I would have done the

same!" replied Her Good Trail, glancing angrily at the weapon.

He looked into her flashing eyes and smiled through his sadness. "My war horse," he said gently, "was the best horse I have ever ridden. I have other war horses, but there will never be another like that gray. There was only one of him." He allowed the memories to dance behind his eyes for a few heartbeats. Then his eyes turned hard. "Not so with the holy iron. There are many. Too many, I am afraid. And they are all alike. Each one will have a power that can take over the mind of the man who owns it. And it is a power that each man, each warrior who takes up a holy iron must face. If a man is strong inside, he will win. If a man is weak, with nothing to guide him, the holy iron will win.

"Instead of hiding it, I should have let each warrior in our village use it for a while, so that each of them could face the power it has. But I was afraid of it. I was afraid the holy iron would win. I did not give my fellow warriors the chance to face it for themselves. I decided for them, by hiding it."

The woman nodded and touched her husband's hand. A smile came into his eyes when he felt the warmth in her touch.

"The holy iron is coming," he went on. "At the trade gathering you told me of, there will be white men with holy irons to trade. There will be other trade gatherings, other white men. Perhaps it will be like a flood."

"But if you give up the war lance, and you are no longer war leader, how can you fight the flood?" she wanted to know.

"We cannot fight a flood," he replied, "we can only try to swim. Some will drown. Some will not. I can only do what I think is the right thing. My father and my uncle taught me the way of the true warrior. They taught me that the power of a true warrior begins and grows inside. That is where the fight will be against the holy iron—inside of each warrior. For some of us, it will not be a difficult fight. For others, it will be the struggle of a lifetime. It will depend on how strong the way of the true warrior is inside of each of us."

"Our son," she whispered, "will it be difficult for him?"

He shook his head. "I do not know," he replied, nodding toward the holy iron. "I will give him that . . ."

Like fleeing birds, Her Good Trail's hands went to her mouth.

Whirlwind continued, "He must face it, like everyone else."

She sighed and nodded. "Yes. I know he must." She threw a dark glance at the encased weapon, but her face softened as she looked back at her husband. "He comes from a long line of true warriors. The holy iron will not claim him."

Before either of them could say anything more, footsteps crunched on the snow outside, and someone scratched at the door.

"Come in," said Whirlwind.

It was the warrior Good Hand. He shook the snow from his buffalo-hide robe and entered, smiling. "Uncle," he said, "it is good to see you. I have news."

"You are smiling, so it must be good news."

Good Hand chuckled as he took the seat offered by Her Good Trail. "Yes," he replied. "Good news. I traveled south to the Running Water River with Caught the Eagle and Spotted Horse. We did not see any enemies or signs of them in our country. And we saw buffalo. Many of them. There is a very large herd wintering in the grassy sandhills, like they did three winters ago."

"That news is worth a smile," observed Whirlwind. "Perhaps we should plan a hunt. Fresh meat is good, and I have not hunted buffalo on snowshoes since . . . three winters ago."

Her Good Trail smiled to herself as the two men tried to hide their excitement over the coming hunt. She would rather her husband hunt buffalo than ride the warpath. However, a twinge of sadness went through her as she glanced up at the war lance. She glared at the holy iron hanging in its case on the next pole.

In a while the men finished their planning. Good Hand spoke his thanks for the tea and left. Her Good Trail worked quietly for a time. She could feel her husband's eyes on her as she moved about.

"Mother of Walks High," he finally said, softly. "I am honored that you have joined your path to mine. And thank you for such a fine son."

She crossed the lodge and joined him as he reclined against the willow backrest. Her eyes were bright. "I did not bring him into this world by myself."

The sun announced its departure by piercing a thin line of clouds with strong red shafts. The Wolf Tail people were down to forty-two lodges, but at nearly every one a war horse was already picketed for the night. Many of the smoke flaps were closed part way. Large snowflakes were falling.

At the lodge of Long Shawl and High Hawk, their daughter Walks Straight finished moving the pole to the smoke flap and came around to the door. She gasped softly at the unexpected sight of a young man standing at the door, with an elk-hide courting robe over his shoulders.

"Tell your sister that I am here," he said, "and that I hope she will talk to me."

Walks Straight's eyes grew bright. She smiled and went into the lodge. Inside she removed her outer robe, looked toward Sun Rise Woman, and cleared her throat. "There is a very tall young man standing at our door," she said. "I know him to be a brave warrior. He is wearing an elk-hide courting robe."

Sun Rise Woman looked up from the string of turnips she was rebraiding. Long Shawl and High Hawk glanced knowingly at one another. "It is a cold evening," High Hawk said to his wife. "It would be warmer if two were standing under that elk-hide robe." Long Shawl smiled toward her eldest daughter.

Sun Rise Woman put down the turnips and crossed over to the door. Her father gave her a nod of encouragement when she looked back.

The door opened and closed, casting a bright, warm glow over the snow for a moment or two. Walks High opened the robe and covered her as she stepped into the protective circle of his arms. Yet again he understood the long, lingering looks that passed between his mother and father. He searched for the right words.

Before he could speak, her arms wound around him, and she pulled him close. "I was afraid something would happen to you and you would not come back."

"Do not worry," he said, gently kissing the top of her head. "I will always come home to you."

The fire burned high in the council lodge as the circle of old men listened patiently. De la Verendrye, now called Beard, sat among them. With reluctance, Walks High told of his near encounter with Bear Heart. His grandfather, Stone, White Crane, and the others listened with great interest. And with sadness. Still, there was no judging, no blaming. Sometimes, a man could not help what he was. But because of who he was, fully eleven other lodges had followed when Bear Heart had left the winter encampment of the Wolf Tail band.

As Walks High finished and took a seat, his father entered the council lodge. In one hand he carried the lance of the war leader, in the other the holy iron in its elk-hide case. Stone motioned him to the back. Whirlwind took his place and remained standing. "Grandfathers," he said, "I hope you will let me speak."

Murmurs of assent moved through the lodge.

Standing with the lance and the holy iron, Whirlwind

looked around for a moment. "There is much that is in my heart," he began. "I hope that I can find the words to put it all before you. First, the white man who sits among us is an honorable man. I do not know about others of his kind, but I do know about him. He is a good man, and he has much to offer us. We have much to learn from him, if he will find it in his heart to tell us what he knows—about other kinds of people, other ways of thinking. I do not say that we will like what he can tell us. I do say that it is important to know these things. As all of you have taught us, knowledge is a warrior's best weapon. The more we know about white men, the better we can defend ourselves if they become our enemies."

Whirlwind paused and held up the holy iron. "This is one of the things we should learn more about. We should not turn our faces from it, because even if we do, it will still be part of our lives. Soon, I am afraid . . ."

White Crane looked up at Whirlwind. "Nephew," he said, "your words are true, and I know you have more to tell us. But I wonder if you will let me speak, for a short time."

Whirlwind nodded and took a seat, still holding the two weapons in his hands.

"Thank you, Nephew," White Crane went on. "While you were gone, two young men from the Mniconju Lakota came. They spoke of a trade gathering up along the Great Muddy, in the spring, a gathering to be held by white traders. I have been thinking about that gathering. Sometimes I think we should go; sometimes I am afraid of what will happen to us if we do go. To travel to that trade gathering is more than a journey from here to the Great Muddy. It is a journey into change, into a new way. Like going into a land we do not know.

"I am afraid because of what I have seen. I have seen that my nephew Bear Heart and the one who killed the mother of High Hawk are the same in one way."

A few of the old men stirred a little, a few throats were nervously cleared. White Crane nodded, knowing he must choose his words carefully. "Hear me," he went on. "I say that the holy iron has blinded my nephew Bear Heart—with its power. As Beard has shown us, it is only something to be used. It is more powerful than the bow but not better. The bow does not give you a feeling of power over others. The holy iron does.

"Our war leader is right. It has two kinds of power. One we can see and hear. The other is what it does to the man inside. Although Bear Heart does not have one, the holy iron has done something to him. In that way, he is the same as that white man who killed the mother of High Hawk."

Spotted Calf held up a hand and looked at the old men sitting in two rows around the fire. "I am afraid that my cousin is right," he said, draping his robe over his left shoulder. "But we would be foolish not to trade for the holy iron ourselves. Bear Heart did speak the truth when he said we must change. The holy iron will come. It is part of our lives now. If we do not have it, we will have no power over how it changes our lives. We cannot let that happen. So we must find a good way to face this change."

An old man closest to the fire loudly cleared his throat and pulled his robe high over his shoulders. His name was Bear Looks Behind, and he had been war leader before High Hawk. "Everything we have heard this night, here in this council lodge, is true," he began. Everyone fell silent. Bear Looks Behind had earned over eighty eagle feathers in his lifetime, a number no other Wolf Tail Lakota warrior had yet surpassed. He cleared his throat and nodded toward the warrior Caught the Eagle, sitting in the back row near Red Lance and Walks High. "He who married my daughter is a fine warrior. He does not turn from a fight and always thinks carefully. That is how a warrior should be. And that is how we should look at this thing with the holy iron. I will never carry such a weapon. I am old, my eyes dim. But the strongest reason is that I am from a different time. Our war leader, Whirlwind, understands that time, and it has guided his thinking. He is wise to be afraid of it, and I feel his fear. Because I, too, know that the holy iron is more than a thing, a weapon. It is the front edge of a new time, like the sun just before it rises, with a new day waiting behind it. The holy iron is bringing change. And as my cousin, White Crane, has said, it can change a man inside. There is where the most important fight is, for even if only one man is changed, we will all feel that change.

"The Mniconju who came brought word of change, and I think we must do something about it. That trade gathering is the beginning of the fight we must not turn from, but we must go into it carefully. I do not think it would be wise for all of the people to strike their lodges and go. I am in favor of sending a few warriors, to be our eyes and ears. So I have spoken."

Bear Looks Behind nodded and pulled his robe up to just below his eyes. It was an old custom, a way to say without words that one was being cautious. Three or four of the old men did likewise, showing their agreement with the old warrior.

White Crane looked toward Whirlwind, and then around at the others, resting his gaze briefly on Bear Looks Behind. "Good words," he said, "from a wise man. I agree that it would be best to send just a few to the trade gathering. Yet there is something inside which tells me we should take our people as far away from white men as we can. But there is no place where change cannot follow us. So we must hope that most of the white men are like the one who sits among us now."

Some of the old men nodded in agreement. Walks High, Lone Elk, and Red Lance glanced nervously at one another as Bear Looks Behind and two other old men pulled their robes up over their heads. Only the soft crackle of the fire could be heard for a time, and as White Crane spoke again, the three old men lowered their robes. But they had shown their hearts where the white man among them and all white men were concerned. To them, white men were a reason to mourn. It was white men who had traded holy irons to the Ojibway. The one now called Beard knew and understood these things, and he kept his eyes down, waiting for the moment to pass.

"I think," White Crane said, "that my nephew has something further to say." Whirlwind nodded. "But before he does, I think that one of those who goes to the trade gathering should be our war leader. And he can choose who rides with him."

Murmurs of agreement rose and fell as Whirlwind stood to address them. "Grandfathers," he said, "yes, the war leader should go with a few to the trade gathering." He drew in a deep breath, let it go, and then stared down into the fire for a short while. "But that war leader will not be me."

Every eye looked toward the warrior standing at the back of the lodge. The firelight gave shadows to his face, shadows which matched the heaviness in his heart. Whirlwind stood the encased holy iron on end with his left hand. In his right he held the war lance, passed to him by the old men leaders who now waited quietly for him to speak his heart.

"This," he began, looking at the holy iron, "until about one moon ago, was hidden away in my lodge—hidden because I was afraid of what it might do to my people and our way of being warriors. I looked at this thing only through my own fears. That was wrong. I kept it to myself, hoping that if it were not seen, it would be soon forgotten. Yet even if I threw it into the deepest river I could find, the thought of the holy iron would still be in our minds. And it will not go away. Grandfather Bear Looks Behind is right. We should not turn away from this holy iron and what it means. We must face up to it, but with great care . . . the same way we approach a bear or a buffalo which has fallen from our arrows. One careful step at a time."

Whirlwind looked around at the two circles of men, mostly old and wise warriors with their life's journey well behind them but some young warriors with their journey still ahead. His gaze lingered briefly on his father and then on his son. In his father's eyes he could see the depths of wisdom. In his son's eyes burned the flame of reckless courage. There were the answers he should have seen. He took a deep breath and spoke again.

"Four winters ago, a white man with this in his hands nearly killed me," he said, raising the holy iron for a moment. "From that moment on, there have been questions in my mind— about the holy iron, about white men. Some questions about both have been answered. We must be careful about both because both can be dangerous. We must deal with them one careful step at a time, both together as a people and separately in each of our own hearts and minds. By hiding this in my lodge, I stood in the way of that. Perhaps if I had not, then some of the things that have come our way would not have happened. So on this night, I must do two things. One I do with no regret, the other with many, many regrets."

A few nervously cleared their throats, and a heavy silence descended on the lodge as Whirlwind paused for a time.

He held up the encased holy iron. "This," he said, "I give as a gift . . . to my son, because it will be a part of his world and his life from now on. Perhaps one day, his children's grandchildren will hold it in their hands and tell its story. And I pray that it will not be a sad one."

Walks High rose to his feet and reached out for the weapon. He had picked it up several times before, when his father and mother were gone from the lodge. But now, it was suddenly much heavier than he remembered it to be. He held it awkwardly as he rejoined Red Lance and

Lone Elk. Red Lance nodded while Beard leaned over and whispered, "It shoots high, but I will show you how to deal with that."

Whirlwind stood tall as he grasped the war lance with his hands. It was made of chokecherry and was nearly as long as a man was tall. At the top end was a flat and narrow point of gray flint, as long as from the bottom of a man's hand to the end of his middle finger. From the sinew and rawhide lashings, which held the point in place, it was wrapped in buffalo hide—hair side out—nearly to the other end. A strip of red-dyed buckskin, as wide as a man's thumb, was stretched from the top end to the bottom, sewn into the opposite ends of the buffalo-hide wrap. From that strip of buckskin, dyed red for the color of honor, hung eleven eagle feathers, each from the tail of the great white-headed eagle. A new feather was added each time a new war leader took up the lance of the Wolf Tail Lakota. Whirlwind was the eleventh.

He began to speak, in order, the names of each warrior who had carried the lance—the first going back to a time long, long before the coming of horses. After each name, every warrior in the council lodge gave a single, strong affirmation of honor: "*Hau!*"

"Wolf Tail! Many Deeds! Has the Fire! Good Voice Eagle! Long Runner! Bear Eyes! Chases in Winter! Star! Bear Looks Behind! High Hawk!"

Whirlwind paused and lifted the war lance. "Those men carried this with honor," he said. "I have done my best, though I am afraid that my pitiful efforts do not come close. But I am honored that you asked me to carry it. Now, with sadness in my heart, I pass it back to you. There are many good men here who are worthy of it, much more than I."

Stone labored to his feet, as a deep silence once again crowded the lodge. He took the lance from Whirlwind. For a long while he studied the face of the younger warrior. "In my lifetime," he finally said, "I have known four of the good men who have carried this, beginning with my father's cousin, Star, when I was a small boy. You have done no less than any of the other three. No less than any of the rest of them. Judge yourself how you choose. That is your right. But one day your name will be spoken with the rest. And it will be spoken with honor."

Twenty-Six

Whirlwind could not move his arm. He looked down at the useless thing hanging at his side as the Arikara warriors rode closer and closer. They would surely kill him this time. His lance was ten paces away. Too far. Pounding, galloping hooves grew louder, like relentless thunder. Glistening lance points were aimed for his heart. There was nowhere to run, nothing he could do. A sharp pain seared his right shoulder. He called out a name. Yellow light pushed through the pain, and he found himself staring into the low flames of a fire. A soft voice spoke.

"Husband, I am here," said Her Good Trail.

The dream, again. He sat up from the willow backrest and rubbed a hand over his face.

Her dark eyes studied the wound just below his collarbone. She rearranged the poultice so gently that he hardly felt her fingers moving. "How long did I sleep?" he asked.

"A long time," she told him. "It is nearly sundown."

Whirlwind glanced toward a backrest in one corner of the spacious lodge.

"He is gone," she said. "He and Beard. With their . . . holy irons. And Red Legs, too." She stared at the backrest for a moment. "I heard the old men have asked him to ride to the trade gathering up on the Great Muddy, in the spring."

Whirlwind nodded.

"He is not going alone, is he?"

"No," he assured her. "He will go with Caught the Eagle, Red Lance, Lone Elk, and Beard. Caught the Eagle is to lead."

"I have heard some talk," she said quietly. "Some of the people want to go. Some will, I think. They are very curious. When the two Mniconju were here, they told about the many different things the white men will have to trade. What will happen to us if some more of our people leave?"

Before he could answer, a distant boom shattered the stillness of Spring Creek Valley. They both gazed toward the empty backrest. "The trade gathering will more than likely be for only a short while," he said, glancing toward the door. "For a short time, I think . . . there will be no great danger from our enemies."

Her Good Trail nodded. "What other things do white men have? Will everything they have be confusing to us, the way a holy iron is? I know we can protect ourselves against the Pawnee, or the Kiowa, or the Arikara. We know about them."

Whirlwind glanced around. At one side of the lodge were the things he used as a warrior: Two buffalo-hide shields, his war lance, two buffalo hunting lances, war clubs, and several bows and quivers of arrows. The bow he had made while pursuing the white man was hanging with the others. He remembered the day Walks High had tried out the new sinew-backed bow made for him by his grandfather, and how his son had shattered a dirt clod tossed in the air . . . with an arrow. Could he do that with a holy iron? Perhaps.

Whirlwind looked at his wife. "I am afraid that some of our people will strike their lodges and go to trade with the white men," he said. "The things they bring back will be new to us. Not Afraid is painting the holy iron on our Winter Count robe. We will always know this time as the Winter of the Holy Iron. What will we call the times yet to come?

Perhaps we will name them for other things that are new to us, that do not come from our being, our ways, and our spirits. I do not know. As for me, I will always go to the hunt or ride the warpath with the lance, and the bow and arrows. That much, I can say to you."

BOOM! Once again, the voice of the holy iron filled the quiet valley. Whirlwind grabbed his winter robe and stepped out of his lodge. Her Good Trail followed him out into the cold, fading day. The sun was about to fall behind the dark western horizon. Lodges and trees cast long, sharp shadows on the whiteness of the land.

The last echoes of the shot faded into the distant draws. An uneasy silence returned. Most of the Wolf Tail people were outside their lodges, looking east toward a small group of men and boys at the base of a hill. Whirlwind could see Walks High and Beard in the middle of the group.

Walks High was preparing his holy iron to shoot again. After a few moments, the young warrior lifted the weapon to his shoulder, taking aim at a dead, gray tree some eighty paces to the north. The boys in the group covered their ears.

Her Good Trail reached for her husband's hand. They waited. The uneasy silence grew oppressive, falling like a heavy robe. Small children pushed against their mothers. BOOM!

Children, horses, and dogs flinched. Whirlwind squeezed his wife's hand as the sound of the holy iron slashed through the valley. It was a new voice, not of the land. It was the voice of a stranger. One that would speak more and more. For Whirlwind, it would always bring memories of the first time he ever heard it. For him, it would always be the voice of death.